Alone Together

A Romantic Comedy

Lindsey Jesionowski

PUZZLES
Publishing

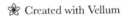

For my girls.
Don't just dare to dream; dare to begin.

Author's Note

Readers, please be advised that this book contains on-page description of a panic attack. It also discusses the deaths of parents and a significant other.

Chapter One

On his thirtieth birthday, Max took his first water aerobics class.

Okay, he wasn't so much a participant as he was an observer, but close enough. While he watched a bunch of little old ladies jig around to oldies music while they yammered on—rather loudly—about the latest gossip to hit the senior citizen rumor mill, something incredible happened. Something he wasn't sure he should blame or thank his best friend, Johnny, for.

"Hey, old man. Let me get that chair for you. Don't want you to break a hip or anything," Johnny had said a mere half hour before the class began.

Max's best friend always had a custom greeting each time they met. He wished he would have kept this one a little more hush-hush, though; he wasn't interested in everyone knowing today was his birthday.

"I'm only thirty. And you're four months older than me."

"True, but I have the buff body and virility of a much younger man." He chortled, comically puffing up his chest.

Max shook his head and took a seat next to his friend.

1

He filled out page upon page of paperwork under the bright fluorescent lights of the fitness center lobby while the bass notes from the nearby aerobics room boomed through the speakers. "I may be coming off an ankle injury, but I'm pretty sure I could still hold my own in the weight room with you, buddy."

"Didn't seem that way when you were hobbling around on crutches the last few weeks. I almost surprised you with a cane for your birthday," Johnny joked, egging his friend on.

Max couldn't argue. He'd looked fairly fragile as of late. "I'm here now, aren't I? Good as new, according to my doctor." He wiggled his foot as proof.

"Not so fast," his friend responded, trading his joking tone for a much sterner one. "If you reinjure yourself on day one, I'll get fired. We agreed on slow and low-impact, so it's the pool for you today ... and nothing more."

Since when did his best friend become Mr. Responsible?

But his plan was probably for the best. Besides, he'd still get in a good workout. Memories of off-season baseball conditioning workouts in college sprang to mind. They were no joke—he'd leave the pool exhausted and nurse fatigued muscles the entire next day. And sometimes the day after that. He grimaced when he imagined the havoc those workouts would wreak on his body now that he was a decade older.

"Do anything fun today? I mean, it *is* your birthday, after all," Johnny asked. "I know you don't like to go out. I just thought maybe this year you'd be up to it. No pressure." He was the best friend a guy could ask for, and his offer reminded Max that he was there to talk, if needed. Johnny understood his buddy's birthday hadn't been the same since that horrible day exactly three years ago. A day

2

Max would trade his birthday wishes for the rest of his life to forget.

"Not this year, Johnny. It was a good day, though. No one at work even acknowledged it was my birthday. Aside from a few texts and Facebook messages, it was a pretty regular day." Just like he wanted.

"Well, you sure you don't wanna go out tonight? Get a bite to eat? Grab a drink somewhere?"

"Nah. I'm good. I think I'll just go home and relax. Maybe I'll even unpack a little." It was pretty much what he'd done every year since that fateful night. He didn't feel like seeing people. And since he'd just moved into his new apartment ten days ago, there were enough boxes to unpack and drawers to organize to keep him plenty busy.

"Fair enough. So, I'll just give you a tour of the gym, show you where the locker rooms are, and you can get yourself ready. There's a water aerobics class at 4:30, but they only use the front two lanes of the pool for that. The back two are open for lap swim and walking. It's the best time to get in the pool because it's not very busy."

Max usually got off work at 4, so the timing was perfect. He'd work out and then go home to relax and pass the rest of the evening doing nothing. A birthday tradition.

After a brief tour and a quick change in the locker room, Max walked into the pool area. The sound of splashing water and the hum of the hot tub greeted him, and the floor-to-ceiling windows on the longest wall gave a spectacular view of the outside. It was strange seeing snow scattered on the trees while he was getting into a swimming pool. The end of February in West Virginia was skiing weather, not swimming weather, as evidenced by the thick blanket of white that covered the ground.

He hung his towel on a hook and slowly entered the water. If you could get high off the smell of chlorine, he'd already be *so* gone. His eyes burned from the smell but

3

rubbing them with his wet hands probably wasn't a good idea. At least he could assume the water was clean. Good thing, considering the gym had swimming classes for toddlers in the mornings. He didn't know at what age children stopped wearing diapers, but he doubted the attendees of these classes were proficient in bathroom usage.

While Max walked laps, he noticed a small group of older women congregating by the steps of the pool. They held onto one another as they each made the descent into the water, and he smiled in admiration of their teamwork. He was lucky to have a handful of people who held onto him and supported him through one of the darkest times of his life.

But when he overheard one of the ladies say something about tucking her tits in her pants this morning, his trip down memory lane was over as quickly as it began, and he continued with his laps.

Just then, the one who told the inappropriate story waved vigorously in his direction. He hoped she was signaling to someone else, but he was the only one in the vicinity. She looked vaguely familiar as he squinted to get a better view of her from across the pool. Was that his parents' neighbor? A swim cap and goggles covered most of her face, so he wasn't sure. But her enthusiasm was undeniable. He waved back sheepishly, not wanting to be associated with the loud bunch of old ladies, especially since they continued to stare at him and whisper. That couldn't be good.

Max's shoulders lowered as the warm water melted away the stressors of his day. He enjoyed having the walking lane to himself. After weeks of hobbling around on crutches and subsequently limping in an air cast, he felt almost back to normal while the water helped carry some of his weight and gently push him along. As he moved back and forth through the lane, he felt the heat of eyes on

4

him. Sure enough, he'd once again caught the attention of the senior citizen crew who, he assumed, was there for the water aerobics class Johnny told him about.

"Is Hannah teaching class today?" a taller lady asked another as she bobbed up and down in the water. Though the women were on the other side of the pool, the acoustics in the aquatic area carried their voices straight to Max's ears.

"She's on the schedule, so I assume she is," a woman in a swimsuit the color of a neon yellow highlighter responded.

"Good," the woman said, looking relieved. "I know she was sick last week, but, Nancy, that ninny they had to replace her was a nightmare."

Neon Nancy shook her head. "Ninny?"

"Short for nincompoop."

"Roberta!" Nancy snapped. "That's not a very kind thing to call a person. I'm sure he was doing his best. And besides, your trash talk is embarrassing. I don't think people have used that word in decades."

A third lady, whose head barely stuck above the water, sloshed over to join the conversation. "You talkin' bout that Nathan? You hear what he made us do?" Whatever it was, this lady was clearly not a fan.

"Oh, I dunno ... jumping jacks? That jogging series we hate?" Nancy guessed.

Roberta scoffed. "Worse than that. He made us stop talking!"

Nancy clutched her chest. "Shut. Your. Mouth."

The small woman nodded her head so rapidly, Max feared for the joints in her neck. "That's exactly what he said to us."

"Now, now, now," Roberta interjected. "He wasn't that rude. But he did shush us."

Nancy gasped. "He really was a nanny then."

5

"Ninny," Roberta and the small lady barked at her.

And just like that, Max lost count of how many laps he'd walked. Johnny said to do no more than twenty-five, but between *The Flirty Over Fifty* crew that whispered and waved earlier and the bickering ones in the pool just now, he didn't know if he'd walked five or five hundred.

And now here they were, distracting him again. This time with loud cheers and clapping. He looked up to see what had gotten them all excited, and, while he was pretty sure it wasn't from the strenuousness of his workout, he momentarily found himself short of breath.

This must be Hannah.

Every sound he heard before, muted. Even the water seemed to still. All sights vanished from view, and he saw nothing but her. A woman with long, golden hair that shone as brightly as the smile she gave to her elderly admirers entered the pool area.

And it rendered Max motionless.

But wasn't he supposed to be walking laps? In fact, there was a huge *Keep Walking* sign at the end of his lane. But he just stood there. Like a doofus. And now the woman stared at him.

Oh geez.

He put his head down and willed himself to move a little faster than before. The quicker he walked, the less awkward the last sixty seconds would seem, right? That's what his subconscious told him, anyway. The woman strode into the pool office to drop off her gym bag, and he blew out a long exhale. *That's it. Deep breaths, buddy. In and out. Let's not pass out in the pool.*

The instructor came out and greeted everyone in the class with a smile so warm, a flare of heat radiated throughout his chest. Or was he having a heart attack? No, this feeling was vaguely familiar, a sensation he hadn't felt in a long time. One he didn't think he'd ever feel again.

She wore a shirt with a smiling piece of Swiss cheese on it that said: "Be the reason someone's cheesin'." Little did she know that after just barely surviving the last three February twenty-eighths, she had given Max his first reason to smile on his birthday since the night his girlfriend died.

~

HANNAH's favorite part of her job? Teaching the 4:30 water aerobics class on Tuesdays and Thursdays. The ladies treated her like a rock star every time she entered the pool. Since she made the schedule, she kept these classes for herself.

Her students loved hearing about her life as much as she enjoyed hearing about theirs, though their mouths usually got more exercise than the rest of their bodies. But she didn't care. She was so proud of these women for getting out of their homes and moving in the water to various aerobic mashups. Together, they had so many laughs, they were more winded from the hilarity than the actual exercise most days.

Hannah's least favorite part of her job? Gym class creepers. It never failed. At least once a week, some guy would show up to a class they had no interest in. Well, that's not *entirely* true—they had interest in either someone teaching or taking the class, but no interest in the actual *content* of the class. They'd pretend to follow along while their eyes locked-in on their newest conquest. And the pool was the perfect place to prowl. Since the back two lanes were for walking or lap swim, the creepers could stalk their prey, just strolling back and forth in the water. Oh, and the bathing suits the instructors wore were a bonus. Perverts.

Gym class creepers didn't normally attend the 4:30 water aerobics class, though. The average age of the participants was about sixty-five, so that time slot was usually a creep-free zone. But not today, apparently. There was one lone male in the walk lane. While he didn't look like someone Hannah would have categorized as a creeper, he *was* staring. And not subtly. And now he wasn't moving. Like, at all. Was he having a medical emergency?

Hannah breathed a sigh of relief when he started to move again. Maybe he just had a cramp. But that didn't explain the staring.

She watched him for a moment to ensure he was okay. Her eyes fixed on his tousled dark hair, a stark contrast to her golden locks. When paired with his perfectly groomed stubble and broad shoulders, he was a cross between a GQ model and a lumberjack. And wow—he must chop a lot of wood to have a body like that. Or else he worked out on a regular basis. Yeah, that was probably it. There weren't many lumberjacks in these parts, so he must have been a regular at the gym, though she'd never seen him at the pool before. His tall frame, which was very much over six feet tall, stuck well above the top of the four-foot pool, so Hannah got a *good* look at the vastness of his back and all the muscles that went along with it.

And now she was staring. *Real professional, Hannah.*

She clapped her hands to get the attention of her students and break herself from her trance. "Okay, ladies, who's ready to start?" The class responded with a cheer she'd come to both expect and enjoy, and she cranked up the music. Today's choice: a medley of ABBA songs she put together specifically for them. She knew they'd love it. Honestly, Hannah did too. It was nothing she could ever play in her Spinning or Step Aerobics classes, and there was set music for Zumba. The freedom she had with tunes in the water aerobics class was something she enjoyed, and she liked to make the playlists special for the women.

"Somebody's got an admirer," Renee, one of the class regulars, said to Hannah loud enough for her to hear over the music. Loud enough for anyone in the complex to hear, actually.

"What, uh—what are you talking about?" Hannah's flaming cheeks and stutter betrayed her attempt to appear innocently oblivious.

"Oh, honey, if I've gotta spell it out for you, you're even more blind than Lois."

"Hey!" Lois barked. "I may be half blind, but I'm not deaf."

They weren't even two minutes into warmups and Hannah had already lost control of the class. It was typical, though. The ladies liked to meddle, and they *loved* gossip. And the juiciest topic to them was Hannah's love life. Or at least it would have been if she had one. The ladies desperately wanted to change that.

"I don't know what you're talking about," Hannah lied, her eyes deliberately looking at anything but the handsome man in the walk lane.

"Bull," snickered Renee so that only the two of them could hear her.

Renee was like the grandmother Hannah never had but was named after. From the stories her mother had told her, Hannah's grandmother and Renee had a lot in common. In a way, she was like family to her—all the regulars were. That's why she gravitated toward this class. She'd lost practically every family member she'd ever known, so she clung tightly to anything that felt remotely close to that feeling of togetherness. And this group of women was as close to that as Hannah could get. That's why she loved them so much.

An hour later, class was over, and everyone got out of the pool. The gym class creeper left about halfway through the hour-long workout. He so obviously tried not to look up as he rounded the pool toward the locker room, Hannah would have bet good money he'd walk headfirst

9

into a wall. Luckily, he made it to the locker room unscathed.

Unluckily for Hannah, she didn't go unnoticed.

"I saw you checking out that tall drink of water in the pool during class," Renee chirped, grabbing her towel.

Hannah shrugged. "I, uh, don't really know what you're talking about."

"Honey, clearly from these wrinkles, you know I wasn't born yesterday. I mean, if circumstances were different and I was thirty years younger, I would have followed that man right into the locker room."

"First of all, that's against locker room policy. And secondly ... *thirty* years, Renee?"

"Okay, forty-five, but that's not my point, and you know it," she said, pointing a crooked, wrinkled finger at her.

Hannah did know it, but the problem wasn't the man. He was gorgeous, no doubt. She thought about the shy look about him, and it made her second-guess her assumption that he was there to creep on the class. There was something endearing about him, and it had nothing to do with his muscled upper body. Well, that certainly didn't hurt. In fact, every time Hannah caught a glimpse of him, she thought about dunking her head under water to soothe the heat in her cheeks.

No, the problem wasn't the guy at all. Since she'd taken this job and moved to Wheeling last summer, Hannah hadn't dated anyone, much to the dismay of the water aerobics ladies. Coming to a new town was a way to start over and leave the past in the past. But she still couldn't take that first step. It felt like learning to walk again. But with cement blocks on her feet. Big, heavy ones. She knew she needed to put one foot in front of the other.

She just had to figure out how.

Chapter Two

Max went to the gym after work the following day but found out there was no water aerobics class on Fridays. Bummer. The entire pool was his, which he didn't mind. The laps seemed to take longer without the entertainment of the old ladies, which he *did* mind. And he kept looking at the door, hoping Hannah would appear, which made him lose track of his lap count once again.

Yesterday, he'd noticed Hannah had a loveable rapport with the ladies in her class that went beyond a usual teacher/student dynamic. He couldn't hear everything the women said to her, but she laughed nervously more than one time in the half hour he shared the pool with them. He wondered what that was all about. The women seemed to adore her, and the feeling was obviously mutual. And for the second time in as many days, he found himself smiling in the fitness center's pool.

The next day, Johnny came over for what he kept calling "B Day." Max had to ask, because, as usual, he wasn't on the same page as his friend. Apparently "B Day" stood for bros, basketball, beer, and boxes—he was coming over to help unpack and watch college basketball. First task on the agenda—unboxing the television.

His friend looked around the living room and scratched his jaw. "So, let me get this straight ... you've lived here almost two weeks, and you still haven't hooked up your television?"

"That is correct," Max said matter-of-factly.

"Why the heck not? What have you been doing here?" he asked in a slightly judgmental tone.

That was a good question because, clearly, with the mounds of boxes surrounding them, he hadn't been unpacking. And that's when Johnny must have noticed the guitar leaning against the wall in the corner.

His eyes widened. "Dude, have you started playing again? This is huge."

And that's exactly why Max hadn't told him that piece of information. He knew he'd make too much of it.

When his girlfriend died, a piece of him did too. In fact, *many* pieces of him died that night. And while a lot of people chose to handle grief by expressing their emotions through music, he didn't. It was far too painful. Courtney loved listening to him play. Sure, he played for others, but he hadn't needed to. He got all the satisfaction he'd ever crave from watching her stare lovingly at him with a look he remembered so vividly it made his heart ache. So, he stopped playing ... until about a week ago.

"I got bored a few nights ago, what with no TV to watch or anything else to do." It wasn't a lie, but it wasn't the whole truth, either. He'd had a particularly frustrating day at work and needed something to distract him from the previous eight hours. He came home to an apartment of mostly unopened boxes, and he had two options: start unpacking one of the fifteen boxes labeled "Misc." and dig for something to entertain himself or pick up his guitar for the first time in nearly three years.

It was one of the few items he hadn't boxed up in the move.

So, he'd hesitantly reached for it and slowly plucked a couple strings. And as he did, something happened that he never imagined. All this time, he'd avoided playing because he thought it would hurt too much. But as he strummed, a wave of peace poured over him. The neck of the guitar rested in his left hand so naturally it felt like an extension of his arm, just like it always had. And when he closed his eyes, he didn't see a montage of the tragedy like he assumed he would. Instead, his mind treated him to happy memories of a woman he loved. And that's how, for the first time in three years, Max felt a little like his old self.

"Whatever the reason, bro, I'm glad to see you're playing again." Johnny gave his best friend a hug with a pat on the back.

"It really felt good. I forgot how much I loved it."

He decided this was the year he'd start being himself again. But when the clock struck midnight, ushering in the year 2020, he felt the same as always. Unchanged. He learned he couldn't force himself to feel a certain way just because he told himself it was time. Life didn't work that way. But he promised himself to be more open to the signs that he was ready to get his life back. One step at a time. The guitar unboxed in the corner was sign number one.

Of course, he'd never be the same man he was before he lost Courtney. He couldn't meet his soulmate at age eight, lose her, and then go about life as someone who wasn't missing half his heart. That was impossible.

"Did you hear back from the headhunter yet?" Johnny asked, interrupting his thoughts.

"I did, actually. A web design company in Dallas showed some serious interest in me. I'm on a short list of candidates for a position at their firm."

"You gonna take the job if they offer?"

Max popped the top off two beers and walked toward his friend. "Ah, that's the million-dollar question. I'd actually have to move to Dallas. There are no remote positions available."

Johnny looked up from the television cables in his hands and regarded his friend with scrunched brows. "I thought that's what you wanted."

It was. But lately, he was less sure. On a particularly depressing afternoon a few weeks ago, he'd put out feelers for jobs out of town. Leaving was the only way he could think of to escape the shadow of grief that followed him wherever he went. But now that his ticket out of town was within his grasp, he didn't know if he still wanted to reach out and snatch it.

He took a long pull of his beer. "I don't really know."

"You've got a lot to think about. Why don't you come out with me tomorrow night? A bunch of us from the gym are going to watch the WVU game at TJ's."

Tempting, since he didn't know many of the people Johnny worked with. Definitely a good thing. He wouldn't have to endure the sad looks and tilted heads of concern he always got because most of the town knew him and, therefore, knew about his past.

For a while, he couldn't go anywhere without someone asking how he was and telling him how awful they felt. While their concern was sincere, it made him feel worse. Every time he almost stopped thinking about what happened (because, let's face it, he never *completely* did), someone would stop him at the grocery store or out on a walk, and it would rehash the whole tragedy.

"Where are you guys meeting up?"

"You're kidding me. Are you really gonna come?" His friend bubbled with the enthusiasm of a kid on Christmas morning.

"Yeah. Why not? Besides, there's some virus they say is

14

coming our way. We might not have another chance to go out like this for a while."

"Yeah, what are we gonna do? Hole ourselves up in our apartments for months and wait this thing out?"

They both laughed out loud.

"Regardless. I think I need to get out more. And, hey, maybe it's time to have a little fun for a change and meet some new people."

A sly grin crept up Johnny's face. "It's interesting that you mention meeting new people ..."

"WHAT THE HECK ARE YOU WEARING?" Hannah asked as her best friend stood in her doorway, striking a pose like a contestant on America's Next Top Model. While Hannah was so excited to see her, Angie was only asking for trouble wearing a Pitt shirt to a bar where everyone was meeting to watch a WVU game.

"I'm making a fashion statement and adding a little class to the group tonight." She mock-strutted into the apartment.

Hannah laughed and shook her head. Her best friend was always making some kind of statement, even if her lips weren't moving. But that was rarely the case. She always had something to say. Her larger-than-life personality more than made up for her small stature.

Since Hannah had moved to Wheeling from Pittsburgh, the two of them hadn't seen each other as much as they'd like, which was sad, because the two cities were just over an hour away. But they'd been roommates together in Pittsburgh, so major withdrawal was setting in. Hannah was glad to have her bestie in town, if only for the weekend.

"You look different," Angie said as her eyes slowly scanned her friend. Nothing ever got past her.

Hannah shrugged. "I have no idea how." Her hair was a little longer than usual these days, her busy work schedule not leaving time for an appointment at the salon. But that was the only change she could think of since they'd last seen each other.

"You look good, don't get me wrong, but there's something about you. I don't know." She paused with a shrug. "You look happy. And that's saying a lot for someone who has crap all over her shirt."

Hannah gasped and frantically looked to see what she may have unknowingly spilled on herself. She quickly realized the "crap" her friend referred to was the bold West Virginia University logo emblazoned on her hoodie.

While not an alum, Hannah did attend a small college in West Virginia for undergrad, so she had some connection to the state. And now that she lived here, it was best to fit in. These people were serious about their love of the Mountaineers. They were also serious about their hatred for the University of Pittsburgh Panthers, which was why her best friend was in for some major heckling tonight. But Hannah suspected that's exactly why Angie wore the shirt. She enjoyed standing out … and causing a stir. Even if the Panthers weren't playing tonight.

The bright lights of the sports bar smacked them in the face as soon as they opened the door. Hannah spotted the gym crowd right away. They had a couple of tables together, but the chairs were empty. They were all too busy playing the arcade games that covered the entire bottom floor of the building. Flashing lights accompanied the ringing bells and cheers of people who relished the chance to feel like a kid again. It was still a half hour until tip-off, so the girls each got a beer and joined the fun.

The Skee-Ball game caught their attention first.

Hannah hadn't played games like these for as long as she could remember. The buzz in the atmosphere was contagious, and the excitement of a small child percolated inside her. She grabbed a wooden ball, swung her arm back, and rolled it right into the hole that earned her zero points. Her second throw earned her ten points, and her last toss got her a whopping fifty. Not a notable score by any means, but she couldn't remember the last time she had this much fun—until she saw the hoop shoot game.

Now, Hannah had only played basketball through junior high, but she *dominated* at free-throw shooting. Summer afternoons spent draining shot after shot from the charity stripe didn't earn her a spot on the varsity team, but they did earn her bragging rights on hoop shoot games. She deposited her coins, the whistle blew, and before she knew it, she was draining buckets like the NBA equivalent of an arcade game pro. When she finished, lights flashed on the screen, signaling a new high score.

"Dang! You're wasting your time teaching aerobics. We should have you running our summer hoops camp," a familiar voice boomed behind her.

"Hey, Johnny. It's good to see you." She enveloped him in a huge hug. When they separated, she noticed Johnny's eyes trained on her best friend. Why wasn't she surprised? He always kept an eye on the women at the gym. He claimed it was his job to make sure they were using the equipment properly, and it was. But he seemed to take that part of his job a lot more seriously among the gym's female clientele.

"Eat shit, Pitt." He chuckled as he looked at Angie.

"Start your tractors," she quipped back, jabbing a rather unfair insult to the state Hannah now called home. She'd lived in West Virginia for nine months now and had literally seen only two tractors the whole time she'd been here.

17

Watching Angie and Johnny interact was akin to conducting a science experiment. Because they were so similar, Hannah didn't know how they'd react. Whether they'd sizzle with chemistry or combust was anyone's guess. But given the looks they exchanged with one another, Hannah's hypothesis was the latter.

"So, *Hannah*," Johnny said, deliberately turning away from Angie and solidifying Hannah's theory. "How are things in the aerobics world?"

"Really good, actually," she answered proudly. "Our attendance numbers are way up, which is always the case at the beginning of a new year with everyone's resolutions. But we've been maintaining steady numbers even now at the beginning of March."

"That's really great to hear. I'm sure your hiring was a huge reason for that. Everyone loves your classes and some of the new ideas you've started. I hear a lot of chatter on the floor." She'd heard Johnny was a flirt, but he never flirted with her. She didn't know if he respected her too much as a coworker or if she was below the caliber of women he usually hit on, but his comments always seemed genuine.

"That really means a lot, Johnny. Thanks." It really did. She was proud of what she'd accomplished in less than a year.

"You're most welcome. Hold on." He glanced at his ringing phone, and his brows turned down. "I need to take this." He placed it to his ear and walked away.

Hannah and Angie spent the rest of the night, chatting like old times. When the basketball game ended, they stopped at Kroger's to pick up way too much ice cream and went to Hannah's for a grown-up version of a sleep-over, complete with junk food, laughs, and boy talk. But like she tried to tell the ladies at the pool, Hannah insisted she wasn't interested in anyone.

"What about that Johnny guy? He was quite studly," Angie said with a wink. Hannah laughed. Who talked like that?

"Nah. Not my type."

"Seriously? He looks like that Captain America guy from the movie. That isn't your type? Do you have a pulse?"

"I do, but Johnny's just a friend." And a good one at that. They were the same age, and he'd taken Hannah under his wing when she started working at the gym. He knew she wasn't from the area and didn't have any friends in town, so he offered to help her move in and assemble furniture. Because she was too proud and thought she could handle anything (girl power, after all), she declined his many offers. Although, in hindsight, she wished she hadn't—putting together her new furniture took up more time than her actual job.

"Just because you happened to date someone who turned out to be the jerk of the century doesn't mean they're all gonna do ya dirty, you know?"

Again, who talked like that? Her best friend made a good point, but Hannah had put all her eggs in one basket, so to speak. She tied up all her relationship hopes and dreams with someone who, instead of promising her a happily ever after, took her out to dinner to tell her he had accepted a job five states away. And that was it. He dropped her like a hot potato. Unfortunate, because Hannah was a fan of spuds in any form. Now whenever she saw them, she thought of Pete.

"I feel like it's such a struggle letting people into my life anymore, you know?" She stifled a sniffle. "I've suffered enough loss and heartbreak. Is it really worth opening myself up enough to let someone in when I know so well how it all could end?"

When Pete broke all his promises of a life together with

her over a plate of chicken parmesan at a fancy restaurant, her world came crashing down around her. And she panicked.

And thus began a chain of events that not only prompted her to leave her hometown but also forced her to leave her life as she knew it. She was nothing if not compelled by gut reactions. When it came to fight or flight, she always flew because it was far less painful than the alternative. And she'd dealt with the alternative enough times to know. She was an expert, in fact. If she kept her distance—from people and even places—she wouldn't hurt again. A lesson she'd learned the hard way. Several times over.

"I understand, it's hard, Hannah. But you're depriving yourself of so many good things that could come your way just because you're camping out in your safe zone."

Hannah acknowledged what her friend said, but even Angie didn't totally understand what a battle this past year had been for her. The extent of her anxiety was something only known to her and her therapist—a therapist Angie didn't even know her friend saw. She wanted to tell Angie, but that might worry her. This was something she needed to handle on her own. She knew herself well enough to know she needed control of her life, and the only way to really control it was to tread lightly with love and remain in this comfort zone she created for herself in a town far from any of the painful memories of her many losses. The people she loved the most always ended up saying goodbye, so it was easier for her to not even give them the chance to say hello.

Chapter Three

"Don't lie to me. Are you really at the tire store right now?"

Max could see how Johnny might believe he'd bailed on him last night. His social interactions the past few years were sporadic at best. But this was the truth: he'd actually gotten himself ready, psyched himself up for a fun night, and went out to find he had a tire flatter than the pancakes he'd made himself that morning for breakfast. Although that wasn't saying as much as it should. The pancakes shouldn't have had so many lumps in them, should they? His mom's never did. He really needed to learn how to cook. So, this morning, he had a digestible breakfast of cereal and a banana and then went to the local tire shop to get a new one put on.

"I'm really here. And I really was coming out last night. I kid you not." He appreciated his friend's enthusiasm regarding their attempted night out, but on the phone last night, he got the feeling Johnny was more bummed than he should have been that he couldn't make it. Maybe he just *really* wanted his buddy back. Or maybe he needed a wingman. Johnny had made that joke about

Max leaving him alone with all the ladies since he couldn't come. Whatever his motive, Johnny finished the call by promising to let him know the next time he was going out.

Max spent the second half of the weekend unpacking. Again. A couple boxes he didn't know what to do with were candidates for the spare bedroom, so he stacked them in there and called it a win. He'd officially moved in. While he originally shopped for a one-bedroom apartment, when a two-bedroom became available at a too-good-to-be-true price, he jumped on it. Since he did a lot of work at home, he had plans to make the spare room an office. Now, it looked more like a storage closet. Maybe a "cloffice" was more practical, anyway.

By the time Thursday rolled around, he was ready to hit the pool again. He hadn't meant to skip his workouts for most of the week, but between issues with his internet, a late night at work, and an appearance at his niece's soccer game to cheer her on—he was her number one fan, after all—the week flew by in a blink.

He got to the pool the same time he did last Thursday, and while he wasn't ready to admit it to anyone but himself, he really hoped Hannah was there again.

The familiar sounds of the various pumps humming and water trickling filled his ears as he hung his towel on the hook, but a loud squeaking noise caught his attention. A huge bin on wheels, nearly as tall as he was, slowly rolled his way. He assumed someone was pushing it, though because of its height, he couldn't see who. PVC pipe and bungee cords failed to contain the pool noodles that hung out over the top and out the sides of the makeshift container. A feat of sound structural engineering, this was not.

As the mobile contraption got closer to him, one of the noodles that stuck out from the side fell to the ground, catching under a very rickety wheel. The entire thing toppled over, spilling about thirty pool noodles all over the ground.

"Seriously?" a defeated voice echoed through the aquatic center as Max bent over to help clean up the mess. When he looked up, he looked into the deepest blue eyes he'd ever seen. They belonged to the water aerobics teacher.

His mouth went bone-dry, his palms slicked with sweat, and he suddenly couldn't remember why he had an assortment of pool noodles in his hands. They stared at each other for several seconds until she smiled at him.

"Hi," he said. His voice trembled so badly, he felt it best to stick to single syllable sentences. She was even more beautiful up close, which from his spot in the pool last week, he'd have deemed that impossible. As she shyly glanced down, he noticed a dusting of freckles that danced across the bridge of her nose to cheeks that were the lightest shade of pink, like the inside of a rose.

"Thank you," she said, gesturing to the noodles he'd picked up. Was it just his imagination, or did she seem nervous? Maybe it was in his head. Her opening sentence was twice as long as his, after all.

"Let me help you with this." He lifted the bin back to its proper upright position. It was such a simple thing to do, but the glowing smile on her face conveyed her gratitude. She had no idea, but he would do anything to see that smile over and over.

"Yeah, so this is on my list of things to look into—a new way to store the noodles. After this fiasco, it has officially moved to the top of the list." She chuckled. "I'm Hannah, by the way," she said, extending a hand. When they shook, her eyes traveled up and down his body.

"I'm Max," he responded. While her eyes homed in on an area south of his face, he quickly remembered he was half naked. Obviously, he was going in the pool, and his wardrobe was appropriate for the occasion.

Hannah quickly looked away like he'd caught her doing something she shouldn't. "Well, thanks for helping me out," she said, avoiding eye contact as she scooped up the rest of the noodles as fast as she could, redness creeping up the back of her neck.

As she picked up what she must have thought was the last noodle, she took a step back. Her foot landed right on one lying behind her, and she lost her balance. As if happening in slow motion, the noodles she held flew into the air, her leg shot up to the sky, and she fell backwards … right toward the pool.

～

By the time Hannah realized she was falling, it was too late to attempt to shift her weight, and she headed right for the water. She was a goner. Her flailing arms, filled with noodles, probably gave the illusion that she had three times the appendages she did. Like she needed anything else to make the event look more ridiculous than it already was.

But out of nowhere, a long arm swooped around her waist, and something cradled the back of her legs. She wasn't moving anymore. At least not on the outside. Once she realized she was in the arms of the shirtless, handsome guy who minutes ago was helping her clean up pool noodles, her insides were anything but still. Her heart pounded, her breath quickened, and everything inside her shook. But that had to be the result of the near-fall, right? Some kind of post-traumatic response to a near-tragedy. That was a thing, right? Surely it wasn't, because possibly the most gorgeous man she'd ever seen was holding her like a fireman carrying her out of a burning building. And smiling down at her.

24

No, it had to be because of the fall.

"Wow," she said, still trying to catch her breath. "That was an impressive save."

"I thought you were worth saving," he responded and then rolled his eyes back as the tips of his ears reddened. Sure, it was cheesy, but Hannah ate it right up.

"Well, I'm glad, because you also saved my clothes," she quickly added so he wouldn't think too much about his post-rescue dialogue. And she was serious about the clothes. She only had what she was wearing, and the bathing suit underneath, with her today. If she'd fallen in, she would have had a cold ride home in the chilly March air later tonight. Plus, she loved this shirt. A small carrot with its fists primed to fight a head of broccoli and a caption bubble that said "Come at me, bro-ccoli" was graphic tee perfection.

Max must have realized he was still holding her and quickly began to put her down. But then he froze.

"Is your ankle okay? I saw you twist it when you tripped over the noodle."

Well, that was thoughtful. She wondered how long he'd hold her if she said it was a little sore? For a second, the temptation to tell him it was killing her nearly won out.

"I'm totally fine. Just embarrassed," she responded, thinking better than to lie to her rescuer.

He gently lowered her to her feet, his eye contact as steadying as an anchor. And when he still held her gaze and calmly said, "You have nothing to be embarrassed about," she swooned.

He picked up the last few noodles, gave Hannah a smile, and then padded to the other side of the pool, presumably to walk as he had the last time she noticed him here. She couldn't stop watching him. The late afternoon sun pouring in through the windowed wall perfectly illuminated him, and it brought attention to the defined muscles that did not need the help of the sunlight to stand out. Yes, he was gorgeous, but there was something in the way he looked at her that made her knees feel like Jell-O. No one had ever looked at her like that before.

Before she knew it, her pool posse crowded around her. They had a front-row ticket to the show, and Hannah was in for it.

"Are you okay?" Roberta asked with an urgency in her voice, as though Hannah had been involved in a shark attack.

"Oh, I think she's doing just fine," quipped Renee. Hannah's cheeks reddened for the second time in less than five minutes.

"If I fling myself toward the pool, do you think he'll come back and wrap his arms around me like that?" Nancy asked, eyes googlier than any Hannah had ever seen before.

Hannah shook her head. "If you fling yourself into the pool, *I'll* have to rescue you. So, remember that before you do something ridiculous in the name of running your hands all over that poor man."

"Look at that—even his muscles have muscles," Nancy chirped, clearly paying Hannah no mind.

"I can't see a damn thing," Lois barked. "Ooh! Paint me a picture with words."

"Alright. Art class is over," Hannah interrupted. "This is worse than men's locker room talk." She gestured to the now-upright container of aquatic props. "I was just about to get these noodles out for us. I thought they might be fun for a little resistance in the water. Something to get our arms ready for tank top season."

"Our hunky hero over there looks ready for Speedo season."

Hannah suppressed a gag and cranked up the music, betting that a few extra decibels would quell any comments or questions about Max. It seemed to work ... until he got out of the pool.

Just as he had last week, he left halfway through the class. The difference this time? He made eye contact with Hannah. On second thought, it was more than just eye contact. His milk chocolate eyes fixed themselves on her, and the corner of his mouth tipped up into a half-smile that made the already humid air feel about ten times thicker. For a moment, Hannah forgot where she was. His attention rendered her speechless. Which wouldn't have been a big deal if she wasn't currently teaching a class.

Cough. "Arms down above your head." *Cough.* "I mean up—up above your head." *Cough. Cough.* "Grab a set of, uh, the uh, water weights."

The fake cough didn't cover the stuttering. And it sure as heck didn't fool the ladies. To make things even worse, she saw Max smirk as he walked into the locker room. Apparently, it didn't fool him, either.

Chapter Four

Max skipped to work Friday morning. Okay, it wasn't quite a skip. There was a noticeable hop in his step, though. And in the grocery store Saturday morning, he smiled at people he didn't even know. Since his encounter with Hannah at the pool Thursday, he was a smiling fool. And honestly, that worried him a little. Okay, a lot.

While he unloaded groceries back at his apartment and hummed a happy tune to himself (seriously—who was he now?), someone knocked at his door.

"Well, hello. I'd like to speak to the gym hero who saves damsels in distress from certain death in the pool." It was Johnny, with another one of his personalized greetings, standing in the doorway. The smile on his face took up over half his face. A bit Joker-adjacent and a little scary, if Max was honest.

"Wait, how did you know about that?"

Johnny barked out a laugh. "Oh, so it *was* you. I only guessed because you're just about the only guy in there during 4:30 water aerobics. But dude—you're the talk of the gym."

Max groaned. Ever since Courtney's accident, he'd been the recipient of a lot of attention he didn't want. And even though this attention was different, he still wasn't a fan.

He invited Johnny in, and they both took a seat at the kitchen table.

"Geez, I don't want people talking about this," Max complained as he grabbed them each a bottle of water from the refrigerator. "I just did what anyone would have in that situation," he quickly responded, though he knew his generic summary of the incident wouldn't be enough to satisfy his friend.

"Spoken like a true hero. But from what I hear, it was quite the dramatic event." Johnny grinned and took a sip.

"It really wasn't. I only stopped her from falling into the pool. And worst-case scenario—she would have fallen into a pool she was about to get into anyway. So, it's not like I saved her life or anything like that."

"Not the dramatic event I was talking about, buddy. A few of the seniors were talking in the lobby after water aerobics, and word going around the gym is Hannah couldn't take her eyes off you. She forgot cues in her class and was fumbling all over the place."

Max had little control over his face these days, it seemed. He smiled broadly at Johnny's info dump.

She couldn't take her eyes off me?

So, he hadn't imagined it.

"I hate to burst your bubble, Johnny, but as flattering as that is, I'm just not in a position to start anything with anyone yet." He was open to going out a little, maybe casually meeting people in groups, and things like that. Those were small steps he felt comfortable with right now. Whatever he felt when he caught Hannah was no small thing. An hour after he left the gym, he swore his skin still felt hot where her body had touched his.

No, Hannah was not a baby step—she was a jump out of a plane. And Max wasn't sure he knew how to work the parachute.

"You know I love you, bud. You know I know you better than just about anyone in this world. That's why I've gotta say this—I think it's time. And deep down, I think you know it too."

Silence stretched more than a few beats. Max did know it, but that didn't help the conflicting feelings waging war in his gut right now.

He couldn't betray someone who wasn't alive anymore. But why did it feel like that's exactly what he was doing? He couldn't stay single and alone for the rest of his life. So, why did it feel like he should? He'd been committed to one person for over half his life, the only person he'd ever committed himself to, and deep down he wondered if it would ever feel right to devote himself to someone else. He'd be willing to get to know her, a step much larger than any he'd taken so far. But just thinking about it, simultaneously gave him hope and gutted him.

"I just don't know." He took a long sip of his water to buy himself a minute to try and organize his thoughts. "You know how long it's been since I've been on a date. Do you realize how long it's been since I've even been on a *first* date?" He and Courtney grew up on the same street and had been friends since elementary school. So, when they both found themselves single and wanting to go to their junior prom, they decided to go together. And the rest, as they say, was history.

But for the purpose of this conversation, it was *ancient* history.

"I don't even know how to talk to women, Johnny," he said with a heavy dose of exasperation. "When Hannah nearly fell, I made some lame comment about how she was worth saving and, frankly, I wished I'd died on the spot to put me out of my misery. I have no game anymore. Actually, I'm not sure I ever had any." He ran his hands through his hair and tugged at the ends. Was it too early to start drinking something stronger than water for this conversation?

"Maybe you don't need it. Because you're right, you never had game." They both chuckled because it was true. "But, as it turns out, you don't need it when you meet your person. I mean, look, you got Courtney to stay with you for nearly ten years. When it's right, I don't think game matters." He sighed audibly and pointed at his chest. "Look at me—I'm oozing game because I have to force something with other women that came so effortlessly for you with Courtney."

"Good point." Being with Courtney was as natural to him as breathing. That's probably why her death sucked the life right out of him. Was it possible for someone to hit the jackpot twice in their lifetime? It seemed unfair and selfish to hope that it could. And Max doubted it. But the grief he had been carrying for years was converting to loneliness, and at times that was a heavier load to bear. Max was getting tired.

He raised his bottle of water to his friend. "Maybe you could give me some pointers." If anyone could coach him on women, it was Johnny.

"Nah. I have a feeling Hannah has a thing for your particular brand of flirting, not mine. Besides, she seemed pretty smitten when she told me about what happened with you at the pool."

Max's jaw dropped. "Hold on—you two were talking about me? Are you friends with her?" It wasn't a huge gym, but Johnny and Hannah worked in different departments. He never gave much thought to whether they interacted, but of course they did—everyone knew everyone in this town. Why did this surprise him?

31

"She may have blushingly told me about what happened, with a twinkle in her eyes like a fairytale princess who'd just been saved by a prince."

Max's eyes rolled back so far, he could almost see his brain.

Johnny continued. "Yes, we talk. No, she doesn't know you and I are friends. And if you're wondering if it was a coincidence I suggested you start walking in the pool on Tuesdays and Thursdays at 4, it was not."

Well, then. There it was. All of it.

"Seriously, Johnny? What the heck?" He'd been set up. And how hadn't he seen this coming? Johnny was the opposite of subtle in just about every aspect of his life.

"Look, I think Hannah is great. She's smart, incredibly sweet, and obviously gorgeous. I don't think I could choose a better person for you if I picked someone out of a catalog. And I know you've repeatedly told me not to set you up on any dates, but technically, I didn't. I just made sure two people I think are suited for each other happened to be at the same place at the same time. That's all. And I'll go on record that if and when you ever *do* decide to 'get out there,' I don't think you could do that with someone better than Hannah."

Max didn't know what to make of all the info that Johnny had dumped on him in the last ninety seconds. From someone who dated around and wasn't a mushy guy, that was certainly a heartfelt thing for him to say about a woman. And then a thought sprang to mind. "Did she turn you down? Why didn't you date her?"

"Nah, Max. I didn't even try. I knew it the moment I met her—she's for you."

Chapter Five

The next week at the gym was anything but typical. For weeks, everyone talked about a virus that was quickly making its way around the world. No one knew much about it, so making preparedness plans was a guessing game at this point. Hannah favored routine and predictability, so this added to the stress she was already feeling.

Her boss called her in to so many meetings to discuss what this potential pandemic could mean for the gym and how they would handle it should it become an issue. It was unlike anything she'd ever managed before. The scarier part? Literally everyone felt the same way. Definitely not a good thing for Hannah's anxiety.

"What are the odds we'll have to close in the next few weeks?" Johnny stood behind her in the break room, pouring a cup of coffee. She prayed that wouldn't happen. While her paycheck was mostly for her social media expertise, she got her greatest payoff from the part of her job that allowed her to teach classes. The community she shared with her students and the physical activity she regularly got were her greatest weapons against anxiety. Her medicine. And going off meds cold turkey, prescription or not, was never a good idea. She needed this job in more ways than anyone knew. No one at the gym would believe the troubled thoughts that could swirl around her mind at the drop of a hat. The smile she constantly wore made sure of that. She wanted to keep it that way.

"I really hope this all passes quickly. In times of stress, exercise is such a huge help to so many of our members. It'd be a shame for that to disappear when they need it most." She hoped Johnny didn't catch on to her allusion that she probably needed to be here more than anyone.

"I guess we'll just have to wait and see. At least there'd be a silver lining—you can't fall into the pool if you're not here." He walked away chuckling. Why couldn't he let that go?

The week was exhausting, and by the end of it, Hannah just wanted to spend her Friday night sacked out in front of the television, watching QVC. Though Angie teased her for her shopping channel addiction, Hannah didn't care. It was mindless entertainment, the deals were good, and most of all, she enjoyed the company. The presenters on the network seemed like they were talking right to her, particularly on late nights when she couldn't sleep. And besides, it was a lot more cheerful than the news, especially lately.

Just when she thought of the news, her cell phone pinged. A text from her boss said that as of Monday, the gym would be closed until further notice in an effort to slow the spread of the Coronavirus.

She blew out a defeated breath and walked to the kitchen for a snack. As she passed the end table with her favorite houseplant, a gift from Angie when she'd moved to Wheeling, her eyes fixed on the message tag that peeked out from underneath one of the leaves. "Be-leaf in yourself," she read aloud to herself. "I'm really trying to, Chan-

34

ning," she mumbled to the plant. Did talking to a plant make her a little crazy? Not really. A lot of people talked to their plants, right? Did naming her houseplants after hunky Hollywood actors earn her that distinction? Perhaps. But she didn't care. Channing was a good listener. And if this lockdown lasted, she'd probably be having a lot more chitchats with him. And Chris. And the other Chris. And the Hemsworth sibling succulents in the bathroom.

She poured herself a glass of wine and watched a shopping show featuring renowned designer, Isaac Mizrahi. With each gorgeous piece of clothing the host presented, Hannah imagined where she'd wear it.

That one would look cute for work presentations. I could wear that for Easter dinner with Angie's family this year. That would make a perfect outfit for a date.

And when she thought of dating, she thought of Max.

This was nuts. He only came to mind because she hadn't seen him all week. That's all. In fact, she hadn't seen him since the Big Rescue. Pandemic preparedness meetings took up most of the past few days. She even had to get Nathan to cover her water aerobics classes in her absence. And now, thanks to the gym closure, she didn't know when she'd see Max again.

Was he at the pool this week? Did he care I wasn't there?

Okay, that was the wine talking now.

Hannah knew she couldn't date him. She was finally feeling herself again. She was happy. The fragments of her shattered self that Pete left at the restaurant that night were all cleaned up and put together again. Sure, the cracks would always be there, but light was shining through them. She felt like herself. It had been a long time since that was the case. Besides, despite Max's more-than-capable physique, she didn't want to saddle the poor guy with all her past relationship baggage. It dragged her down enough, as it was. No need to bring him down with her. Even if he looked strong enough to lift just about anything.

Stop thinking about his muscles, Hannah.

She couldn't help it. Thoughts of him had crept into her mind all week long. And it wasn't just thoughts of his brawny physique—though they'd snuck in periodically too. Not that she was complaining. But she also remembered the way he rushed to her aid. The way his strong arms cradled her like she was too precious to let go of. The way his eyes smiled at her, which she didn't even know was possible. But she was sure she'd seen it.

So, she missed seeing him at the pool all week. Big whoop. It didn't mean anything. He was a tall, muscular stud in swim trunks that she got to check out while doing her job. And part of her job *was* to check him out … she had to make sure no one in the pool drowned, after all. It didn't necessarily mean she wanted to date him. But just because she wasn't interested in buying anything at the store didn't mean she couldn't window shop. Right?

She sighed and took another sip of wine. A crush. That's all this was. And now that she wouldn't see him for a while, she'd have time to get over whatever this feeling was that made her stomach seem like a home to no fewer than a thousand butterflies. Everything would go back to normal. She had to stay in control. Her mental health depended on it. The last man she dated nearly destroyed her. She felt too good to let anyone take away what months of work had given her.

Maybe this break would be just what she needed.

~

MAX SAT on his new couch and wondered what was happening. Between a virus taking over the world, people in a panic, and the news reporting customers buying obscene amounts of toilet paper, he wasn't sure if this was real life or some crazy movie he was living in. It seemed the whole world had gone crazy. And to top it all off, he had a brand-new leather couch that, although insanely comfortable, let out a loud fart sound each time he sat on it. *Lovely.* Hopefully that would go away. And soon.

Worst of all? He'd missed his chance with Hannah. He set his mind that he was going to ask her out. Well, that was the plan anyway. He was going to see if she'd like to grab a cup of coffee. Nothing elaborate. Something she could easily decline. And he anticipated that. Between his inability to be coherent around her and Hannah clearly being out of his league, this had "epic fail" written all over it.

But he couldn't fail at something he didn't do. As fate would have it, he didn't even get a chance. Hannah didn't teach class either day this week. He overheard that she was in meetings regarding the virus, and some dude was teaching class in her place. Her students seemed lost without her, quiet and bobbing around aimlessly in the water on autopilot mode. And clearly the guy didn't want to be sloshing around in the pool to oldies music. Then on Friday night, Johnny texted him that the gym would close until further notice. So, if all of this was any sign, he clearly wasn't meant to go out with Hannah. That was that. Loud and clear.

Maybe he'd set all this bad energy into motion when he decided to ask out the first woman he'd wanted in over a decade. Had he shocked the universe so much he'd triggered the end of the world? He doubted the universe cared that much. The timing was an eerie coincidence, though.

Well, there wasn't much he could do now. Perhaps he could get her info from Johnny. That seemed a little stalker-ish, though. He'd just have to bide his time. He was good at being alone. He'd manage.

But he wasn't alone for long.

"Uncle Max," a voice boomed as his niece ran through the living room, curls bouncing with every step she took, to give him a hug.

"You have a key already?"

"Well, since I'm kind of living here now, Mom gave me hers." She smiled, holding up her copy.

Max's older sister called him yesterday asking if Quinn could stay with him. There were so many unknowns about this virus, but one thing most agreed on was that it was a respiratory illness. Quinn had severe asthma, and since both of her parents worked at the hospital (her father was a doctor, and Max's sister a medical technologist), they asked Max if Quinn could stay with him since they had a higher chance of virus exposure. And because Max's office decided to let everyone work from home, his apartment was the perfect place for her to quarantine. As long as she didn't mind sleeping in the "cloffice". He'd volunteered to let her take his bed, but his sister insisted he sleep there since he was still recovering from an ankle fracture. Not that sleeping in his bed would help much, but his back would thank her later.

"I'm glad you're here." He really meant that. The large age gap between Max and his sister resulted in him having a niece who wasn't much younger than he was. Quinn was sixteen, but she had the maturity of someone much older. Though he was her uncle, he often felt more like her big brother, a role he very much loved. Since just about everyone in the country was on "lockdown" and unable to go anywhere, it was nice to have company. Maybe she could keep him from thinking about how much he wanted to see Hannah.

"I'm glad I'm here too. I really appreciate this. I know I'm crashing your bachelor pad," she said with a laugh.

"Oh yeah. My hoppin' bachelor pad. It sucks I had to

cancel all my major ragers I planned to host." He playfully nudged her with his elbow.

"Nerd. Okay, well, I'm going to go unpack and call Ciarra." She glanced behind him. "That's a really nice balcony, Uncle Max."

He followed her gaze. He'd forgotten about the balcony. The freezing weather he'd experienced since moving here wasn't exactly porch-sitting weather. But the sun was out in full force today, and the previous owners left behind brand new furniture he hadn't had a chance to use yet. Quinn went into her new room, and he decided it was time for a little warmth and fresh air.

His view from the balcony was breathtaking. The mountains of West Virginia had always captivated him. They were the perfect canvas for every season. In winter, the tops glistened with pure white snow; in the fall, they looked regal in bold colors the autumn sun magnified. Spring was just around the corner, and the faintest hints of buds that promised the start of a new season would soon pop in the trees with the sounds of birds as the soundtrack to accompany the majestic view.

As the late afternoon sun highlighted the vast land-scape, he thought about how lucky he was to live here. There were few things more beautiful than his home state. As he glanced at the balcony of his next-door neighbor, he had to focus on breathing. It was then he realized the most beautiful thing he'd *ever* seen evidently lived on the other side of his wall.

Chapter Six

The outdoors brought Hannah peace. The sun on her face, the picturesque view from her fourth-floor balcony, and the birds singing calmed her mind and allowed her to breathe a little slower. The heady scent of green tea in her favorite mug mixed with the smell of fresh air. It was one of the first warm days of the season, and even so, she needed a hoodie and long pants to feel comfortable. She was grateful to have her hot beverage to cuddle up with as she tucked her knees to her chest on the wicker couch. She breathed deeply to let the tension of the past week release with her exhale as the sun warmed her upturned face.

Cheering and laughing from children in the open lawn below grabbed her attention, so she got up to see what they were doing. Two young boys, probably preschool-aged, kicked around a ball in a loose attempt at playing soccer. One of the boys got so tired of missing the ball each time he kicked, he finally grunted, picked up the ball, and heaved it into the makeshift goal. She giggled at the sight.

But hers wasn't the only sound of laughter filling the air. And it wasn't coming from the boys, either. No, this was a man's laugh, and it seemed close by. Her eyes darted in all directions, and when she glanced to her left, she did a double take.

If a blizzard had instantly dropped six inches of snow on her balcony at that very moment, she would have been less surprised than when she saw who looked back at her. There he was—his dark hair blowing in the soft spring breeze, his warm smile making her knees all kinds of wobbly, and those unmistakable deep brown eyes entrancing her in his stare. She was standing a balcony away from someone she figured she wouldn't see for weeks, and she couldn't believe it. But there Max was—and she nearly lost her balance.

Luckily, she'd just practiced a few cleansing breaths because right now it was all she could do to keep air moving through her body at a pace that wouldn't cause her to pass out.

Max is my neighbor?

She knew someone had moved into the empty apartment a couple weeks ago. She never would have dreamt it was him. She pictured a musician living there but hadn't given much thought to her neighbor beyond that. His nightly acoustic performances were something she looked forward to. Though muffled by the wall between them, she could tell her neighbor had a smooth voice. It had the uncanny ability to make Hannah relax after just a couple of sung words.

"Hold on to that railing. If you start to fall now, there's no way I'd get there fast enough to rescue you this time." His half-smile was on full display. It was a little crooked, which made him even more attractive. Despite the chill in the air, she felt warm all of a sudden.

"Very funny. But if you attempted a rescue, I think you'd be violating the social distancing guidelines they're recommending," Hannah quipped back.

41

"All the more reason to be careful over there." He seemed much more relaxed than he had at the pool last week. His shoulders were low, his grin playful. He was the first person Hannah had talked to in person in about three days. She craved human interaction, and if these past few days were any indication, this lockdown wasn't going to be easy. Knowing that Max was just next door made her feel a little more relaxed. But why? She wasn't sure, but it was a welcomed feeling. Although they were on separate balconies, there was only about eight feet of space between them. She'd bet his apartment was the mirror image of hers.

"How are you enjoying your new place?" she asked.

"It's nice, but I've been so busy with work and running errands to get things set up, I haven't had enough time to relax and enjoy it. But I guess with the mandatory stay-at-home order, that's *all* I'll have time for."

Everyone was pretty much on house arrest at this point. About the only things you could do were go grocery shopping, get carryout, and go out for a walk (as long as you stayed six feet from everyone, that is).

"Maybe this will be over soon. I hope so, anyway. They closed the gym, as I'm sure you've heard by now. Are you still working on site?"

"No. My office is having everyone work from home. And I'm going to miss the gym. I was really enjoying regular workouts."

"Well, if we quarantine for fourteen days, that'll mean we're virus-free, and you could come over and work out with me if you'd like."

Wait—what?

Why had she said that? Just being neighborly. That's all. This was a global pandemic, for heaven's sake. She was trying to be nice in a time of crisis. It had nothing to do with wanting a sweaty Max in her apartment.

He'd say no. And he should. She was coming on way too strong. Imagining him in her

apartment, flexing those muscles she couldn't stop thinking about, wasn't helping.

Breathe, Hannah.

"I'd actually enjoy that." The apples of his cheeks reddened as he smiled. "I'm coming off an ankle injury and physical therapy, and I'd like to keep progressing. If you're offering, I'll accept."

His response surprised her. She figured he was just being nice because they were neighbors. After all, how awkward would it be if he rejected her offer to be workout partners in a pandemic? And then they'd have to see each other in the hallways of the building. Or maybe he was seeking her out for exercise training and advice. Besides, Hannah doubted he'd even remember this offer in two weeks, anyway.

But when she looked over at him flashing that half-smile that made her feel half-drunk, she got the feeling maybe it was something he *would* remember in a couple weeks' time. And Hannah mentally began counting down the days. She knew it was something she would not only remember but was truly looking forward to, as well.

OKAY, what just happened? In a matter of moments, Max discovered the woman he was crushing on lived next door to him, *and* he had an exercise date to look forward to. He'd all but given up on his shot with her, at least until the pandemic slowed. But there she was, literally, on the other side of his wall. Was this a sign? It was hard to deny that it was.

The next couple days dragged by. Warm weather in mid-March was a rarity in Wheeling, a fact made crystal clear by the drop in temperatures over the early part of the week. He so badly wanted to see her again, but he couldn't think of a way. He hadn't had the courage to get her number when they were on their balconies, and although he knew exactly where she lived, he couldn't exactly go knock on her door and run halfway down the hall to be at a safe distance to chat. That would seem desperate. And weird.

No, the new plan now was to wait for another warm day and hope that she would go out onto her balcony. But judging from the five-day forecast that displayed behind the chipper weather anchor on the evening news, it was going to be cloudy and cool for the rest of the week.

He sat at his kitchen table and began his latest work project. With Quinn in his office, he moved his supplies out there. The table was big enough for them each to sit and eat. It wasn't like he was a gourmet chef in need of lots of space to prepare fantastic meals, a fact made apparent with a second batch of lumpy pancakes. Quinn, the sweetheart she was, choked them down. It took her about three glasses of water to do so, but it was sweet she tried. For dinners, he relied heavily on delivery pizza and a couple of leftover meals his mom sent before the pandemic started. He'd smartly stashed them in his freezer and was grateful he had. As for what they'd be eating for dinners the rest of the week, he wasn't sure. He probably should have given that a little more thought, or at least watched a couple internet cooking tutorials.

Sometime after lunch, his phone rang. He was expecting a call from his boss, so it was a pleasant surprise when Johnny's name flashed on the screen.

"Hey, buddy!" his friend shouted through the phone. "How's it going?"

"This working from home gig isn't so bad. Having to plan meals because I can't keep ordering pizza for Quinn

44

isn't my favorite thing at the moment. How are you doing? Any news about the gym?" He felt bad his buddy was essentially out of work for however long this shutdown lasted.

"Actually, I've got some great news. I'm gonna be able to do some virtual training with my clients online, so I'm at least able to do some part of my job. I just got off a call with Hannah, and she's going to start livestreaming workout classes on the gym page, so that's good news too."

At the mere mention of her name, Max blushed.

This was the perfect segue to fill his buddy in on something he still couldn't quite believe himself. "So, um, about Hannah … as it turns out, she's my next-door neighbor."

"No. Freaking. Way. Are you kidding me right now?" Given their last conversation about Hannah, his response wasn't surprising.

"I'm not kidding at all." He proceeded to tell his buddy about the balcony encounter and subsequent workout proposal.

"Well, you know this is happening now," he said so loudly, Max had to move his phone away from his ear.

"Um, *what* exactly is happening? We can't get within six feet of each other, and my only hope of seeing her is if she happens to go sit on her balcony." It was in his nature to be positive, but even he had trouble seeing an upside to this situation.

Johnny sighed deeply. "Max. Listen. All along you've told me how you need to take your time, take things slow, take baby steps, blah, blah, blah. This whole situation is a gift. You have all the time you need to take it slow. This lockdown business is at least going to be a few weeks. Slow it down. Go out on the balcony if it's nice. If it's not, don't. Neither of you are going anywhere. This is your game. Slow and steady, buddy."

He made some good points. At a time when he didn't

feel like rushing in, he didn't have to. Besides, why would people want to rush something like this? Falling in love with Courtney was something he couldn't help himself from doing. But each little thing he'd learned about her, each new "first" they did together, and every stolen glance he got of her was something he deeply cherished. And at the end of it all, these little memories were the only things he had left. How much he'd have missed if they'd rushed in.

"Well, we'll see. I still have no idea if she likes me as anything more than a friend or even just a neighbor. But there's a comforting feeling just knowing she's nearby."

He then heard a knock at the door and told Johnny he'd check in with him later. The only person who ever stopped by unannounced was just on the phone with him, so he couldn't imagine who the unexpected visitor was. He looked through the peephole before opening the door. Oddly, no one was there. When he opened it, no one was in the hallway, either.

He was just about to shut the door when a piece of hot pink paper by his foot caught his eye. He picked it up and read it.

Hey, Neighbor!

I'm making a batch of tacos for dinner tonight and will have more than enough for just me. Knock twice on the wall if you'd like me to drop some off at your door later. I'd be more than happy to share.

-Hannah 😊

Had he hit the neighbor jackpot? Had she also been thinking of him? He sure hoped so. He'd definitely been thinking about her. A lot. In the days since they'd met on the balcony, all he wanted was to see her again. And now she was offering him a meal. He wished he could share it with her, but baby steps. Whether this was a good neighbor thing or an "I kinda like you" thing, he didn't know. But whatever kind of gesture this was, it truly touched him.

He shut the door, walked over to the wall that separated their apartments, and gave it two loud knocks.

Quinn walked out of her bedroom. "What are you doing?" she asked as she saw him beating on the wall like a caveman.

He smiled at how silly he must have looked to her. "Getting us dinner for tonight."

Really, he was taking the first step toward something he hadn't wanted in a long time.

And it wasn't tacos.

Chapter Seven

Hannah wasn't an amazing cook. She'd probably made more messes than successful meals in her lifetime. But she could make the heck out of tacos. They were something simple she could reheat after teaching later classes at the gym, and she had them at least once a week. That's why she had a freezer with assorted varieties of ground meats.

Her preparedness paid off because getting groceries with the lockdown was becoming quite a process. She was glad she'd gone on a bulk grocery shopping trip earlier last week. When she grabbed the meat out of the freezer last night, she took a chance and put more in the fridge to thaw than she normally would have. She kept thinking of Max. He'd just moved in a couple weeks ago, and he probably didn't even have all the kitchen supplies he needed for normal circumstances, much less a pandemic.

And then she heard him playing his guitar. She'd cursed at the thin walls when her old neighbors would have loud dinnertime sex seemingly against the wall they shared with Hannah. But when Max played his guitar, she was thankful for the paper-thin divider. It was a secret serenade she doubted he knew she could hear, but she was glad she could. He was truly talented.

"So, are you starting your campaign for Neighbor of the Year? Or maybe it's Girlfriend of the Year."

Hannah looked over at her tablet and caught the tail end of Angie's question, complete with a suggestive eyebrow waggle.

"Neither. I mean, I know it's not right to assume, but if he's like most guys, he probably isn't that kitchen savvy. You remember how thrown my dad was when my mom died—if your nonna hadn't taught me how to cook, we probably both would have starved to death." Hannah's dad was good at a lot of things, but cooking wasn't one of them.

"Nonna and I would have never let that happen—you know that," Angie responded. "This is so like you, though. Remember how you'd go home on weekends in college and make enough food for a few meals for your dad and stick them in the freezer, even though he told you not to?"

Hannah smiled. "I believe his exact words were: 'stop coming home and start having fun.'"

"But you always think of others. You always have."

As Hannah started browning the meat for tonight's tacos, she had a funny thought.

"You know, I haven't cooked anything for anyone since my dad." Sure, she and Angie would cook together when they had shared an apartment, but there was something special about fixing a whole meal for someone to enjoy. And she had never cooked for Pete. He always preferred going out to swanky restaurants. He and Hannah didn't live together, so he always suggested dining out. If he'd paid her any attention, he'd have known a night at home, sharing a meal and watching a movie, were all she needed to be happy. But deep down, she didn't think he cared. From the beginning, it was always about what Pete wanted.

49

How hadn't she realized that sooner? He'd even taken her to a fancy restaurant to break up with her. *Jerk.*

"Well, that's what makes you special, Hannah Banana —your big heart. Just remember to read your labels. Don't go putting cinnamon in the mix instead of chili powder again."

Hannah shivered at the memory. "That's a mistake you only make once." If she closed her eyes, she could still taste the bitterness on her tongue.

She finished the tacos, signed off with Angie, and put the different toppings for the meal into small LocknLock containers. She didn't normally lend those to people because when she did, she rarely got them back. But she knew where Max lived, and she could hunt down her favorite little bins if needed.

The pile of small containers, stacked like children's blocks, definitely needed a bag. Her reusable grocery totes were in the trunk of her car parked outside, and with the rain pounding on her windows, she decided to search through her gift bag stash for something to use. She decided on a bag with a snowman with sunglasses and a saxophone and the script "Have a Cool Yule" at the top, since Christmas bags seemed to be all she had. She was a sucker for anything with a witty saying, which was why she had a rather large collection of graphic tees with various mottos on them. They usually made people smile when they read them, and she lived to make people happy.

As she walked into the hallway, she noticed a bag sitting in front of Max's door. *I guess I'm not the only one taking care of him.* But when she set her snowman bag beside it, she spotted a tag that read "Hannah" perched on top. Surprised, she peeked into the bag and saw a note.

You took care of dinner, so it's only fair I take care of dessert. I hope you like these—they're all I had. They may or may not have been a part of my dinner this evening if you hadn't been so thoughtful to offer me some of yours. So, thank you. Also, here's my number. If you need anything at all, I'd love to repay this favor.

-Max

When she looked to see what was in the bag, she squealed with glee. Max had stuffed about thirty fun-size Kit Kats in it, her absolute favorite candy. She gave a knock on the door to let Max know his food was waiting, and she walked to her apartment. Before she opened the door, she hesitated so she could see him come out to grab the meal.

"Thanks. They're my favorite," she shouted in his direction as she raised the bag.

"Mine too," Max answered. "My second favorite food —right behind tacos." He gave her that signature half-smile that made her stomach do funny things. She returned the smile as she opened the door. Glancing at the note again, she saved his number to her contacts. Then she decided to text him, you know, so he'd have her number. It's what a good neighbor would do, right?

Hey, this is Hannah. I'm sending a customer satisfaction survey for your dinner this evening. Seriously though—I hope you enjoy it!

She made herself a plate of tacos, poured a glass of wine, and turned on QVC while she relaxed to the sound of rain outside the windows of her apartment. With any luck, she'd enjoy her Kit Kats to the musical stylings of the neighbor she couldn't stop thinking about.

Everything was perfect until she thought about how much better the evening would be if Max was on Hannah's side of the wall with her. If they could snuggle and enjoy an evening sharing a meal and watching TV just like she'd always wanted to do with someone. But this time, she didn't want to do that with *someone*. She wanted to do it with Max. Although, the last time she was with a man, she lost herself in him. And it nearly ruined her.

On second thought, maybe she wasn't ready to go

down that road again. Her mental health depended on her being in control. And the way her stomach flipped when Max smiled at her tonight? Clearly her control took a hike when it came to him. They could be neighbors, friends even, but nothing more. She couldn't let him in. Especially not now. Her routine was such a mishmash these days, with not being able to go the gym for work and exercise. Anxiety inched its way in a little further each day. It was incrementally getting worse, but it was still manageable.

But right at this moment, while she thought about how her life had turned upside down in a matter of days and with no end in sight, the anxiety she felt trickling in began to gush.

She took a deep breath to calm her nervous system, but it didn't quiet her mind as much as she wanted. Sweat beaded on the back of her neck, and the pressure on her forehead felt like an unrelenting grip. It tightened with no mercy and caused her head to pound. She closed her eyes and tried to take more deep breaths but felt physically incapable of controlling the speed of her breathing. As its pace increased, Hannah feared hyperventilation was on the horizon.

Just as she reached the point of the attack where she'd usually lose the ability to hear anything but muffled noises and the thumping in her head, music filtered through her apartment.

The strumming of a guitar, the only thing she could hear, stole her attention. The tune was familiar, though she couldn't put her finger on it right away. But the best part? She could actually *hear* it.

Her shoulders lowered from her ears, her jaw unclenched, and her breathing slowed. As Max sang the lyrics to Coldplay's "Fix You," one of Hannah's favorite songs, she started to cry. Not because she was in the throes of a panic attack (and she was), but because she knew, despite all the work she'd done, she wasn't who she used to be. Maybe she was beyond repair. She hadn't had an attack like that since she moved here. But on a positive note, she'd never come out of one so calmly and quickly. With her mind silenced, she closed her eyes and listened to Max.

The past few nights, sleep hadn't come easily to her. So, when she awoke on the couch, in the exact same place she'd had an anxiety attack the night before, she couldn't believe it. As the morning sun poured in through the window, she realized she'd not only slept, but she'd slept through the entire night. She felt rested for the first time since the pandemic started. And when she remembered the last thing she could about the previous night, she heard Max's lullaby in her head. Coming fresh off a time when the closest man in her life caused nothing but stress and panic, she had a hard time believing one could be capable of the exact opposite. But the proof was there. She spent the next several minutes staring at the wall that separated them, wondering why she wasted so much time settling for so much less than what she deserved.

Chapter Eight

The morning sun barely peeked above the hillside, but Max already heard activity in his apartment. He walked out of his room to make his daily brew when he noticed Quinn's breakfast dishes already washed and in the drain rack, her iPad and several books scattered around her on the kitchen table.

"What's going on here?" He didn't think teenagers were supposed to wake up until closer to lunchtime.

"It's my first day back from Spring Break, and I've got virtual class today. A couple of us are going to meet on Zoom early to nail down a few last details for a group project," Quinn responded. Her professional tone had her uncle wondering if she was sixteen and preparing school-work or thirty-five and prepping for a board meeting. Boy, high school had sure changed a lot since he'd been there.

"It's our first attempt at online learning, and I wanted to be ready."

Max shook his head. "Well, color me impressed." He wasn't immature as a teen, but he certainly didn't have the self-discipline Quinn did. She was always at the top of her class, and she worked so hard in the off-season to be at the top of her game each year for soccer. It wasn't the acco-lades she earned that her uncle admired—though they were certainly numerous and well-deserved—but he respected her work ethic. Sure, Max graduated in the top ten of his class, and he'd collected several awards throughout his baseball career. But his biggest takeaway from his high school and college days? He learned how much hard work paid off. Quinn had clearly gotten that message.

"Okay, well, I'm going to get some work done myself." He felt a little extra push to be productive after seeing Quinn's set-up. No need to demonstrate his proficiency in slacking off. Even if his job was slowly sucking out his soul, ounce by ounce, day by day.

Late afternoon turned to early evening much too slowly for Max's liking. He stepped out onto the balcony in desperate need of some fresh air. The monotony of his job was killing him. The change of scenery provided by working from home had helped, but it didn't take his brain long to realize he was still doing the same boring stuff, just in a different place. He sat down on the wicker chair and saw Hannah relaxing on her outdoor couch, snuggling with a fuzzy blanket to keep away the slight chill in the air. She had earbuds in and watched something on an iPad. He assumed whatever she was watching was set to music by the way her head rhythmically moved.

She'd piled her long, blonde hair on top of her head, and had glasses perched on her nose. It gave her a sexy look, and he couldn't take his eyes away. He noticed her cozy sweatshirt and chuckled softly. On it appeared to be several tiny cactus-like plants in party hats and sunglasses with the script "Life Doesn't Suc" across the top. Her appearance, her demeanor, her clothing—everything about this woman made Max smile. Though their interac-tions to this point had been few, he felt this aura of happi-

55

ness surrounding her. The ladies in her water aerobics class must have felt it too. That was probably why so many of them came to her class. And was likely the reason they looked completely disgusted when that sad guy subbed in to teach last week. Even now, after sitting and working at his computer for the past several hours, he magically felt happier just being in her presence.

Her eyes darted up and caught him looking at her. Well, not so much *looking.* More like gaping. Yep, he'd been caught.

"Well, hello, neighbor." The grin on her face definitely said *I saw you staring at me.*

Max looked down, unable to summon the courage to look at her again. "Came out to get some fresh air and a little sunshine. Also, thanks for the dinner last night. You really didn't have to do that, but I'm glad you did. The tacos were delicious."

"You're absolutely welcome. I was happy to do it." Her eyes sparkled beneath the lens of her glasses. "I think we're lucking out with the weather these days, don't you?"

"Oh, definitely. Are you from around here?" He already knew the answer to that. Johnny told him she was new in town, but he needed some way to continue the conversation. The longer they chatted, the longer she'd stay out. And he wanted her to stay out here with him. Badly.

"Not really. I mean I'm familiar with the weather for the area, but I'm not from here. Pittsburgh, actually. You?"

"I'm a Mountaineer," he proudly declared, pointing to the WVU Baseball logo on the sweatshirt he wore. "Born and raised right here in Wheeling. So, I guess I should welcome you, although you've lived in this building longer than I have, so I'm sure someone already has by now." Why did he say such lame things around her all the time?

"Not really," she chuckled. "I've lived here about nine

months, but I haven't had a proper welcome from an actual Mountaineer, so thanks for that. I came down here for work."

"How do you like it at the gym?"

She clasped her hands at her chest and let out a tiny squeak. "I absolutely love it. I couldn't think of a job more perfect for me. I'd originally applied because I have PR experience, but when my boss found out I had group exercise teaching experience as well, he was elated and put me in charge of scheduling the classes I'd be teaching and promoting."

"Sounds like a perfect fit. Have you gotten to go anywhere fun since you've been here?"

"Um, not too many places. I don't know a lot of people here, so I feel silly going out a bunch by myself. I've hit a few of the running trails. I've walked a few at Oglebay Park, but I'd love to go back up there when the weather breaks to visit the zoo and some other attractions. My parents brought me a few times when I was a kid, but I was too young to remember. They loved it there." She closed her eyes briefly, and her shoulders raised and lowered with the inhale and exhale of her deep breath. Maybe she missed her folks? And with the lockdown order, who knew when she'd get back to Pittsburgh to see them, if that was even where they lived. It didn't seem the time to ask, so he didn't.

"It's a beautiful place. I go there a lot. Tons to do and see, that's for sure." He changed the subject. "What were you watching on your iPad? I'm looking for some new shows to binge since we're suddenly stuck inside our apartments now." If the pandemic canceled baseball season, he was going to be both devastated and bored stiff.

"Oh, just watching some workout videos and doing a little research." She bit her lower lip as her eyes dropped to the iPad. "With the lockdown and the gym being closed, I

57

pitched the idea to maybe livestream some classes for our members to keep them moving."

"I heard. That's great news."

She froze and squinted her eyes. "That just got approved yesterday. And it hasn't been made public. I mean, I would know since I'm the media director, and I haven't posted it yet." She leaned forward, one brow rising above the frame of her glasses. "So, how did you hear this?"

He had two options: he could tell her Johnny told him, which would mean they'd been talking about her. Or he could make something up. But what, exactly? He'd never been good at improvising on the fly, so he opted for the truth. She'd already caught him staring at her. He didn't want to add lying to his resume today too. "Johnny told me."

Her eyes rounded. "Wait, you know Johnny?" Hannah seemed surprised. She'd learn soon enough how small towns worked.

"Yep. He's been my best friend since second grade." He did a mental double-take. He'd never really stopped to think about how they'd been friends for over two decades.

"Well, I had no idea. Johnny was one of the first people to befriend me at the gym. He showed me the ropes and introduced me to a lot of people there."

Of course. That was classic Johnny. He knew everyone and even claimed to know people he didn't. By the end of a short conversation with them, he actually did.

"He's a good guy. I'm lucky to have had him as a friend all these years."

Hannah rubbed a hand against her chest. "That must be nice. My best friend lives back in Pittsburgh. I don't see her nearly enough." She shrugged halfheartedly. "She's really all I have right now."

Her best friend was the only person in her life right

now? That was a sad thought, but also … did that mean she didn't have a boyfriend? He'd make a mental note to come back around to that another time.

"Max?" She said his name softly, a pitch or two higher than she normally spoke. "Would you mind if I asked you a small favor?"

Um, I'd do anything you asked. "Not at all. What do you need?"

She glanced away from him and once again bit her lower lip. Why did she keep bringing his attention there? He doubted she did it on purpose, but he didn't need her help for his eyes to linger on the area.

"So, like I said, I'm going to start livestreaming a few classes. I was wondering if you could log on to my first one and watch." She shook her head and waved a dismissive hand. "This probably seems weird, and I shouldn't ask. I don't know—I'm hoping you can give me some feedback. I feel like teaching to a computer screen, seemingly to no one, will be a little tricky. And I've already discovered everything is backwards to the camera." She glued her eyes back to her tablet. "Would you be willing to watch a class and let me know if I'm cueing right and left correctly? And maybe tell me whether or not I look robotic?" She looked up slowly. Her blue eyes reminded him of two pools of water, refreshing and inviting—appropriate since he usually felt a little warm in her presence. They pleaded with him to fulfill this small ask.

Was she for real? In the pool, he worked like it was a fulltime job to keep from watching her teach. He didn't want to seem like Captain Creepy. And now she was asking him to do exactly that?

"I can absolutely do that," he replied. With maybe a little too much gusto. *Reel it in, buddy.*

She blew out a long breath from her puffed cheeks. "Great. I really appreciate it. There'll be participants. I

59

think I've got things under control enough to teach the first one, but a little feedback would help if the classes become a regular event." She smiled. She had no idea what that smile could get him to do.

"My niece is staying with me. I know she's been bummed she can't get out for her workouts, so maybe she'd like to join the class," he noted, hoping to take the attention away from his overzealous response a moment ago.

"Oh, really? So, you're babysitting during the pandemic?"

"No. No. Not babysitting. She's sixteen and probably more capable being home alone than I am." He laughed because it was true. "Both of her parents work at the hospital, and she has severe asthma. They didn't want her to stay at their house in case they came in contact with the virus."

"That's kind of you to let her stay with you."

"Ah, it's no biggie. We're family. That's what families do for each other," he said but almost wished he hadn't. His words pulled a dimmer switch that controlled her eyes, and he didn't know how to illuminate them again. She slowly gathered up her things like she was preparing to go back inside. Then, Max blurted out an idea.

"I feel like we should get to know each other a little better, being neighbors in a pandemic and all," he rattled off quickly. His heart couldn't take her leaving with that look on her face.

"Oh yeah?" A smile returned and a slight twinkle shone in her eyes. "What do you want to know?"

"Well, what if we played a little game? Maybe like 'Would You Rather?' But let's call it 'This or That.' Each night someone can give the other two things to choose from, and that person has to pick what he or she likes most. If you say 'neither,' you have to answer another one." *So lame*, he thought as he heard himself blabber on about the game. But it was the best he could come up with.

"Sounds like it could be fun. I'm in. Who goes first? My vote is you since you came up with this."

"Okay, I can live with that. Let me think. Alright ... Kit Kats or tacos?"

She giggled and snorted adorably when she tried to stop.

"Oh, hun. You know that bag of Kit Kats you gave me? I'm embarrassed to admit this, but it's half gone already." She blocked her face with her hand as though she was embarrassed by the admission and walked to the door. She looked back at him and smiled. "Goodnight, Max."

"Goodnight."

He didn't know what was sexier: her laugh or her legs in those yoga pants she just revealed when she removed her blanket and walked away. One thing was for sure—if she really *did* eat half a sack of Kit Kats, he definitely couldn't see where she was hiding them.

Chapter Nine

Hannah looked around her apartment. She'd pushed the coffee table to the living room wall, and her small couch found a new home a few feet away from its usual spot. Nodding approvingly, she figured this would be enough room for her first livestreamed exercise class. The few practice runs she'd done ended abruptly with her either kicking or punching a piece of furniture. She'd never thought of her apartment as small, but an aerobics studio was much larger, a fact validated by her throbbing foot and fist.

She'd been teaching since her senior year of college and had easily taught hundreds of classes over that time. So why did she tremble with nerves at the thought of what she was about to do later this afternoon?

Oh yeah. Now she remembered.

Why did I ask him to watch?

That was a good question, actually. Johnny could have tuned in and given her a critique. Heck, she could have asked Angie to log on and let her know how it looked. But, oh no. She just had to ask her hunky next-door neighbor. And this was totally different than when he'd seen her at the pool. He had his own workout occupying him then. Today, he'd literally be watching her, like a show on television. She would have kicked herself if her foot wasn't still sore from accidentally kicking the coffee table earlier.

When the clock showed 4:25 in seemingly the blink of an eye, she secretly hoped Max had an urgent work issue and would be unable to catch the live broadcast. Did web designers actually have workplace emergencies? Probably not. She doubted that would stop him, anyway. He seemed like someone who kept his promises.

She took a deep breath, hit the "Live" button on her screen, and waited for viewers to join the feed. The very first person to enter, of course, was her stud of a neighbor. As other names popped up on the screen, indicating they were also watching, she saw a message pop up from a viewer. But not just any viewer.

Max Robertson: You've got this Hannah! :)

Her shoulders relaxed, her cheeks warmed, and the tightness in her stomach from moments ago was replaced with a fluttery feeling that was very noticeable but much more tolerable. She was ready for this.

"Welcome, everyone!" she said to her forty-five viewers … and counting. This was huge! She could never get that many people to safely fit in the aerobics studio for a class, so an audience of this size was unchartered territory for her. But she loved it. She'd always wanted a platform where she could reach more people. Knowing this many were looking to her to help get some endorphins flowing made her heart soar.

Then, she received a surprise message from a familiar face.

Renee Morris: Hannah!!!!! I learned how to use the Facebook for this! Go get 'em, Hannah Banana!

She couldn't believe her eyes. On a pretty regular basis, she'd heard Renee complain about technology. She didn't even own a cell phone. But the fact she learned how to create a Facebook account and log in to the workout meant a lot.

"Alright, we're gonna get this party started. Who's ready to sweat?" Hannah laughed when she remembered she was in an empty room and not her usual aerobics studio. "Okay, well, usually I get a loud cheer as a response, but I'm just now realizing I can't hear any of you." She shook her head. This class, like so many other things in the world right now, was suddenly so different because of the pandemic. She hoped the workout would bring some sense of normalcy to her members ... and herself. "Anyway, I hope you cheered from home."

As she turned to hit "play" to start the music, she heard a loud "oh yeah" from the other side of her living room wall. She laughed and smiled so hard, she thought her face might crack. It was the perfect way to start her class, so she did.

THE PAST WEEK hadn't been the best for Hannah. But this moment right now? Well, it was one she would savor long after the pandemic ended. Not only had she taught what she deemed a very successful class, but over eighty people joined in. Hopefully it would grow once word got out this would be a regular event with the gym closed. For as lost as she felt at the onset of the quarantine, she felt she'd really found herself again. And there was no better feeling.

To her surprise, the person she most wanted to talk to was the only person she couldn't even see right now. The physical distance between them mocked her. And with the rain hammering her window yet again, it looked like a balcony chat with Max this evening was out of the question, as well. Her ringtone interrupted her thoughts, and when she saw the name flash on her screen, her face lit up brighter than the lightning illuminating the dark sky.

"Hi. I'm looking for the instructor who taught the aerobics class on the gym's Facebook page. I don't want to take too much of her time because, judging by how many people tuned in, she's going to be a local celebrity by tomorrow," Max rattled off before she could so much as say "hello" herself. Flattered, she was speechless for a beat.

"You're a sweetheart. But I couldn't believe how many people were there!" The class ended a little over an hour ago, yet the shock remained.

"Is this going to be a regular thing? Because I think with so many people interested, it probably should be."

Hannah nodded. "That's my goal. I didn't get my hopes up too much. I thought I'd get maybe a quarter of that many members to join. I had no idea how many would be open to taking a class in this format, but I'm pleasantly surprised." She never expected this response. This was her idea—she set everything up, promoted it as much as she could in the small window of time she had, and got the music together. This was her baby. And the fact that others were so receptive brought her so much pride.

"I really thought you did an amazing job. It must have been weird not having faces to feed off of, but you were a true professional in every sense of the word." She blushed. He could have said she looked nice, her moves were good, or something more superficial, but he chose to compliment her professionalism, and that meant more to her than anything else he could have said. And she wanted him to know that.

"Hold on a sec." Before she could talk herself out of it, she hit the video call button on her phone. When Max answered, she was not at all prepared for what she saw. Oh no, what she saw was a gorgeous man with his signature, impeccable 5 o'clock shadow … and no shirt.

65

"Oh, I'm sorry. Am I interrupting something?" she asked, her face burning hotter than that time she and Angie spent all day on the lake with no sunscreen to "get a little color." Blood red was definitely a color. "I should have asked first before I video called you. I just wanted to thank you for watching and also for the message before class started. That really helped me relax and settle in." The shirtless man on the screen had the opposite effect, a fact demonstrated by her rapid speech.

He flashed a smile that resembled the one she probably sported when she read his message. She smiled back to buy her a minute before she spoke. Coherent thoughts eluded her at the moment. She couldn't see much of him, but his chiseled chest and muscled shoulders were enough to scramble her brain.

"First, don't be sorry. I'm happy to see you. I figured we'd catch each other on the balcony, but it seems Mother Nature had other plans. Second, you're not interrupting anything—I just took a shower because I was pretty sweaty." He raked his hands through his damp hair, the pieces flopping perfectly back into place. She wished her phone had the capable technology to reach through the screen and run her fingers through it as well. "And last, I'm glad the message did exactly what it was intended to do."

Now *she* was the one sweating. Knowing he cared how she felt did something funny to her insides. But wait … did he say he was sweating?

"Max … did you actually *do* the class?"

"Of course! You asked me to critique it. How could I give a thorough analysis of a class I didn't take?"

Hannah's eyes widened, and her brows disappeared into her hairline.

"But, Max … it was an aerobics *dance* class."

"While I wasn't aware of that *before* class started, I certainly am now," he said with a laugh. And then he wasn't the only one busting a gut. The thought of all six foot, four inches of a ruggedly handsome Max booty shaking and shimmying was too much for Hannah to handle, and literal tears rolled down her cheeks as they both laughed for the better part of a few minutes. She hadn't laughed like that in a long time. Maybe ever. Boy, did it feel good.

"Thank you for that. All of it. Thanks for the laugh. Thanks for the support. I still can't believe you did the class, but I'm truly grateful. And I heard your shout out through the wall just before class began. It was great."

"Oh, so I better watch what I say if you can hear me so easily," he said with a chuckle.

"Well, that's the only thing I've heard so far. Aside from your guitar playing, that is."

His smile disappeared so quickly, it was as though someone hit the *delete* button.

"You, uh, you can hear me play?" He rubbed his stubble with his free hand.

Oh geez. Should she not have mentioned that? Too late now.

"Yeah, I mean, I kind of look forward to it." She fiddled with the hem of her workout top. "It's the highlight of most of my nights if I'm honest." Omitting the part about his music pulling her out of one of the most intense panic attacks she'd ever had was probably for the best. Better not to spook him, especially since the mention of hearing him play seemed to earn a negative reaction from him. But the firm line of his mouth melted like chocolate warming on the tongue, and the smile that appeared on his face was even sweeter.

"Well, I didn't know I had listeners, but I guess since I do, I'm glad it's someone who enjoys it," he said as his chin dipped down and he rubbed the back of his neck.

"I love it," Hannah blurted.

67

He looked up at her on the screen. His eyes twinkled with something Hannah couldn't quite decipher. And although the picture on her phone wasn't perfectly clear, she swore they appeared a little glassy. He looked at her like she'd told him something that touched a tender place in his soul. And if that's truly what happened, she'd tell him she loved his playing over and over just to touch that spot again. But when he cleared his throat, she realized he actually was a little emotional. And because he'd been such a gentleman the other night and changed the subject when he sensed she didn't want to talk about her parents, she extended him the same courtesy.

"Hey, Max. I've gotta ask, you know, for getting-to-know-your-neighbor purposes as well as a gym member survey: this or that—walking in the pool or dance aerobics?"

He laughed without abandon as he shook his head and looked up at the ceiling.

"You know, that's a tough one." He made a show of tapping his finger on his chin. "I'll have to take the dance aerobics class a few more times to see how my butt improves," Max said, still chuckling.

She bit her tongue. Hard. She didn't want to blurt out that his plump rump was perfection, something that had made her speechless at the pool.

"You're an amazing teacher, though. The class was fun, exhausting, and everything you'd want in a workout class. You're a natural, Hannah." Then, Max let out a sigh. "But to answer your question—if I had to pick right now, I'd say I'll take any class where I get to see a smile like yours while I'm taking it. It makes any workout enjoyable."

Before that moment, Hannah would have said it was physically impossible for internal organs to melt. But try telling that to her heart as it puddled on the floor around her.

Chapter Ten

Max sat on his couch watching *Good Morning Football* while answering work emails and sipping his coffee. Finished with the mug, he reached forward to place it on the coffee table and stifled a moan.

"What's wrong with you?" Quinn asked in a tone that sounded, frankly, a little judge-y. He apparently hadn't suppressed his whine enough. And also, he hadn't realized she was in the room.

"Oh, uh, just a little sore." He would have shrugged, but his shoulders hurt too much.

Quinn laughed. "From what? Hannah's exercise class? That was three days ago."

True, but clearly the moving and shaking he did that afternoon woke up muscles he hadn't worked in a while (if ever), and they were obviously ticked at him. The morning after the workout, parts of him ached, others burned, and everything moved in slow motion. He was ashamed his college athlete body was betraying him in this way, but it was apparent his thirty-year-old physique was not the same as it was in his early twenties.

"Yea, I'm sorry I can't just jump out of bed like a Pop Tart flying out of a toaster like you, dear niece who is half my age," he grumbled.

"Need I remind you I'm in off-season training? I might have a slight advantage over you these days. Plus, you're just coming off your ankle injury. In fact, you might want to come with me for some extra training at Hannah's. We think it would be a fun time."

Anything with Hannah would be a fun time.

"Whoa, wait—what do you mean? You're going over to Hannah's? Since when did you talk to her … or even meet her for that matter?" It's possible he hadn't been keeping an eye on his niece's whereabouts as much as he should.

"Yesterday afternoon while you were on that Zoom call for work. I went out for some fresh air and to read for my English class, and she was out there. We got talking about Shakespeare, she helped me start my essay for my lit assignment, and we hung out a bit. She's awesome."

He was well aware. And his lack of a poker face must have been glaringly obvious to his niece. She crossed her arms and narrowed her eyes at him, a slow smile building on her face. Why did it feel like an interrogation was about to take place?

"What's that goofy grin, Uncle Max? Do you *like* her?"

Well, that was a loaded question that was a little tricky to answer. The simple response was "yes," but nothing in life was simple. He thought he was ready to slowly step back into dating, but when Hannah mentioned the other night that she'd heard him play numerous times in the few weeks he'd lived there, he suddenly felt raw and exposed, emotions he hadn't experienced in quite some time. It was an intimate moment Hannah didn't even know she was sharing with him. She didn't know what he'd been through in the past few years. And she certainly didn't know she was the first person to hear him play since Courtney died.

Then he remembered his first and only love and whether he truly was ready to take this step. He contemplated not just whether he was ready but if he even could.

"She seems like a great person," he answered curtly, fully knowing she wasn't going to leave this alone. She was more a sister to him than his own, and although his actual sister had been by his side to comfort him through his grief following the accident, Quinn had been there for him just as much as Johnny.

"I think my English teacher is a 'great person,'" she said, holding up the novel he'd assigned. "But my face doesn't do whatever yours is doing when I think about him."

Max wrinkled his nose. "Isn't Mr. Bell like sixty? He was there when I was in high school."

"Not the point, and you know it. Seriously, though, it's okay if you do like her. I mean, you're allowed."

It was silly she'd even have to say something like that, but part of him felt relieved at hearing it. She had been close to Courtney too. Since Quinn always hung around Max's parents' house after school until her own parents could pick her up, she was around Courtney a lot when she'd stop by, which was quite often since Courtney lived two doors down and was best friends with her uncle. She knew how much Courtney meant to Max, and she also knew how hard the past three years had been for him.

"I thought I was ready. I really did. Johnny's been trying to get me back out and meet people, and I was ready to try. I even intended to go out a couple weeks ago, but I got a flat tire."

"That's great! So, what's the problem?"

"Quinn, I haven't been on a first date in ten years. And part of me thought when I did take that step, it would be with just a regular girl who I was minimally interested in, we'd have an average time, and that would be it. The mile-

71

stone would be merely something crossed off a list. There'd be no fireworks, no chemistry, and therefore no buildup … and no letdown."

"Wow," she deadpanned. "Good thing you don't write romance novels." She chuckled softly before she continued. "Hey, maybe God's throwing you a bone. After the hell you've been through, you deserve something good. Maybe something great."

His eyes stung, and Quinn's features blurred. "Do you know when I first saw Hannah?" He paused, still unable to get over the irony. "My birthday."

"Well, then it was God's birthday present to you. Even better."

Max saw the moment she put the pieces together. "Oh my."

And then he wasn't the only one in the room with watery eyes.

"The other night, she said she'd been listening to me play. She said she loved it." His voice dropped to just above a whisper. "Quinn, I haven't played for *anyone* since Courtney died. And here, I've been playing for her for weeks and didn't even know it."

She opened her mouth to speak but then paused for a beat. "Well, okay. Is that bad?"

"Uh, no. It's just when she was telling me how much she enjoyed it, her eyes lit up in a way I haven't seen eyes light since Courtney's did when she'd listen to me." It wasn't even the way Hannah looked at him. It was the way he felt when she had. It sucked the breath from him, and he suddenly had a visceral impulse to run down the hallway and rush into her apartment just so he could put his arms around her. Just so he could be near her. Like a magnet to a fridge, an unstoppable force pulled him toward her, and he couldn't stop it if he tried.

And that's how he knew dating Hannah wouldn't be

the casual first date experience he was hoping to have this first time out the gate. There was nothing ordinary about the way he instinctively felt about her. And, frankly, that scared the heck out of him.

"Look, I'm no relationship expert, and I'm not going to pretend to be," Quinn started, interrupting his thoughts. "But maybe all these signs are pointing to you taking that step. Meeting her on your birthday. Finding out you're next-door neighbors. Being practically quarantined together. If you were looking for the right time or right circumstances or the perfect sign, I think you're blind if you don't see how ideal this all is." She rounded the kitchen island to put an arm around him. "All I'm saying is why don't you channel your inner Ross Geller, stop leering over your Rachel, and grab a spoon?"

It was just like her to have the perfect thing to say to make him smile. And referencing a scene from his all-time favorite show was a great way to do that. Yes, there were many flavors of ice cream in this world, but the only flavor he wanted was on the other side of that wall.

He looked down at his computer screen and noticed the date in the corner. They'd both quarantined for twelve days, meaning on day fourteen, this Friday, they'd be free to see each other face to face and be within six feet of each other.

He was grabbing that spoon.

Before a tiny part in his brain could convince him otherwise, he reached for his phone and opened the text box.

Max: *Do you have any plans Friday evening?*

He took a deep breath and blew it out in a long exhale, figuring he'd have to wait a while to hear back from her. But to his surprise, the three little dots danced on his screen, and he'd never been so happy to see them.

Hannah: *If this is my "this or that" question for the day and you're asking if I'd rather sit in my apartment alone or spend the evening hanging out with you, I'll answer by asking what time, and should I bring tacos?*

It was a small step for most people but ginormous for Max. The excitement buzzed through him like electricity, sparking him to life. He'd all but forgotten Quinn was sitting across the table from him until he looked up and saw a smile on her face that rivaled his in both size and sheer joy.

"Well, there ya go. I'm proud of you, Uncle Max. It's about time you went out for ice cream."

Chapter Eleven

Hannah missed people. A lot. She craved human interaction like most people craved pumpkin-spiced everything the minute the calendar flipped to September. This quarantine really highlighted how much she needed to be around others. Which was why she was *really* looking forward to tonight.

At this point, she would have settled for company with anyone she could strike up a conversation with. Well, anyone who wasn't a houseplant. She'd been chatting poor Channing's ears off—well, if he had ears. But an actual man who seemed as kind as he was handsome had invited her to spend an evening with him, and suddenly this quarantine was looking up.

She spent the afternoon listening to music and cooking the taco meat for tonight's dinner. Now it was time to pick out an outfit. She told herself this wasn't a date. Adding that title weighted the night a little more than she was comfortable with. But still. There seemed to be a little more importance to it than simply two friends hanging out. But really, that's all it was. Plus, she wasn't into dating right now anyway, so calling it one was a thought that needed to skedaddle.

"So, whatcha wearing tonight?" Angie asked from the tablet screen. When the two of them lived together, they pumped music and got ready with lots of lip-synching and hip-shaking. Thanks to modern technology, a version of that tradition continued.

Hannah pressed her lips together and took a step back from her closet to see what she was working with. "I dunno. I want to look put together, but not like I'm trying too hard. How about this?" She held up a graphic tee that said "Let's Taco Bout It." Totally cheesy but totally appropriate.

"You do realize you have a graphic tee collection so large, you have the perfect one for literally every occasion, right? And you know how much I loathe the overuse of the word 'literally,' right? But you literally do."

"You know it. Give me a sec to put this on." She stepped off screen. "Don't want to turn this into a digital get-down."

Angie laughed. "Ah, 'N SYNC—so ahead of their time."

Hannah gave her shirt a half-tuck and added her simple monogrammed gold chain she always wore, a gift from her dad for her sixteenth birthday. She stepped back in front of the laptop screen and struck a pose.

Angie threw up two enthusiastic thumbs up. "Perfect."

Hannah dumped some makeup on the table next to the laptop and squirted some foundation on the back of her hand.

"This is so much different than when you used to get ready for a night out with Pete."

Hannah's foundation brush froze mid-swirl on her hand. "Well, yeah—this is totally different. I mean, we're just friends hanging out."

"True. But that's how you and Pete started out too." Angie dramatically raised a brow.

Hannah thought back to the nights she'd scurry to put together a super chic outfit for a trendy place Pete insisted on going to. And her hands began to shake.

She liked feeling in control of most aspects of her life, but she couldn't control her intruding thoughts and feelings —she could only control how she reacted to them. The anxiety rushed in, but instead of letting it settle inside her, she successfully diffused it, something she would have never been able to do a year ago. She thought of how far she'd come, and smiled. Small victories were still victories, after all.

"Why so smiley? Thinkin' bout your new boo?"

Amid the near-panic attack, Hannah nearly forgot Angie was there. "Huh? Yeah. I mean—no. He's not my boo."

"Whatever you say, Hannah Banana."

"He can't be."

Angie's brows knit together. "Why not?"

"He just can't." Hannah shook her head side to side rapidly. "I couldn't do that to someone."

Angie leaned closer to the screen. "Do what, exactly?"

Where should she begin? "I have a lot of baggage from my last relationship, as you know." In her head, she still heard Pete telling her she was *too much to handle*. He never meant that in a good way. Her anxiety was inconvenient for Pete, and he reminded her regularly. *Why can't you just relax*, he'd say. Like it was that easy. "Max is too sweet to be burdened with all that. To be burdened with me."

"Let him decide that. And who doesn't have baggage in their life? Heck, my back aches on the daily with the load I'm carrying." Her attempt at a joke earned her a chuckle.

She appreciated the effort her friend made, but

77

Hannah still wasn't convinced. Angie didn't know the extent of the mind games Pete played with her. But now wasn't the time to get into all of that.

She grabbed her wand, curled some loose waves into her long, blonde hair, and gave it a quick shake. She did a final twirl for her friend. "How do I look?"

"Happy."

She caught a glimpse of herself in the tiny box at the bottom of the screen.

Well, look at that.

This was the Hannah everyone remembered. She couldn't believe she'd ever been weak enough to let someone almost take that person away, but she was happy she was back. And right then and there, she made a promise that she'd never let someone make her feel the way Pete had so many times in their relationship. Anxiety was part of her, and there was no shame in admitting that —no matter what her ex had continually told her. She just wasn't ready to hash all this out with Angie yet.

"Now, I expect a report of all the juicy deets tomorrow." Angie winked exaggeratedly.

"I promise you there will be no deets to spill, juicy or otherwise. But I'll give you a call, anyway."

She slipped on a pair of ballet flats, grabbed the prepared dinner, and walked next door. After letting out a deep breath she didn't realize she was holding, she knocked on the door.

When it opened, she nearly forgot her name. The last time she'd been this close to Max, she was making a fool of herself and clinging onto him for dear life. She'd never really been able to get a good look at him, and now that she had that opportunity, her mouth seemed broken. Oh, wait—not broken—just hanging wide open. *Smooth.*

"Hey, Hannah."

She still couldn't form words, so she went for a hug.

She was a big fan of hugging, but perhaps a "hi" prior to the embrace would have been a little less awkward. *Get ahold of yourself.* In her defense, she hadn't seen a person in real life for two weeks. Excuse her for wanting some human contact. Some warm, muscled, don't-wanna-take-my-hands-off-him human contact.

Max didn't seem to mind. He returned the hug with one that swallowed her and made her feel happy to be there. It gave her hands a chance to feel his broad back and all the taut muscles that rippled beneath her palms.

"Come on in." He gestured as he opened the door a little wider and offered to take the food from her hands. She looked around at the plain walls. The only thing he'd hung so far was a framed picture of a baseball stadium, which had a small plaque below indicating it was on the campus of West Virginia University. Since he'd moved in just a few weeks ago, he didn't have many other decorations, but he had nice furniture, and that gave the space an immediately cozy feel.

"Make yourself at home. Can I get you a drink? Water? Juice? That's about all I have, unfortunately. I got ingredients for margaritas to go with the taco theme of the night, but I wasn't sure if you drank or what you drank ..." He trailed off. He was jabbering so quickly, she could barely process what he was saying. Was he nervous? During their balcony chats, and even the shirtless Facetime call, he seemed so calm, cool, and collected. Well, to be fair, she couldn't really judge the shirtless Facetime call with the same attention as their other encounters because, well, he was shirtless. That was a lot to process.

"I'm fine with water. That's pretty much all I drink at home. And I love margaritas. I haven't had one in forever," she said a little slower than she usually spoke. She'd learned in therapy that when people talked at a slower pace, it could help to calm others, though she wasn't usually the one doing the calming. It was nice to be on this side of things for once.

"Great. I like them, too, but I rarely make them because I'm by myself, and I feel like I have to make a pitcher, and I really don't need a pitcher of margaritas, ya know?" He relaxed a little but still fumbled with the handle from the bag of food Hannah had given him.

"I totally get it." She helped empty the contents of the bag. "But now you have a quarantine margarita drinking buddy."

He put the food in the refrigerator and walked to the living room, inviting her to have a seat on the couch. She looked at him, and her fingers ached to reach out and brush the stubble of his perfectly groomed facial hair. It straddled the fine line between five o'clock shadow and beard, and it begged to be touched. Maybe that would relax him a little more. But as she held his gaze, a smile crept across her face that mirrored the one slowly making its way across his, and it suddenly seemed like whatever stress he'd been carrying had lifted. The same was true for her.

"I, um, I'm sorry," he blurted. "I wanted to say something, but I didn't know if it would be appropriate, and I don't want to weird you out or anything because I just invited you over here to chill and eat tacos ..."

"Max, it's okay." She rested a hand on his forearm to relax him, and suddenly she was the one who needed to chill. The corded muscle beneath her palm flexed when she touched it, causing her to suck in a breath. Who knew touching the bottom half of a man's arm could cause such a stir? "What do you need to tell me?"

"I, um ... I'm just really glad you're here," he said with an honesty that sent warmth spreading throughout her chest. "I mean, I know I'm living with Quinn right now—and, full disclosure, she's on a group Facetime call with friends tonight but may pop her head in here at any moment—but I've really enjoyed our balcony talks. And I'm just grateful for your company tonight."

She blushed. And not just because he'd blushed as he said that—although that made her like him even more. She felt the same way, and it was nice to be with someone who enjoyed time with her as much as she enjoyed it with him.

"Same. To all of that. Our chats have been a highlight of my days lately." And it had little to do with her not being able to talk to many people during the lockdown. Even if she had the chance to talk to anyone out of a hundred people, she'd choose Max. He was as easy to talk to as they came, and she always left their conversations in a better mood than when they started.

"I'm glad to hear that," he said as a smile with a gradual build lit his face.

The evening carried on, and she couldn't remember the last time she'd had this much fun. Max was hilarious. He'd told her stories that had tears running down her cheeks as she gasped for air, and each time she laughed, his eyes lit up brighter and brighter. She'd learned his parents lived nearby but were older. Quinn was staying with him because his parents didn't even have WiFi, which she needed since she was now attending high school classes online because of the lockdown. Max's parents said they'd lived this long without "highfalutin" internet, and there was no need for it now. They both had a chuckle over that. Apparently "unfancy" dialup service was enough for them.

She initially thought if she kept her head down and continued eating her tacos, the topic of her parents would pass by. No such luck.

"So, tell me about your folks. You mentioned they brought you to Wheeling a few times when you were younger. Do they still live in the Pittsburgh area?" he asked, innocently enough.

Few things could kill a mood faster than her answer to that question.

"They're both dead, actually."

Silence.

"Oh, I'm sorry. I, oh geez … I didn't mean to bring up something so terrible," he said quietly. This wasn't new for her, though. The pity. She got it any time this subject came up.

"It's okay, really," she said, and her hands began to tremble like they always did when she got anxious. She slid them under her legs without him noticing and continued. "They were told they couldn't have children, and they'd accepted it. My mom was a teacher and said she had hundreds of kids, and my dad was a surgeon who kept himself busy enough. Not that it didn't bother my dad, but my mom was devastated she couldn't have kids."

"So, you're adopted then?"

"No. Actually, I'm a miracle, I've been told. Not only did my mom defy the odds by conceiving a child doctors told her she never would, but she did so at the age of forty-five."

"Wow! That's amazing! How lucky they were to have you," he replied.

"It was very lucky. But the irony is my mom waited two decades for a child she only got to spend ten years with because she was in a car accident with a drunk driver and passed away."

More silence. No one could say Hannah didn't know how to kill a buzz.

"That's so awful." His eyes filled with something. Not just sympathy. "Was your dad with her? You said he had also passed." He looked as though he was trying to wrap his head around the bombshell she'd dropped. He ran his hands through his hair and looked a little white—not the

82

typical reaction she got from people when they learned about her past. Maybe he empathized more than others.

"No. My mother was alone in the car. Dad and I continued on—as much as we could, anyway. He really took it hard, but he had his career to keep him busy. And he did everything he could for me. He was the strongest, smartest man I've ever known, which made it so hard to watch him battle Alzheimer's and see all that strength sucked from him and replaced with a shell of a man I used to know. I took care of him until he passed. He got to see me get my Master's. My friend Angie recorded it for him. He died a couple months after that."

Max leaned forward and lightly held her hand. "So, you've been on your own for quite some time then," he surmised. And he was right. Because even though she'd jumped into a relationship with Pete not long after her father's passing, she still was alone. He'd never been there for her in any way that mattered. Her problems weren't his. When she'd talk to him about missing her parents, he'd remind her that there were a lot of people in similar situations like hers. He saw it every day in the hospital, he'd say. He never really showed that he listened to her or that he cared. Not like the man sitting across the couch from her.

Yes, she'd been on her own for some time, and she had friends who saw her through her heartache. But tonight was the first moment in a long time she didn't feel lonely, and it became clear the reason was sitting on the other side of the sofa, turning from her for a second as he wiped a stray tear from his eye.

～

Wasn't it enough that Max was a ball of nerves on his first one-on-one evening with a woman in a decade? Apparently not, because once the edginess wore off and they were having a great time, he not only had to bring up what was the most depressing topic for Hannah to talk about, but he was about to cry.

Say something. Anything. Do something, for heaven's sake.

Understanding what a devastating subject he brought up, his initial reaction was to comfort her. So, he leaned over to simply place a consoling arm around her shoulder because he was afraid to say something else that might upset her. As he leaned in her direction, his couch broke both the silence and the tension in a single, loud, faux-flatulent blast.

"Oh!" Hannah stifled a laugh as hard as she could with her hand over her mouth, but her shoulders violently shook. She wasn't hiding it well.

"It was the couch, I swear!" he shouted as his face heated from his cheeks to the tips of his ears. He should have stuck with crying—it was far less embarrassing than this.

"I know. I know," she said between gasps for air. "It's just the timing. Set to the background of that heavy conversation, it was just what we needed."

As he watched her laugh, he couldn't help but join in. She did so with such joy, it was contagious. And soon, they both wiped away tears that had mixed with those of a sadder topic. He wouldn't have imagined that happening tonight, especially since his couch hadn't done that since the first week he had it. But to see Hannah so carefree and happy made the humiliation worth it.

"I swear, when I first got the couch, every time I sat on it, it had *something* to say. But it hasn't done that in weeks."

She waved a dismissive hand. "I believe you. But for as long as I know you, whenever we reference this moment, it was real. That's the only way we can be even after I made a fool of myself nearly falling in the pool." Apparently one woman's embarrassment was another man's highlight of the month, because there was nothing Max wouldn't give to be that close to her again.

"Deal," he said, to make her feel better. "So how about some margaritas?"

"I thought you'd never ask," she answered with a smile that was ... a little flirty? Or was he imagining things?

They finished mixing their drinks and walked back to the couch. He made sure to sit excessively gently so as not to have another incident. Although, if the sound repeated, it'd prove the couch had made the sound and not him.

Didn't work.

"So, did you ever imagine living through a global pandemic?" she asked as she took her first sip.

"Not in my wildest dreams." He took a sip of his drink, and whoa—how much tequila was in it? He should have known better than to follow a recipe Johnny gave him. The drinks were so strong, he was going to breathe fire soon. That was probably by design. His friend had probably boosted the alcohol in the recipe to help Max unwind during this non-date.

"How are things with Quinn going?"

"It's so easy being a 'parent' to a sixteen-year-old who is responsible enough to live on her own. I know she misses her soccer games, and she definitely misses her friends. At least they get to Facetime. And the other day I think there were several of them Facetiming all at once."

"How lonely would we have been if this had happened to us when *we* were sixteen? No Facetime, no Zoom calls, no online classes. And she's not that much younger than us, but boy, does thinking about this make me feel ancient," she said with a chuckle at that last part.

He gave that some thought. "My best friend lived two doors down, so I guess I would have been lucky enough to have someone to hang out with."

"Well, that is lucky. I would have been on my own with

my dad at the hospital all the time. I'm sure he would have been busy. Much like your sister and brother-in-law are now."

They'd called a time or two each day to check in on Quinn, but the conversations were short and to the point. There wasn't a lot of time for idle chitchat.

"So, what's next for the online exercise classes? Are you doing another dance aerobics one or are you adding more?"

Her eyes lit up, and her knee bounced with excitement. "I meant to tell you. Before I came over, my boss gave me the okay to add more. I pretty much have the green light to add whatever I want. I was thinking of maybe doing a boot camp-style class next."

It was nice to see someone have such a genuine passion for their occupation. Max liked his job, but he figured in a couple more years the stress of it would start giving him those premature wrinkles his sister used all kinds of creams to erase. Maybe she'd lend him a bottle.

"That sounds a little more my style than the aerobics dance class. Not that I didn't enjoy the dance class," he quickly added, not wanting to hurt her feelings.

She giggled. She was so darn cute when she laughed.

"I'm actually glad you said that. This class features various modifications to the exercises so they can fit any fitness level, and it would be helpful to have a couple people demonstrating them during the class." She gave him a sideways look and a half-smile. He started to see where this conversation was going. "Quinn already agreed, so I was hoping ..." She trailed off.

"So, you want to know if I'll help too?"

She gave her best pleading grin, her round eyes peeping up at him through lashes most girls paid money to fake. When she bit her bottom lip, he was a goner. How could he say no to that? Quite simply, he couldn't.

Maybe it was the margaritas. Maybe it was the way he wanted to do anything for her just so she'd look at him that way again. Whatever it was, he'd just agreed to be in his first workout video. And in more ways than one, he wondered what he was getting himself into.

Chapter Twelve

Hannah woke the next morning feeling better than she had in a long time. She was pretty sure of the reason. Last night was exactly what she needed. Conversation wasn't hard for her—she could make friends with a stranger in the checkout line at the grocery store. But talking to Max was the easiest thing in the world, and after some initial jitters shook off, he talked to her as effortlessly as she talked to him.

And he listened. So many guys would nod along and make the squinty-eyed, I'm-listening face. But Max? He *actually* listened. And he cared. She compared him to Pete in her head, but there was no comparison. Max wasn't like anyone she'd met before. He treated her like she was fascinating. What she said and did mattered to him. And after their evening together, a few of the cracks inside her began to heal.

Max asked her to chill and watch TV with him this evening before last night was even over. That meant he enjoyed spending time with her too, right? She hoped, anyway. This time, he was coming over to her place. Quinn was having a virtual sleepover with her five girlfriends, and

Max said they planned to watch romcoms all night while eating popcorn and drinking soda on a Zoom call. You had to admit, that was a creative use of technology.

Hannah's finger hovered right over the brew button on her coffee pot when her phone rang. She looked at the screen and saw Max's name. Calling her the morning after they'd hung out the previous night surprised her, but she didn't care. Guys had these secret algorithms to figure out when it was appropriate to call a woman after a date. She was glad those silly rules, like so many other things, didn't apply to him.

She answered with a breezy hello, but there was a much less easy-going Max on the end of the line. In fact, he was downright frantic.

"Hannah, hey! Can you get over here quickly? Quinn has an emergency, and she says she needs you!"

～

"WHEN YOU GET BACK, we're going to have a nice, long chat about when we use the word 'emergency,'" a now-relieved Max semi-shouted down the hall as Hannah walked with Quinn to her apartment. She looked back and saw him scrub a hand down his face as he walked into his place.

"I'm so sorry, Hannah," Quinn said, clearly embarrassed. "I haven't been out to shop, and we've been ordering groceries and things online. I couldn't have Uncle Max ordering tampons for me."

Hannah chuckled. The whole scenario was just too much. A frenzied Max had greeted her at the door. He'd told her Quinn shouted from inside the bathroom that she was having an emergency. She knew immediately what was going on, and once confirmed, Max turned the same shade he did last night when he "farted" on the couch.

"I totally get it, but … you *did* know this would happen eventually, right?"

"Yeah."

Hannah was always prepared. Her mom passed before she'd gotten her first period. And while her father was a physician and fine with what went on with everyone else's bodies, he became very uncomfortable discussing this particular issue with his only daughter. So, she was always a couple months ahead with her stock. She figured her father would sooner die than make late-night trips for feminine supplies. Luckily for her temp neighbor, old habits die hard, and she had a small drug store supply in her bathroom cupboard.

"Take as much of whatever kinds you need," she said as she showed Quinn to her stash. When Quinn emerged from the bathroom, Hannah waited with a brown paper bag to conceal her supply. There was no need to make her any more uncomfortable with this issue around her uncle.

"Thank you so, so much. You're my hero." She wrapped Hannah in a giant hug.

"Well, I wouldn't go that far, but I'm certainly happy to help in any way I can. In fact, why don't you write down what products and brands you normally use?" Hannah grabbed a pen and small pad of paper from the kitchen table and handed them to Quinn. "This way, I can order your supplies with mine and drop them off to you, and you don't have to talk to Uncle Max about lady stuff that makes you squirm."

Quinn placed a hand against her chest. "Are you serious right now? That's honestly the nicest thing. You're the absolute best." She wrapped Hannah in yet another hug, this one bigger than the last. "I'll send Uncle Max over with money tonight."

"Don't worry about it. We can square up when it's delivered. I know where you live," she quipped. There was something endearing about Quinn, and after the afternoon they spent chatting about literature on the balcony, a piece inside her pinged with delight. She'd always dreamed of having a sister. And for an afternoon, she got to see what that might have been like.

Another couple hugs later, Hannah walked Quinn to the door when her neighbor stopped suddenly and pointed to the card displayed on the entryway table.

"'Happy Birthday,'" she read aloud as her eyebrows drew together. "Wait, when was your birthday?"

Hannah wasn't making a big deal of it because nothing seemed normal these days. They were living in a pandemic, after all. Her closest friend was in a different state, restaurants and stores were all closed—this wasn't the ideal environment for something like a birthday. So, she hadn't mentioned it to anyone. But that's what made Max's invitation to hang out tonight just what she needed. She wouldn't have to celebrate, but she wouldn't have to be alone, either.

"It's today."

Chapter Thirteen

Max had his work cut out for himself. Under normal circumstances, planning a birthday celebration in a day would be tough. During a global pandemic? Almost impossible. With the local bakeries closed, he couldn't get a cake. With shops closed, how could he get a present? He could go to the grocery store, but the last time he went there, the shelves were mostly bare. And the bakery at the grocery store wasn't open, either. He needed to get resourceful. And in a hurry.

It occurred to him that Hannah might want her birthday to fly under the radar. He could certainly understand that. If she really didn't want to make a deal of it, he could pass it off as a thank you for her massive act of kindness during this morning's false emergency. She at least deserved that. He was lucky Quinn went over there this morning. He wouldn't know he was spending the evening with Hannah on her birthday otherwise.

They agreed to order pizza, one of the few take-out options currently available. With dinner out of the way, that still left dessert. He couldn't pass off another sack of

Kit Kats as an after-dinner treat. Besides, it was her birthday. She deserved something special.

He raided the cupboards and found a few key ingredients for chocolate chip cookies, the one and only baked good he'd ever attempted. He was lucky his mom filled his pantry with a few staples for baking and cooking. Honestly, he wasn't sure what to do with a lot of them. He'd be learning on the fly today. As he glanced at the ingredients spread over his countertop, he couldn't believe he had everything he needed. Until he realized he didn't—there were no chocolate chips.

Then he spotted the Kit-Kats.

If he put them in the food processor and pulsed them to a chunky consistency, would they be a decent substitute for chocolate chips? He was about to find out.

Quinn eyed the baking supplies strewn across the kitchen island and watched Max hastily unwrap and put Kit Kats in a bowl. "Do you need help? This looks like it has disaster written all over it."

"Would you mind opening these?" He was running out of time and had officially entered panic mode. "I'll start on the batter and get these in the oven."

"Got it. These for Hannah?"

"Yes. And thank you for telling me about her birthday." He really owed her for the tip.

"No problem. Have you given any thought to a present?"

That was the million-dollar question. He'd given it *a lot* of thought—well, as much as he could in the hour since he'd found out it was her birthday. Nothing seemed appropriate to give her.

"I'm still thinking." But he knew he didn't have much time for thought. It was time for action.

Once he mixed the batter, he poured the Kit Kat chunks in and gave them a stir. This was either the best or worst idea ever, but it was too late to turn back now. He rolled the dough into equal-sized balls, spaced them evenly on the baking sheet, and got them in the oven. He said a silent prayer to his Grandma Rose, one of the best bakers he'd ever known. He begged her to use some divine intervention to help him pull out an edible treat in about ten minute's time, and then he hustled to his room to think of gift ideas.

He searched his room from top to bottom for inspiration but struck out. Framed photos of him with family and friends sat on his dresser, but he and Hannah hadn't taken any pictures together. Framing one was obviously out of question. He could make her a card, but what would he write? And what would he put in it? Not cash. She wasn't his granddaughter. And she deserved more than a homemade card and some questionable cookies on her big day, anyway.

He scurried to the "cloffice," where a few boxes still sat, unpacked. His mind kept returning to the card idea. It was at least a start. His eyes scanned the room as he tried to remember where he put the plain paper when he unpacked. Suddenly, his gaze snagged on a shoebox in his closet, something his mother insisted he take with him when he moved. In this very moment, as much as he'd always rolled his eyes at his mom's unwillingness to throw anything away, he realized the perfect pandemic birthday gift stared him right in the face. He'd never admit it to her, of course, but his mom's borderline hoarding had paid off.

~

MAX SPENT the rest of the morning and all afternoon working on his gift, and he was quite proud of what he'd accomplished. The only gift bag around was the "Cool

Yule" snowman bag Hannah left the tacos in the first time she made him dinner. That would have to do.

He also gave himself a pat on the back for the cookies he made. While he was highly skeptical they'd taste like much, the Kit Kats actually turned out to be a suitable replacement for the chocolate chips. He made a mental note to use them again in the future, given his love for the candy. And what a coincidence they were also a favorite of Hannah's.

Gift and cookies in hand, he told Quinn to enjoy her virtual sleepover and walked next door. This was his first visit to Hannah's place, though he got a glimpse of it when he did her virtual dance aerobics class. But who was he kidding? It wasn't like his eyes were paying more attention to the walls of her apartment in the shot than the beautiful woman standing in front of them. Was she even standing in front of a wall? If she had stood in front of an erupting volcano, he probably wouldn't have noticed.

He tightened his grip on the gift bag handles, now dampened from his sweaty palms. *Gross.* Taking a deep breath, he gave three knocks as he looked down at the bag. He hoped she would like the present, but his confidence decreased with each passing moment.

When Hannah opened the door, they immediately locked eyes. A shade darker than Carolina blue but reminiscent of the clearest water you could imagine, her eyes hypnotically pulled him in. His grip on his belongings loosened as his muscles went limp, but he willed his body to remain steady. He didn't want to drop the surprises he'd worked all day to create.

"Well, what's all this?" she asked as she invited Max in.

"Rumor has it today's your birthday. That's what all this is." He held up the gift bag and tin of cookies.

"Ah, Quinn." A tentative smile appeared on her face and broadened slowly. "I'll get her for this." She chuckled.

But something told him she didn't mind at all that the secret was out, which allowed him to unclench a little.

"I'll just put these here on the table." She placed the cookies and gift bag on the kitchen island. Max scanned the space, and he was right—her apartment was the mirror image of his. It was the exact same layout, flipped. But everything was so much livelier on this side of the wall.

Pink and coral decorative pillows sat on a couch that looked as comfortable as it was vibrant. Bright green houseplants in pots of varying shades of pink and yellow lined the windowsill. Some had little "Hello, my name is ..." tags, while others were simply labeled by type. And framed photos of people with Hannah perched on various surfaces. In short, this apartment was just like her: warm, inviting, comfortable, and of course, beautiful.

To further add to the welcoming atmosphere, she had music playing. Very familiar music, in fact.

Max stopped mid-stride. "Is this Ray LaMontagne?"

She tipped her head to the side "Yeah. Do you know him?"

"Know him? I love him. He's one of my favorite musicians." He played his music a lot on his guitar. Had she ever heard him playing Ray's songs through the wall at night?

"He's great. At the gym, I always play really upbeat, peppy music, obviously. When I get home, it's nice to put some of his music on and chill. And Ray pairs well with wine. Oh, and speaking of ..." Hannah skipped over to the kitchen to pull out two unopened bottles. "I don't know if you like wine, but it's all I have. There's red or white. You pick," she said, extending both options out to him.

"It's your birthday, so I think the choice is yours. Whatever you want, you get tonight," he said, then cringed internally. He hoped it didn't come off as too suggestive.

"Perfect." She opened the bottle of white then eyed

him up and down before turning to grab some glasses. He couldn't help but notice the way she kept holding his gaze tonight, more than usual. He loved the reassuring feeling it gave him, and his heart began to fill with hope. It anchored him in the moment, which was helpful because he could easily get swept in whether or not he should hold her hand, find an excuse to touch her, or lean in for a kiss. He wanted to do all those things, of course, but there was only one thing he needed to do now: relax.

"So, I ordered the pizza. They're running a little behind, and it might be a while. I think they're overloaded, being one of the few places serving food right now. And I don't have wine glasses yet, so I hope this is okay." She handed him a mug filled to the brim. It wasn't your average-size mug, either—it rivaled the giant ones they served coffee in at Central Perk on the TV show *Friends*.

"Well, then maybe we'll need something to tide us over ... and absorb a little of this wine," he suggested. It seemed a little on the strong side, not that he was a wine connoisseur by any means. He was no lightweight, but a giant mug full of this on an empty stomach would go straight to his head. "I apologize for not bringing you a cake, but I did manage to make these cookies. So, maybe I could offer you one?" He pointed to the tin on the kitchen island.

"Max—did you really do this? I can't believe you." She gave him the biggest smile he'd ever seen from her. Note to self: make Hannah more cookies. Many more cookies.

"Well, I didn't have chocolate chips, so I crushed up some Kit Kats. I hope you like them." His hands got clammy again. *Calm down, dude. They're just cookies.*

"I can't wait to try them." She raised the top off the container and pulled out a cookie for each of them.

For the rest of his life, he'd never be able to forget her reaction as she took her first bite of the cookie. She was

97

honest, she was delighted ... and she was unknowingly turning him on.

"Oooooooooh. Oh, God, Max—it's so good."

And just like that, his face turned several shades of red. He prayed she didn't notice.

"I-I-I'm glad you like them so much," he croaked, nearly choking on his first bite.

"These are amazing! I can't believe you did this for me." She came in for a hug. Thank goodness they were standing at the kitchen island, and Max's front faced it. Fortunately, she had no choice but to hug him from the side, saving Max from an awkward situation. She already thought he freely passed gas on couches—he didn't want her to think he was turned on by someone eating a cookie too.

"You deserved something special, and I also owed you bigtime after helping Quinn this morning. I *really* don't think she wanted my help. Like, at all." He shuddered as he recalled the morning's events.

"Like I told her, it's no problem. I was happy to help." Her gaze shifted to the gift bag. "Did you bring me a present?"

"Well, now, don't get too excited," he replied, unexpectedly bashful. "All the stores in town are closed, and with such short notice, I couldn't order something." He shrugged. "So, this is nothing really."

It was "nothing" he'd spent the whole day making, but he suddenly felt shy. Standing here in front of him, Hannah seemed worthy of so much more than the contents of the bag. He'd noticed her beauty the moment she walked into the pool. But now that he'd gotten to know her, her kindness toward not only him but his niece made her luminous. And in that moment, he wanted to give her so much more than what he'd made.

"I'm sure I'll love it," she said. Probably because she was kind. It was in her nature to be gracious.

His hands trembled a bit as he watched her slowly pull his present out of the bag. He'd kind of put his heart into what he'd made, and when she looked at it with eyes soft and glassy, he was glad he had.

Chapter Fourteen

I f she lived to have a hundred more birthdays, Hannah doubted she'd ever feel as special as she did this very moment. Her hands cradled probably the most beautiful thing she'd ever seen, given to her by a man standing in front of her, with his hands behind his back and a smile on his face that conveyed both pride and vulnerability.

"Max, this is incredible," she said, barely above a whisper. It had truly taken her breath away, and speaking was difficult. She held the fragile gift in her hands, rotating to view it from every angle. "Wait—did you make this?"

"I, uh, yeah. It's just paper." His voice was thick with an emotion she couldn't decipher, and she couldn't help but notice him rubbing his hands against his pants.

It wasn't "just paper." No, what she held was a bouquet of intricately formed roses, easily a dozen, folded from several shades of blue pieces. They were bound together by stems and leaves created with the same delicate technique.

"I can't even believe it. I—I'm shocked. I've never seen anything like this. It's absolutely beautiful." Her eyes stung as she sniffled softly. She looked at the bouquet again, noticing the intricate details of each flower. They varied in size, but all had the same shape. He'd used several different shades of blue paper to create an ombre effect that reminded her of the varying colors of the ocean, one of her favorite places in the world. As she continued to admire the gift, she noticed something scrawled in the center of one of the flowers. When she peeked in another, she saw what appeared to be more writing she couldn't quite read.

"Is there something written here?"

"Uh, yeah." He cleared his throat before he spoke again. "So, I wrote a wish for you inside each of the roses. You know, something good that I hope happens to you in this new year. I figured since I didn't have birthday cake or any candles for you to blow out and make a wish on, this was the next best thing." His gaze stuck to the floor like glue. "It's silly, I just, uh ..."

She cut him off with a hug. He wasn't looking at her, so it caught him by surprise, but he immediately enveloped her in his large arms. She hoped the embrace said what she couldn't find the words for at that very moment. No words could do justice for the thoughtfulness he showed her tonight. Her heart pounded, and her whole body shook. He must have noticed because he slowly ran his hands up and down her back in a firm yet soothing manner. No one had cared for her like this since her father passed. She'd forgotten how good it felt and couldn't believe she'd gone this long without this sensation.

He felt so good in her arms. She inhaled deeply, cataloguing his masculine scent so she could recall it whenever she needed to feel the serenity that washed over her body. Behind his natural scent, she caught the notes of Kit Kat cookies on his breath, which only reminded her further how much time and effort he put into making this evening special. Just for her. She reflexively held him a little tighter.

While she didn't want to end the greatest hug she'd ever had, they hadn't spoken for a moment or two. So, she stepped back, still in his arms, looked him deep in those chocolate brown eyes of his, and said the only thing she could bring herself to say with her unsteady breath.

"Thank you."

It was simple but said with such conviction; she hoped he felt the honesty behind the words. As they stood there, still in each other's arms, his eyes lowered to her mouth, and her cheeks heated. His eyes slowly rose to meet hers once again, and he gave her one of his half-smiles that made her legs want to give out. As he tucked a piece of hair behind her ear, his hand brushed along her cheek, bringing to life thousands of goosebumps all over her arms. She hummed contentedly, and as if on cue, a slow Ray LaMontagne song started to play. His grip around her waist tightened, and she sucked in a breath.

Hannah had given a lot of thought to when she might be ready to let her guard down and date another guy. Her gut instinct told her it should be later rather than sooner. But Max proved tonight he wasn't "another guy." And in this moment, she realized that around him, she didn't even have a guard. She didn't need one—this wasn't scary. Maybe she'd been wrong to hold herself back from a relationship. She wasn't totally sure yet, but maybe Max was worth taking that step with. So, she took that step by leaning in closer to him. As she slowly advanced, his breath tickled her lips and their noses nearly touched.

It had taken her so long to get to this place, and the gradual build to this moment had been rising for her since that first day at the pool. But when a loud bang on the door made them jump apart faster than a bullet shot from a gun, she blew out a sigh and silently wished she'd moved just a smidge faster.

"I think the pizza is here."

~

HANNAH HATED PIZZA.

Okay, that was a lie. Before this evening, she'd loved it. It was one of her favorite foods. But since it had just ruined the most romantic moment of her life, she officially loathed it.

What was happening tonight? From the moment the door opened, she kept having these moments with Max. The eye contact, the ease of conversation (even more than normal), the sly grins—something was happening between them. It was like the beginning of a fireworks show—pops of excitement intermittently burst, prompting jolts of excitement and anticipation. And after what had just *almost* happened, she couldn't believe how much the prospect of kissing him excited her.

"That pizza was delicious," she said as she dabbed her mouth with a napkin and pushed back from the table. "Thanks again for everything. This is the best birthday I've ever had." Pete had taken her to the swankiest bars and restaurants for her past couple birthdays with people who were barely acquaintances of hers. He presented her with lavish gifts that, while appreciated, truly weren't her. She couldn't imagine anything making her happier than spending the evening with a pizza, some wine, a paper bouquet, and a man who gave her butterflies. She'd take butterflies and paper flowers over gold necklaces any day.

"So, are you ever going to tell me how you learned to make something like that?" She pointed to the bouquet now proudly displayed on her coffee table.

"Okay, well, we had a foreign exchange student in high

103

school who was really good at origami. Like *insanely* good. He'd whip up the craziest things during our lunch period. Now, I'm not a crafty guy, but I do like doing things with my hands." Hannah looked down at them. She couldn't imagine how hands so large and rugged could make something as delicate as a flower.

Her mind quickly derailed to thoughts of other things his hands could do. The memory of them fixed tightly around her waist just moments ago played on loop in her mind. "Like playing the guitar?" At least her voice stayed in the moment with a suitable, PG response. *Well done, words. Brain, knock it off.*

"Right. So, I took a stab at origami and really enjoyed it. Flowers are my specialty." He laughed and shook his head. "Now, that's a funny story."

"Oooooh, do tell," she prodded as she topped off their mugs of wine, emptying the bottle.

"Well, I was the president of our community service group at school. I'd floated the idea of doing something nice for the women at church on Mother's Day. Not just for mothers—I wanted every woman to get a little something. It's such a complicated day—if you're a mother, you're on cloud nine, but if you're not and you want to be, it's just tough."

"I'm sure that's how my mother felt for all those years she wanted me," she said with understanding.

"I'm sure. And it was hard for my sister for a while. She struggled to have Quinn, and although they wanted a second, it just wasn't meant to be. Anyway, I got this idea to make origami roses for all the women at the church to be handed out after the service."

She was positive he couldn't get more caring, but then there he was, proving her wrong. Again.

"That's seriously so sweet," she told him. "You're truly amazing."

He smiled at her and then began laughing at the memory as he continued with the story.

"I wouldn't call myself amazing. Maybe overly ambitious—or downright dumb." He chortled. "While we had enough supplies and a handful of student volunteers, we grossly underestimated the time it would take to make all the roses. Our helpers started heading home sometime around midnight. Johnny and I were up until 3 a.m. Mother's Day morning, finishing the roses, but we made sure every woman at mass that day got one. Seeing their reactions made the sleepless night worthwhile." He ran his thumb back and forth across the mug of wine in his hand. "So, yeah, I'm *really* good at roses."

"I don't even know what to say. That had to mean so much to those women, Max," she said, in awe of him and his kind, generous heart. He was the good guy all girls hoped to one day find. And marry. How was he single? Or was he? Her breath hitched. They'd never officially covered that topic.

"Ah, we had a fun night putting them together."

"I bet. So, do you have a lot of friends still in the area? A girlfriend?" Did she really just slip that last part in there? The wine was officially talking now, and it wasn't speaking subtly. But after what *almost* happened earlier, she needed an answer. And with a giant mug and half a bottle of wine in her system, she was apparently ready to play detective.

"Um, well, there's Johnny, who you know. I have a few other buddies still in town, but most went away for college and never came back. With technology and social media though, you never feel like you're too far from anyone these days." He paused, looking down. But then he looked up, his face sporting his signature half-smile. "No. I don't have a girlfriend."

Hannah's insides roared to life while she did a little happy dance in her head. She'd spent the past few weeks swearing she was only going to pursue a friendship with Max, but after this evening—after whatever this feeling was—she wanted more. Scratch that. She *needed* more. She couldn't go without the flutter in her stomach, the excitement that pulsed through her veins, and the smile that had been plastered on her face so long, her cheekbones were sore.

Ah, but she promised herself she'd take things slow. Although, she never really defined slow. She wasn't going to marry the guy next week or anything. Perhaps she could just hold hands with him, kiss his inviting lips, run her hands through his thick hair and down his rock-hard chest ...

No—there was still a sour taste in her mouth when she thought about relationships. And she didn't do hookups. That whole Pete debacle was a lesson she wouldn't need to learn again. If she did nothing else, she was going to keep this promise to herself. She deserved that much.

"How is that possible?" she asked with a flirty tone to her voice, courtesy of wine mug number two.

"Well ... I just haven't dated anyone in a while," he answered. "How about you? Do you have a boyfriend back in Pittsburgh? Or have you met anyone here?"

Well, I have a jerk back in Pittsburgh. Does that count?

"Um, no. I had a bad breakup back home," she answered, attempting to convey a neutral façade. She didn't want to get into the dirty details of her past relationship. "That's part of what precipitated this move. I wasn't totally happy with my job back home, anyway, so it really was for the best. But I haven't met anyone here. I haven't dated in a while, either, I guess," she said, trailing off.

"A bad breakup? I'm sorry to hear. That's never easy," he responded with his signature caring tone. *Why couldn't all guys be like him?*

"Eh, no worries," she replied. She needed to shut down

this conversation as quickly as possible so it wouldn't ruin what was an amazing evening so far. "He just wasn't my lobster."

She'd thought nothing of it when the words left her mouth, but when she saw Max's eyes widen, his brows raise, and his mouth smile like a child who'd just heard Christmas is tomorrow, she had a feeling they'd connected on yet another level.

Chapter Fifteen

Max sat at his computer, willing himself to work, and begged his mind to focus on what he should be thinking about from 8-4 on weekdays. But his brain had other ideas. Well, one, really: Hannah.

He wouldn't have believed being stuck at home for days on end would be tolerable, much less enjoyable, but that spoke to his neighbor's ability to take a less-than-desirable circumstance and make it pleasant, a word he'd undoubtedly use to describe her.

The evening of her birthday was better than he could have imagined. Aside from the near-kiss—which would have more than made any evening—they shared so many laughs, his abs hurt the next morning. And that did not bode well for his upcoming boot camp session with Hannah.

Oh, and then she made that comment about her ex not being her lobster, a reference to an episode of *Friends*. He couldn't believe their shared obsession over what they both agreed was the greatest show in the history of television. And she, too, had the complete ten season boxset of

DVDs. "All the cool kids stream everything these days, but the *coolest* own season sets on DVD," she joked as she popped in season one, disc one and they started to watch the series from the premiere episode.

They sat so close, their shoulders touched. He'd never held so still before. He was afraid if he moved, she'd notice their proximity and shimmy away. There was no way he was letting that happen.

When she pulled the softest blanket he'd ever felt across their laps, his bones felt like they'd melted into her couch. Though she admitted to seeing each episode at least a dozen times, her head tipped back as she laughed with her entire body at least twice each show. Her unrestrained laugh at each tagline was contagious, and Max was happy to join in.

He sure wished she was with him right now as he stared blankly at his computer screen. The ring of his cell broke him from his daydream.

"Hey, buddy," Johnny greeted on the line.

Max was grateful for the distraction. It wasn't like he was accomplishing much at the moment. "How are you doing, man?"

"Not too shabby." There was palpable excitement in his friend's voice. "Apparently, people are really into this virtual training thing, and I've actually been really busy. A good busy, but that's why I haven't called." He didn't need to give a reason. Max hadn't called him lately, either. Wait … why *hadn't* he called him? Oh yea, he'd been swept into Hannah Land.

"Yeah, sorry, I've been busy here too," he admitted.

"I know."

Could you hear a smirk through the phone? Because Max was sure he'd heard Johnny's. "What exactly is that supposed to mean?" he asked suspiciously.

"Well, I talked to your girl the other day, and she said

you were coming over to watch *Friends* reruns." He said that last part suggestively, and it made Max blush. He obviously wouldn't turn her away. But he was enjoying just spending time with his neighbor, analyzing each episode as they made their way through the series most nights for the past couple weeks.

"Okay, seriously, we are just hanging out. That's all. She's amazing, and I'm having a lot of fun with her. But right now, she's just a friend." Since the night of her birthday when their faces were centimeters apart, they hadn't gotten intimately close again. He wasn't sure if she didn't feel it, if she'd friend-zoned him, or what. Heck, maybe he was so smitten with her, he hallucinated the whole thing. They sat a lot closer than he imagined friends would when they'd hung out and watched TV, but there was no other concrete evidence that said she was interested in anything other than a friendship. Maybe she sat that close because they only had one blanket to share and he looked cold. There were a lot of options to consider here.

"You said 'but right now,' implying something might happen later, though. You're thinking about it, then." Johnny could moonlight as a mind reader if he wanted. Going out on a date with her was *all* Max could think about.

"I'm open to it."

"Jeez, Max. Is this a job interview?" Johnny laughed. "If you agree to be in a girl's exercise video, you're more than open to it. In fact, if you make her an origami bouquet, which you and I both know takes *hours* to complete, you are one hundred percent ready for it and working on it."

Max nearly dropped the phone. "Whoa … how did you know about all that?"

"She asked me some questions about proper terminology for cueing different moves in the boot camp class she's streaming this week—starring Max Robertson—when she called yesterday." He laughed again.

A lot of planning sure went into these classes. Max never gave much thought to how much work went on behind the scenes. Hannah said she wanted the classes to be equal parts fun and educational, because it was as important for the clients to know the proper technique for the moves as it was for them to enjoy themselves. There was a science behind the sequencing in each class. How she kept track of all the routines was beyond him. He could barely keep track of what food he needed to order from the grocery store for the week's meals.

"So, you guys were talking about me." That was a good sign.

"I didn't do much of the talking," Johnny admitted. Max found that hard to believe, given his friend's chatty nature. "She said you made her thirtieth birthday something she'd never forget."

So, she was thirty. Same as him. She'd never said, and his mama always told him not to ask a woman her age. But this made him even happier that he celebrated with her, and she didn't have to spend a milestone birthday by herself. "I just did what a good neighbor would do."

"Ha! Mr. Rogers is a good neighbor. You, on the other hand, seem to be a neighbor falling in love with the girl next door."

"Uh … falling? Nah that's not what's happening. I've known her for just over a month, and we've only been hanging out for a few weeks now. You can't fall for someone in that amount of time. And don't even get me started on the love part." Even with Courtney, they were friends for *years* before they dated.

"I don't know, buddy. You're friends with me, and I never got an origami bouquet. If that's what people get when they're friends with you, consider me officially hurt."

The more he thought of it, he wondered if his buddy was on to something. He told himself he'd be totally fine if he and Hannah were only ever friends. What if Johnny was right, and that was a lie? He knew he had a crush on her, and she was attractive. Very attractive. He spent most nights staring at the ceiling, thinking about how attractive she was. The fact they hadn't shared any more moments like the night he'd given her the origami roses made him a little uneasy, and a weird sensation churned in his stomach. He didn't realize how much he wanted more with her until he realized he may not get it.

The next morning, it was Saturday, the day of the boot camp practice run. Max didn't know what to expect. Hannah just told him to come in regular gym clothes and tennis shoes. He threw on a T-shirt with the sleeves cut off and gym shorts, his typical workout uniform.

He wondered what she'd be wearing and prayed it wasn't what she wore this morning. Quinn put Hannah's live Zumba class on the living room TV, and he had to leave. He'd only seen his neighbor do dance aerobics and water aerobics classes. What little he saw of the Zumba class did more for his cardiovascular system than any workout he'd ever done. And he was only sitting on the couch.

He never imagined the gorgeous-looking, sweet girl next door he harbored a crush for could move like that. The way her hips gyrated to the music, the booty shaking—oh, and her outfit? One thing was certain— gone were the days when he wondered what was under the graphic tees and hoodies she always wore. The yoga pants she donned did things for her curves he didn't know clothing could do for a body. The top she wore wasn't a sports bra—he knew what those were now that Quinn left them flung over the shower rod to air dry. This was a little longer, but it still offered enough glances of her toned stomach to make him imagine what it would feel like to wrap his arms around it. He left Quinn to do the class in the living room alone while he went to the kitchen for a cold glass of water. He was sweating suddenly.

Max and Quinn knocked on their neighbor's door. She'd changed, but her outfit still did something to his insides. It wasn't as tight-fitting, but his body didn't care. He willed himself to imagine an old lady in the same outfit to save himself from embarrassment. He was standing there with his niece, for crying out loud.

"Hey, guys. Come on in."

They followed her into the apartment.

"I was just clearing the living room to give us some space, but I think I need to move more. I'm used to doing these classes myself."

The coffee table and cozy recliner were now in the hallway that led to her bedroom. *How strong was this woman?* He made a mental note to keep doing her online classes because they obviously kept her in tremendous shape. He saw the slight definition in her arms, not bulky by any means but definitely toned. His eyes traveled down to the curve of her glutes—yes, he called them glutes. He was there for an exercise class, and that was the technical term for the beautifully curved, tight muscle below her hips. Okay, now he was just staring. Quinn gave him a look that said *what the heck?* His face felt like it was on fire.

"Uh, can I help with anything else?" She could clear the rest of the space herself—he knew that. But he wanted to be a gentleman, especially after his niece caught him not acting much like one. What a fine example he was setting for her.

"Sure. Go ahead and move the end tables, and that should do it." She seemed really excited for this. He was, too, but he desperately needed to tell certain parts of himself to be a little less enthused. Otherwise, this was going to be a long afternoon.

~

WHY DID he have to look so sexy? It was a valid question, one Hannah kept asking over and over in her head, oh you know, every time Max moved. Holy cannoli, he was in shape. She'd seen him shirtless in the pool, and she felt how hard he was when he grabbed her from falling. But it was a totally different experience watching his muscles in motion. It was physiological poetry, for heaven's sake. Perhaps it was her imagination, but she got a little light-headed when he did the push-up circuit of the class. He busted through them like it was as easy to him as breathing. And in that moment, Hannah almost couldn't. That long pep talk she gave herself the other night about taking things slow? The memory of that was long gone, and an image of a chiseled Max now took its place. She was in trouble.

"So, for the next part, we'd typically use weights if we were at the gym. But since we aren't, I got creative—just like the participants doing this in their homes." She handed out canned food and bottles of water she pulled from the pantry. "These won't be much resistance for either of you, but a little is better than nothing. I'll reiterate that during the live class."

Max and Quinn looked at the stash and each chose two props, one for each hand.

"We'll do a little triceps work now." Hannah bent her knees like she was sitting in a chair. She wasn't sure, but it felt like Max was looking a little more intently than needed to fully understand the exercise. Was he a good student, or was he staring? She hoped it was the latter.

"Is this more of a squat?"

Hannah startled. She nearly forgot Quinn was even in the room. Now she was really embarrassed.

"Sort of. You'll want to hinge forward and put your arms behind you like you're skiing down a hill," she said, demonstrating the posture. "From there, you'll move your arms up and down. Make sure to flex your triceps as you lift." She didn't need to add the flexing comment for Max's sake. He was flexing the heck out of this exercise. What she wouldn't give to be that can of soup in his hands.

"Do we do a set amount of these, or is it timed?" he asked as they continued with the exercise. Hannah had no idea how long they'd been doing it because clearly, his arms had put her in a trance. His muscular, hard, flexing …

"Um, uh, times up," she blurted. They may have done a week's worth of triceps exercises in the time she was gawking at his deliciously brawny arms. Hopefully, neither of them would be too sore in the morning. She assumed Max wouldn't be—nobody got arms like that by working out with canned goods.

"That was some full body work," he said as he placed the soup cans out of the way. "In that chair squat, my legs were starting to burn in that little bit of time." She didn't want to tell him he held the position probably three times longer than he was supposed to. But she wanted to seem professional—unlike the ogling fool she played now—so, she kept that part to herself.

"That's one of my favorite exercises, but the next one is the best—a plank series." She lowered herself to the floor.

"Ah, I hate planks," he grumbled. "It's not natural to sweat so much without moving." Until today, she would have agreed with him. But she was sure she broke a sweat watching him do push-ups earlier. So, what did she know?

"This good?" Quinn asked, easily getting herself into position and holding it like a champ. Fitness must have run

115

in the Robertson family because she was a picture-perfect example of planking. You could have put a teacup on her back, and it wouldn't have moved.

Hannah looked over her student. "Impressive."

"Class pet." Max smirked as he got into the posture he despised.

Hannah joined them in planking and then gave her next instruction. "From here, you'll move into a side plank." She lifted her arm and transitioned into the pose.

"Wait, what?" Max asked, his brows knit in confusion as he dropped onto his knees to see what she was doing. "How the … do we twist … what?" He unnaturally contorted himself, and while the girls both found it amusing, Hannah didn't want him to hurt himself.

"Hold on there. Get back into the basic plank," she instructed. He did, easily. "Now, raise your left hand up toward the ceiling as you open your chest and keep your weight on your right hand." He still wobbled as he shifted his weight from hand to hand, trying to figure out how to perform the exercise.

"Open what, now? How does one open one's chest, exactly?"

She grabbed his shoulders to initiate the twisting motion for him. As she touched the smooth skin of his arms, now damp with sweat, she couldn't help but let out an exhale that was a prelude to the moan she was, thankfully, able to stifle.

"It helps to breathe deeply when you're doing these exercises," she quickly added. It was also helpful to breathe when you were in the situation she was, and she reminded herself to keep the air flowing through her lungs. It seemed her body had forgotten how to do that involuntarily.

"There you go, Max." She congratulated him as he finally made his way to the side plank. She let him revel in his victory for a beat. He'd need to get back to a regular plank and then another side plank with the other arm next. Besides, this gave her a chance to examine his form. After all, it was her job to make sure he did the exercise correctly.

He wobbled a little, and she placed an arm to the middle of his back to steady him. She got lost in the feeling of heat radiating from his body and the smell of his sweat. His cutoff shirt gave a clear view of the entire side of his body. *Well, what do you know … it's toned as well. Big surprise.*

But then she noticed something that was a bit surprising. Max had a tattoo. It wasn't shocking that he had one —just surprising that she hadn't noticed it at the pool. Then again, its location didn't make it instantly visible. It was on his side, over his ribs, and his left arm covered it when it was down, which it currently was not. It was a simple outline of a notebook, with something scrawled in the center of it.

2*28*2017

She wondered at the date's significance and what it had to do with a notebook. Did he have something published? Was he a writer on the side, and his career in web design was just a way to pay the bills? He probably would have mentioned that before, though. There had to be a story. But asking would disclose that she'd been staring inside his shirt for a while now because, apparently, she didn't time these exercises anymore.

She quickly stood. "Okay, so I think you guys get the idea with the plank series."

"These exercises are great, Hannah," Quinn said with a smile. She hoped that his sweet niece didn't see her gawking at the inside of her uncle's shirt, but the smirk on her face told her she had. "I can't wait to do this live. It's going to be fun. Right, Uncle Max?"

117

"Um, yeah. Looking forward to it." He rubbed his arms and breathed a little heavier than a typical plank series would warrant. Maybe he wasn't in as good of shape as Hannah thought. Her eyes scanned his body again. Who was she kidding? Of course, he was. She still had the image of his abs in side plank burned into her memory. Probably forever.

"Great. I really appreciate your help with this. We'll go live next Saturday morning. If you have any questions about anything before then, just let me know." She pushed pieces of furniture back in their proper places. Could she have waited until they left? Yes. But she needed somewhere for her eyes to go instead of finding their home on Max's arms. How did they look better now than they did when he first came over?

"I actually have a question," Quinn chimed in. "What's all this? Are you doing arts and crafts later?" She pointed to the cut elastic pieces and scraps of random fabric scattered about the kitchen table.

"Sort of. I'm gonna try my hand at making masks for friends and people in the community who need them. Soon, we might not be able to go out without them." She had scraps from other projects, so she ordered some extra fabric and planned to put her sewing machine to work. She enjoyed making little crafts here and there when she had the time, and now *all* she had was time. Besides, keeping her hands busy was a great way to keep her mind calm.

"Do you need any help?"

Hannah smiled. "Actually, I'd love the help and the company, if you're offering." She genuinely enjoyed spending time with Quinn. "How does tomorrow afternoon sound?"

She looked at her uncle. "Is that okay?"

"Hey, as long as you have your homework done, it's

fine with me. I have that big presentation Monday morning, so I could use tomorrow afternoon to prepare."

"Perfect. I'll see you tomorrow. Thanks for offering to help." She walked Max and Quinn to the door.

"My pleasure. Uncle Max and I were just talking about what a sweet person you are. It's so like you to do something like this for others."

He gave his niece a strained smile. To Hannah, it looked like a silent signal to get his niece to stop talking. Immediately.

Hannah sensed if he wanted her to drop the topic, there must be more to this than she was telling. "Oh, so you two have been talking about me?"

"We talk about you all the time."

With that, Max unsubtly whisked his niece away as he shouted, "Thanks for the workout." They scurried down the hall, leaving Hannah wondering what the two of them talked about. And why did their talking about her intrigue her the way it did?

Chapter Sixteen

Cozy with a mug of warm hot chocolate in hand, Hannah spent the afternoon snuggled on the couch, watching a new series she found only moderately interesting, but it was enough to hold her interest for three straight episodes. She had nowhere to go and hadn't for a few weeks but decided to blow-dry her hair and put on a little blush and mascara as a pick-me-up. It was the most makeup she'd put on since her first night hanging out with Max. Although, she suspected he preferred her unmade-up face.

A ping from her cell phone took her eyes away from the television. She'd planned to Facetime with Angie tonight, but it looked like that wasn't happening.

Angie: *Hey, Hannah Banana! I hope you're doing okay. I'm gonna need a raincheck for our date tonight ... my mom's neighborhood is without power, so I'm packing up some things at her place for her to come spend a couple days with me. We'll catch up soon, k? Hope you're staying out of trouble! JK!*

So much for her big Saturday night plans. She picked up the remote and looked for more shows to binge.

When nothing piqued her interest, she grabbed her

phone. She didn't dislike social media. It was part of her job, after all. But she disliked the anxiety it gave her. It started with mindless scrolling, but then she couldn't stop. It sucked her in, and she didn't realize she was uneasy until it was too late. So, what started as something to do out of boredom turned into something that caused the exact opposite of the relaxation she tried to achieve by opening the app.

A notification lit, and she innocently tapped the icon. The heading read: "On this day three years ago" and below it was a photo of her—with Pete.

A picture can bring back a flood of memories, but in this case, it was a deluge. And Hannah started to drown. A friend had snapped the shot the night she and Pete decided to go from friends to more than friends. She couldn't even say they'd gone to boyfriend/girlfriend status because, for the life of her, she couldn't remember one time he'd referred to her as his girlfriend. But there she was, holding to him tight like he was the last life preserver, which was ironic because the girl in that photo wouldn't believe their relationship would sink like the *Titanic*. And with so much loss.

Without thinking, she clicked on Pete's name, which went straight to his profile page. There stood her ex, holding tightly to a woman who was holding her left hand out to show off a diamond so large, it was impossible to miss in the photo. Hannah's eyes must have deceived her. There was no way Pete was engaged already. She choked on her hot chocolate and cursed when she coughed it up on her screen.

Then the photo blurred. Tears rushed down her face, and she couldn't believe she was back in this place again—Pete was still bringing her to tears. Wasn't she past this point? And how had this happened so quickly? Hannah spent so much time fixing herself after the number he did on her, and he was going out and getting engaged? Hannah's life ground to a halt, and Pete was moving on as though nothing between them had ever happened? This only solidified something she thought so many times since he left her—she wasn't enough.

She closed her eyes and started thinking of her calm place. The beach was her go-to. But without consciously willing it, her mind took her right to the couch where she was falling apart. Only, in her mind, she sat next to Max.

He put his hand on her back and rubbed her in large, slow circles with a firm touch. He told her she'd be okay and he was right there over and over until she realized she was no longer shaking and her head no longer throbbed, though she still had a headache.

She had so few people left in her life that she could trust. Was her subconscious telling her Max was one of them? Did it mean something that she felt at peace thinking of him? Perhaps. "Relying on too many people is too dangerous," she said to an empty room. Well, not totally empty. Channing sat in his pot, looking a little peaked, himself. Maybe he needed a little more water. She filled the small watering can. "People are always leaving me, buddy. It's not healthy to rely on people who may one day be out of your life." She shook her head. "I mean, I'm not going anywhere, Channing," she said as she put a fertilizer stick in the soil. "It's just better if I keep to myself, isn't it?"

So many questions. Too many unknowns. For someone who liked to have answers and control, this was pure hell. How could she plan for a future she couldn't see clearly? The simple answer: she couldn't.

A knock on her door startled her. She knew she looked like crap after the attack, so she kept quiet and hoped whoever was there would go away.

"Hannah, it's Max. Are you there?"

122

Seriously? Why is he here? She stilled with the watering can mid-pour. A million thoughts raced through her head. She couldn't pretend she wasn't home. She'd told Max this afternoon about her virtual plans with Angie. She didn't need a mirror to show her that after her sobbing, she could pass for Alice Cooper's doppelganger. Max told her she was pretty the other day when she wasn't wearing makeup, but this was far scarier than going au naturale.

She tiptoed to the bathroom. If he heard the shower running, she wouldn't have to face him, and she could hold on to the smidge of dignity she had left. Well, that was the plan, anyway. But like so many of her ideas as of late, this one went downhill in a hurry.

～

A NAIL polish explosion in Max's bathroom, thanks to his niece and a bottle of dropped and shattered lacquer, brought him to Hannah's apartment door. Quinn didn't have enough nail polish remover to clean the mess, so instead of asking a neighbor for a cup of sugar like most people, he was here to ask for a bottle of remover. He heard a loud shriek shortly after he knocked, and his blood went cold.

"Hannah! Are you okay?" When there was no response, he wondered how long he should wait until he attempted to break in.

Luckily, he didn't have to wait long. The door flew open, revealing a soaking wet Hannah with eyes wide and manic. She held a bathroom fixture in her hand that looked like a shower knob. Max's demeanor shifted from worried to curious.

"Max, I need help! The Hemsworths are drowning!" She circled her arm like a third-base coach waving a baserunner to home plate, signaling the disaster was in the

123

bathroom. There was a lot to take in: the broken dialogue, the makeup running down her face, the panicky tone in her voice. And what on earth did the Hemsworths have to do with this?

He moved as fast as he could to keep up with her as she sprinted through the living room and slid into her bathroom a la Tom Cruise in *Risky Business.* He heard the water spraying before he entered the now-soaked room. She scurried around the bathroom like a chicken with her head cut off. Between gasps for air, she told Max she'd turned on the shower and the knob fell off the wall. She scooped up delicate succulents from the counter like a mother shielding her children from impending doom.

"I'll go get a bucket!" she shouted like she had a solution to end world hunger. Before Max could tell her that wasn't necessary, she vanished into another room, plants in tow. Though his plumbing knowledge was limited, he knew enough to turn off the bathroom's shutoff valve. Within seconds, the geyser stopped.

Hannah sprinted into the bathroom with a small bucket and one of those mugs she used as a wine glass the last time he came over. How long did she think those vessels would hold the water at the rate it was shooting from the pipe?

"Hannah, watch out!" he warned. But it was much too late. The slick tile made the bathroom floor akin to an ice rink, and in her soaked socks, she didn't stand a chance. Before his mind realized what his body was instinctively doing, he found himself underneath a drenched and startled Hannah on the hard, wet ground.

"Oof," she moaned as she fell right on top of him. Chests pressed together, he felt her heart pounding against his as their eyes locked in a stare that immediately grounded him. In less than two minutes, he'd been through every emotion from worry to panic to relief. And now he lay on the floor, holding Hannah closer than he'd held anyone in a very long time. With wet hair plastered to her face, he gently pushed the stray pieces behind her ear and dove deeper into her deep blue eyes. Though beautiful, they didn't have the same light he usually saw. He felt in his bones something was wrong. His bones also felt sore after the fall, but that was secondary at the moment.

"Are you okay?" He rubbed a firm hand in slow circles on her back. Had she hurt herself? He tried his best to cushion her fall, but they both hit the ground pretty hard.

She took a deep breath and closed her eyes, the first time either of them had broken eye contact since they landed on top of one another.

"I will be," she whispered softly. Her timid smile was much different than the large, unbridled ones she usually wore. "I'm sorry. I'm crushing you."

She pushed herself off him, her eyes still locked on his. He hoped she couldn't read the disappointment on his face. The only thing getting crushed right now was his desire to stay in that position on the bathroom floor. Although, there were more hygienic places to cuddle. And far drier. His entire body was soaked, but never mind that. She was keeping something from him. If she was the least bit vulnerable or upset, he couldn't make a move. She had to know he was there for her in any way she needed. Her comfort and happiness were his priority. His needs could wait.

"Look, I'll help you clean this up, and I can run out in the morning to get the part to fix the shower. Everything will be back to normal in no time."

The last part was the biggest lie he'd ever told. After whatever just happened, he doubted anything between them would ever be normal again.

125

Chapter Seventeen

So, this is what happens to liars.

Well, technically, Hannah didn't lie. She just tried to fake a shower to get out of seeing her neighbor. A man who was next door, changing out of wet clothes because he saved her bathroom from flooding. A man who was packing up chicken noodle soup for her dinner because he said she needed some after being so cold and wet.

"I'm trying my crock pot for the first time, so don't expect much," he'd said before he left.

Don't expect much.

When it came to Max, no matter what she expected from him, he blew those expectations to smithereens with his caring, thoughtful heart. And lying on top of him, drenching him with tears—as if the poor guy wasn't soaked enough already—he'd rubbed circles on her back. Like he'd done in her mind when she settled down from a near-panic attack earlier. In that moment, she had exactly what she needed.

She finished straightening herself up. The ruined mascara proved a challenge to wipe off, but she got the job done eventually. Doing so was therapeutic, in a way. She wiped away the past and what made her unhappy. She decided it was time she pursued happiness. Yes, she'd made a promise to herself to move slowly or avoid men altogether, but she couldn't help how this man made her feel. Max made her happy. And it had been a long time since she'd truly been happy.

When she heard the knock on her door, she leapt from her couch. She couldn't open the door fast enough, though it'd only been twenty minutes since she'd seen him last.

"You're dry and not holding a shower knob. This is already going better than last time I came over." He chuckled.

And then it was her turn to laugh. He now sported a shirt with two bowling pins on it that said "Split Happens."

He looked down at his shirt and then back at her. "Alright! It worked." He pumped a fist in the air. "I know you're a fan of punny graphic tees. I hoped this one would get a smile out of you." How did he always find new ways to make her happy?

"I love it." She couldn't stop laughing. He carried a large bowl of soup that was much too big for one person as he walked into the apartment. When she saw him grab two bowls from her cabinet and pair them with two cups from the drain rack, she knew she wouldn't be eating alone tonight.

"You're staying?" An uncontainable smile spread across her face. Earlier, he mentioned making dinner for himself and Quinn. Hannah assumed he'd eat with her.

His hands froze as he set the table. "Ah, I forgot you had your chat with Angie tonight. You know what? Let me just get your soup ready, and then I'll get out of your hair."

She reached out and grabbed his arm. "Stay." She blurted it without a second thought. She cleared her throat and still held his forearm tightly, unwilling to be without the warmth that radiated from the point of contact. "I mean, if you'd like to. Angie couldn't talk tonight."

"Is that okay?" he asked, a touch of hesitancy in his voice. "I told Quinn she could have one of her Zoom dinner dates with her friends. I know she'd rather eat with them than her old Uncle Max." He placed one soup bowl in front of her and then used that hand to cover hers still on his arm, rubbing the back of it in slow circles with his thumb. "I'm not a mind reader or anything, but I sorta thought you'd like some company tonight. Unless you'd rather have some time alone. I totally understand if you do." She wrapped her arms around him and took her first deep breath in hours.

Tears pricked her eyes, but she willed them away. She'd cried for the last time tonight. "I would love for you to stay. Let's eat this soup before it gets cold." She released him and walked back to her side of the table. He stayed frozen in place, never taking his eyes off her. Like he wanted to watch her every move to make sure she was really okay. Why did she feel so visible to him? Like he saw every part of her? She'd shown some unflattering parts, yet he was still there. He didn't run away. He didn't tell her to be a little less anxious or a little less Hannah. He stood here with her, wanting her just as she was.

They chowed down on the best chicken noodle soup she'd ever had and then cleared the table together. "Wanna pick up where we left off in *Friends*?" she asked as they walked to the living room. She popped a DVD out of its case and bent to pop it in the player.

He lightly grasped the back of her arm, and her breath caught in her throat. "Do you need to talk about why you were upset earlier today? Or are fully-clothed showers a new self-care ritual I've never heard of?" His attempted joke lightened the mood a bit. She didn't want to peel back the truth, but she couldn't lie to him. No, if she wanted to let him into her life, she had to tell him everything. Even if it sent him running for the hills. And that started with a confession about this afternoon's chaos. No matter how embarrassing.

She steadied herself with a long, slow breath. "Well, I tried to turn the shower on quickly, and the dang nob came off in my hand. And I was in clothes because I really wasn't going to take a shower." She bit her lip. This was bad.

His brows knit together. "I'm not following."

"I didn't want you to see me because I was crying. Like full-on, ugly crying with a capital 'U.' I thought if you heard me showering, you'd leave. But then I broke the shower and needed you, and now I feel like the biggest idiot on the planet." She hung her head, unable to bring herself to look at him. She waited for his disappointment to pour into the apartment. But when he took both of her hands in his, it was the last thing she expected. The last thing she deserved.

"Don't call yourself an idiot," he said a bit authoritatively. His eyes pleaded with her to listen.

"*That's* what you got out of my confession?"

"No. Not all. We'll circle back to the rest." He offered a small smile. His eyes bore into hers. "I just don't like people saying bad things about people I like." She couldn't believe what she heard. She just told him she avoided him, but somehow, he knew that wasn't the point of the story.

His gentle hand stroked her face, and a soft thumb wiped the spot where tears had been just a couple hours prior. "If you don't want to talk about why you were crying, that's okay. But if you need a hand to hold, an ear to listen, or just a big guy to lean on while you watch your favorite show, I can be whatever you need, Hannah. Just, please"—his eyes rounded as he looked at her—"let me be whatever you need."

MAX MEANT WHAT HE SAID. If she needed, he'd climb the highest mountain for her. Although, given his fear of heights, he hoped it wouldn't come to that. Apparently, she needed him for hugging, and he was happy to oblige when Hannah threw herself into his lap and wrapped her arms around him. He was a good hugger. He held her extra tight, a silent sign that he would protect her. Under his nose, a whiff of her shampoo flooded his senses. The mixed smells of vanilla and citrus were the perfect blend for Hannah: bright and comforting, just like her.

She shifted in his arms, and when she let go, her eyes were red again, just like before.

"I, uh—I'm not sure how to really say this." Sensing her distress, he held both of her hands in his. He felt the slight tremble and rubbed the tops of her hands with his thumbs as he had before because it seemed to help earlier. "Tonight, I was scrolling social media, and I saw that my ex-boyfriend, who dumped me not even a year ago, is now engaged."

What kind of idiot would dump a gorgeous, wonderful girl like Hannah? He guessed if he ever saw this ex of hers, he'd get to see what a moron looked like.

"That was hard to see, I bet." He had a feeling there was more to the story. He hoped she wasn't still hung up on this nimrod.

"It was, but it's not like I still have feelings for him. I mean, I have feelings for him, but they're more like the feelings Carrie Underwood sings about when she keyed her boyfriend's truck and then took a baseball bat to the head-lights. And I have reason to believe he was cheating on me with his new fiancée. The caption for the photo said some-thing about the past eighteen months with her being the best of his life." She scrunched her nose. "I'm no mathematician, but by my calculations, there was some overlap, seeing how we've only been broken up about twelve."

That son of a ...

The only thing Max was calculating was how many blows to the face it would take to teach this idiot what happens to cheaters. But those barbaric thoughts immediately left his head when he saw tears trickle down Hannah's cheeks.

"Hannah, don't cry over him," he said soothingly as he tried to wipe the tears away, but they came much faster than his thumbs could wipe.

"These tears aren't for him. Or maybe they are. I don't know." She fanned her face to dry her cheeks. "I'm trying to find the right words."

"Take all the time you need. I'm not going anywhere." He wasn't sure why, but a slow smile appeared across her face. She inhaled deeply, and on her exhale, she calmly stated something that rocked him to his core.

"You see, it's not that he's engaged that upsets me. That just triggered a flood of emotions I wasn't prepared to handle." She looked down at the floor. "I was in an abusive relationship."

Max. Couldn't. Breathe.

He swore he tasted blood. Probably because he bit his tongue. Hard. He needed a couple of beats to calm himself before he roared something about her ex. But no. He couldn't do that right now. This wasn't about him. It was about Hannah and her needs. What she didn't need was someone becoming emotionally unhinged on her behalf. Although, restraining his emotions became one of the harder things he'd ever had to do in his life.

"He hit you?" he choked. Imagining anyone laying a hand on this beautiful woman was more than he could take. Acid churned in his stomach. He felt ill.

"Oh, no. Nothing physical. Pete's abuse was the

emotional variety, though. After he dumped me, I realized emotional abuse leaves scars that aren't visible, but they can be just as damaging as physical abuse."

He saw red. His nails bit into his palms and a vein in his temple pulsed with every beat of his pounding heart. This clown hadn't hit her. That was good. But Max needed to call his high school to amend his senior yearbook—with the thoughts running through his head about this Pete character, he no longer deserved the class superlative "Nicest Guy."

"I am so sorry."

"Max, I have an anxiety disorder. I guess I've always had it, but it reared its head when life got tough. Like, really tough." She fidgeted with the ring on her finger that spun each time she stroked it with her thumb. "When my dad died, my anxiety reached a level it never had, and I got scared." Her voice cracked slightly. He scooted closer to her and wrapped his arm around her shoulders. "Shortly after that, I met Pete through mutual friends. We hung out in groups, and then it was just the two of us. He gave me attention I needed at that time. I was lonely, and honestly, being with him seemed better than being alone. At least initially." Max didn't like where this was going, but he listened anyway.

"I suspect he liked having me around, too, but for different reasons. He liked taking me to fundraising events for the hospital, out with friends, and to these posh happenings around the city. He'd buy me outfits, accessories, and jewelry. At first, I thought it was a sweet gesture, but I couldn't quite shake the feeling he was trying to make me something more worthy of being with him. Like being me wasn't enough. Until I was too much." Her nostrils flared as her face turned red. "Any time my anxiety would kick up, he'd shush me like a baby. He'd say I was being 'too Hannah.'"

"*Too* Hannah?" Max repeated in disbelief. "The only Hannah-related issue I have is that there's not enough Hannah in the world."

A small, watery chuckle escaped her mouth as she wiped a few more tears.

"I've spent the past year in therapy, trying to repair the damage he did. All the times he told me to 'shelve' my anxiety 'for later' when we went to his big galas, his insistence that my teaching exercise classes wasn't a worthy occupation and just a hobby to bide my time until I found what I was good at—he chipped away at who I was until there was nothing left of me but broken little pieces he had no interest in putting back together. The small pieces were more manageable for him." She cleared her throat. "He found me vulnerable after my father passed, and I was the perfect prop for 'The Pete Show.' I was embarrassed to admit I needed therapy, but I'm grateful for it each day. Although, you're the only person who knows I go. Well, you and my therapist, obviously." She took a deep breath. "I want to be clear: I'm not upset that Pete is engaged. I'm upset that he's been able to move on, unscathed, while I had to enlist professional help to move past what was undoubtedly one of the worst times in my life."

Max swallowed. This was a lot to digest. If he'd had a chance to gather his thoughts, he could have used his brain to create a helpful response. Without the luxury of time, however, he had to speak straight from his heart.

"You know, when Quinn was a baby, my mom constantly reminded my sister that it takes a village to raise a child. My sister tried to do everything on her own. I'm sure you can imagine how overwhelming that was. We all chipped in and helped because, well, it really does take a village." He leaned closer to her, taking her delicate hands in his once again. They trembled lightly under his touch. "But what happens when the child grows into adulthood

133

and faces challenges more difficult than diaper rashes and skinned knees? If you ask me, *that's* when you need a village."

She sniffled. "Well, I don't really have much of a village anymore." A lonely tear trickled down her face, pausing on her rounded cheek.

"Then move to mine." He smiled and let go of her hand just long enough to wipe the tear away. "We're good people in my village. Although, if you asked any of them, they'd probably vote me the village idiot." He laughed at his own joke.

"Hey!" She playfully punched his arm.

He made a show of rubbing it like she'd caused him bodily harm. "What the heck was that for?" A smirk crept up his face.

"I just don't like people saying bad things about people I like."

His smile widened. "Oh, so you like me? I would have never guessed from your strong right hook." He rubbed his arm again as he grinned.

She laughed and shook her head, eyes rolling up to the ceiling. When her gaze met his, she placed a hand over her heart. "Of course, I like you, Max." Her voice was as soft as silk, but its message spoke volumes to him. "Isn't it obvious? Geez, I mean if you didn't pick up on that, maybe you really are the village—"

"Don't you dare say it," he said, cutting her off and covering her mouth with his hand. He felt her soft lips move into what he guessed was a smile because her eyes crinkled at the corners. He slowly lowered his hand, and the pads of his fingertips ever so softly lingered on her bottom lip. He wasn't sure who moved toward who, but in the timespan of about two breaths, they were as close as two people could be without kissing. And, oh, how he wanted to kiss her. Now that he'd touched her pillowy lips with his fingers, all he could think about was what they'd feel like on his mouth. He'd claim them as his. He'd convey with a kiss what he failed to say with words tonight.

Tonight. *Ah!* He couldn't do this. Not after the emotional rollercoaster this woman was on today.

When he kissed her, he wanted it to be without reservation. He wanted her to kiss him because she was dying to kiss him as much as he was dying to kiss her. Because she felt what he was feeling and not because she felt sad or hurt. He couldn't kiss her like this.

He cleared his throat. "Look, you've had a tough afternoon." His voice sounded gravelly. "I don't want to take advantage—"

"Oh, no. Yeah. I understand," she quickly interrupted, scooting away from him.

"Do you, though? Because I don't want you to think—"

"Think what?"

"That I haven't stopped thinking about this moment since the day you walked into the gym and I forgot how to walk."

"*That's* what happened? I thought you were having a medical emergency like a heart attack or something." She burst with laughter.

He shook his head. "Nope, I was just an ogling doofus, apparently."

She moved into his side and rested her head on his shoulder. He wrapped his arm around her and pulled her closer in one fluid motion. He grabbed the blanket from the back of the couch and draped it over them.

As he looked down at her, resting her head on his chest, he knew she was someone special. Pete hadn't broken her. And she was brave to put together pieces of her he'd tried to smash. If he was honest, it only made her more beautiful. Like a stained-glass window, she was comprised of

135

many pieces that, when separate, didn't show a complete picture. But when the pieces were bound together, they were not only stronger, but they told a story through beauty and light. And as he watched the woman curled into his side, he made a silent vow to do everything he could to keep her beauty and light from ever dimming again.

Chapter Eighteen

"**W**hoa, whoa, whoa—let me get this straight ... you got a boyfriend in the middle of a pandemic, and I'm just now hearing about it?"

"Uh, pump the breaks a little, Ang. He's not my boyfriend." Hannah told her best friend all the events of the past couple weeks: the *Friends*-watching, the impromptu birthday celebration, the shower incident, and the heart-to-heart they had last night after she told Max about her past. Angie became so still on the screen, face unchanged for so long, Hannah thought the app had frozen.

"Are you there?"

Angie blinked slowly, her first sign of movement in several long seconds. "I know you've filled me in on bits and pieces of what's been happening, but I feel like you skirted over a few details in our daily texts."

"I'm just not sure what to make of everything right now, and my head is spinning, if I'm honest." Hannah rubbed her temples. Guilt was an unwelcome, invisible guest in this chat. It was time to confess something she should have told her best friend long ago. She didn't regret telling Max. But the hollow feeling in her stomach told her she should have told Angie first.

"Ang, I have something to tell you. I know I shouldn't have waited so long to do it." Worry lines crossed her friend's forehead. "I've been in therapy for six months. I had pretty regular and consistent panic attacks after Pete and I broke up. And while I know I could have confided in you, I was embarrassed. I decided I was better suited for professional help." She took another deep breath, eyes trained on the coffee table, unable to look at her friend on the screen. "I just hope you're not mad I kept this from you."

"Mad? Hannah, honey, I'm relieved."

Hannah let out an exhale that had half a year's worth of tension enveloped inside it. She should have known her best friend was only concerned with Hannah's best interests.

"I have prayed every night that you would do whatever it took to be happy again. As you well know, I wasn't a fan of Pete." She grimaced, like his name tasted sour in her mouth. "It was so damn hard to watch him dim you, day by day, one put-down after another. When you moved, it broke my heart. But I knew you needed to find happiness, and you sure weren't going to find it here in the shadows of all you've lived through. I hoped you'd confide in someone to help you get your groove back." She exhaled audibly. "I'm so proud of you, Hannah Banana."

The dam broke, and Hannah blubbered. She considered grabbing a glass of water. At this rate, dehydration was a definite possibility. "Thank you." She snorted loudly, unable to manage a ladylike sniffle at this point. She was too deep in ugly-cry territory to help it. Forget that—she'd blown past ugly crying and was well into grotesque crying at this point. "I figured you knew most of this. You've always had an uncanny ability to know what I'm thinking, sometimes before I even think it."

Her friend nodded slowly. "I did. Though I wish I didn't know. Wait—scratch that. If I'm wishing things, I wish it would have never happened in the first place."

That made two of them.

"Although ..." Angie continued, dragging out the last syllable of the word. "If it never happened, you wouldn't have found out how tough and capable you are of handling the roughest obstacles life can muster." The corner of her mouth tipped up. "And if it hadn't happened, you never would have moved next door to your new *lov-ah*. So, see? Things have a way of working out exactly as they're supposed to."

Hannah's head snapped back as she laughed with her whole body. "'*Lov-ah*?' We're not posh, middle-aged socialites having afternoon cocktails while lusting after the pool boy, Ang!"

Angie cackled so loudly, Hannah worried she'd blow the iPad's speaker.

"And more importantly, Max is not my lov-ah."

"Yea, I know," her friend admitted. "It's just been so long since I've seen you this happy, I thought for sure you'd slip and confess that you've been playing tonsil hockey between those episodes of *Friends*. Please tell me you've at least shared a peck. I'll even settle for a tiny peck-ette."

If only Angie knew how much she wished for any and all of those things. She mentioned how close they came to kissing yesterday, both on the bathroom floor and when she told him about Pete. When she mentioned how quickly he stopped and why, she watched her best friend turn into the human version of the heart-eyed emoji.

"Oh. Just. Stop. Could this man be any more perfect?"

She blushed at her friend's response. It's not like she could disagree with her.

"Does he have a single brother, by any chance?" She flashed a mischievous grin and waggled her perfectly groomed brows.

"Only a married sister. He does have a single best friend who is *like* a brother to him."

Angie pulled a face. "You mean that turd we met at the sports bar the weekend I visited? Hard pass."

She knew better than to convince her friend she was wrong about Johnny, especially since it was unlikely they'd see each other any time soon. It was even less likely her stubborn friend would change her opinion of the man.

"Listen up, Hannah, because I'm about to drop some truth bombs here. You see, guys are like … formal gowns, if you will." Hannah wanted to disagree, but she was more interested in seeing where her friend was going with this analogy. "Some are unappealing, others are loud and too in-your-face, and a few can make you itch." *Gross.* "A lot seem lovely until you see they do nothing for you—they actually steal your beauty. But, boy, when you find The One—the gown that fits in all the right places, makes you feel comfortable, pretty, yourself, one that complements you rather than stealing the spotlight—you hold onto it and don't let go. Because once you've found that perfect fit, nothing will ever make you feel as wonderful as you did when you found yourself something that was made just for you."

HANNAH SAT behind a sewing machine while Angie's gown analogy played on loop in her mind. And speaking of the "gown" her friend referred to, its niece stood across the table from her.

"So, I just use this pizza cutter then?" Quinn asked, holding up a rotary cutter.

"Yes, but you'll need to put the cutting mat down first so you don't mark the table. Just move those papers to the couch. You'll have enough room then." Fliers promoting a fundraiser the gym sponsored every year cluttered the table. The rather large event was going to be a little different this year because of the pandemic. Coordinators agreed on a virtual cocktail party and silent auction, offering everyone the chance to get out of their yoga pants and sweatshirts, the unofficial uniform of the last several weeks. It was an excuse to get a little fancy, even if the only thing others could see was the waist up.

"Are you going to the virtual gala?" Quinn asked as she moved the fliers to the living room.

"Sure am. I'm on the planning committee."

All gym employees took part in some capacity, but Hannah would have helped with the fundraiser anyway. When she heard it was a benefit for MADD, a cause that was near and dear to her heart given how her mother had passed, she asked for more responsibilities. She soon found herself one of the event's coordinators.

"No way. Uncle Max is on it too. Wonder why he didn't mention you."

"Oh, really? He probably doesn't know I'm involved. I'm in charge of promotion, so I'm only working with people putting up fliers and spreading the word on social media. Maybe he's doing something else." She ran another piece of fabric through the sewing machine.

"He's usually in charge of the food. But now that the event's virtual, I don't know what he's doing." Quinn shrugged and placed the scrap of fabric on the cutting mat. "So, how big are these pieces supposed to be?"

"Hold on." Hannah scurried over to the other end of the table and grabbed a piece of cut cardboard. "I made a template. Just put it over the fabric like this." She placed the cardboard on the piece. "Then, take the cutter and run it alongside the edge. Hand both pieces to me, I'll put the elastic between, and once it's through the machine, it's finished. Easy peasy, lemon squeezy."

"You sure are handy," Quinn said with admiration in her voice.

"Ah, I wasn't so handy yesterday when I pulled the shower knob off the wall and water sprayed everywhere." She could laugh at the memory now, especially since the Hemsworth sibling succulents hadn't perished during the fiasco. "Your uncle is my hero."

"So *that's* why he came home soaking wet. He just hopped in the shower, packed up soup, and told me he was having dinner with you, which was fine by me. I needed to finish up a paper for Mr. Bell before I could come over today. This time yesterday, I hadn't even started. Uncle Max sure is strict."

Why did an authoritative Max make Hannah's cheeks hot?

"Well, I'm glad you finished. I think I bit off more than I can chew with all these masks we're making." She figured they could make a half dozen or so. But then she thought of all the places around town she could donate them, and she couldn't stop. "What was the paper about?" she asked Quinn, whose tongue hung out of her mouth as she slowly ran the rotary cutter over a piece of fabric. She'd let the cutter get away from her once already and made the pieces about twice the size they should be. Hannah didn't have the heart to tell her.

"It was a cool assignment, actually. Mr. Bell assigned us a Shakespearian sonnet we've studied this year to compare it to a modern-day song with the same meaning. I thought it was a little far-fetched, at first, but themes from poems from 400 years ago are still applicable today—who knew?"

142

"That's really cool." Hannah admired teachers who found out-of-the-box ways to connect with students' interests. "I remember doing something similar in high school, except with movies. We had to compare a modern movie to a Shakespearian play with a similar message."

"Do you remember which you picked?"

"Oh, I remember it like it was yesterday. And it was *far* from yesterday." They both laughed. Hannah realized when she was in high school, Quinn was a baby. It was less funny now. "I compared *Romeo and Juliet* to *The Notebook*."

"Oooooh, I'm *very* familiar with *The Notebook*." Her eyes had an unfocused gaze to them, and Hannah wondered what kind of memory connected to this particular movie. "Uncle Max's girlfriend made him watch it every Valentine's Day. He acted like he did it begrudgingly, but we all knew better."

Hannah thought it a bit strange that she was aware of her uncle's Valentine's rituals. And how many Valentine's Days did Max share with this woman to have a tradition even his niece knew about? She tried to piece together these bits of information about a part of his past he'd never shared with her. He only said he didn't have a girlfriend. Right now. Maybe this was someone he still wasn't over. Hannah didn't want to feel self-conscious, but she couldn't help it now.

But then realization hit her like a bolt of lightning.

The tattoo.

"Oh yeah, he got that done shortly after she died," Quinn said as Hannah's mind reeled at the connection.

She knew the notebook tattoo on his side was too random to not have some sort of meaning.

Wait, what did Quinn say? Had Hannah shouted tattoo out loud?

"Wait ... who died?"

Quinn narrowed her eyes. "Uh, Courtney?"

143

"No, sweetie. I'm Hannah."

"No. *Courtney* died ... Uncle Max's girlfriend," she said slowly, realizing Hannah wasn't following this conversation. "He *did* mention Courtney, didn't he?"

"He didn't."

Quinn rose slowly from her seat at the table and began pacing. "Oh crap. Should I not have mentioned it? I just figured he told you." A light sheen of sweat materialized above Quinn's brow.

"I wish he had," Hannah whispered.

"When I saw the fliers for the fundraiser, I assumed Max had told you everything about her." She frantically pulled her hair up in a messy bun. It was the third messy bun she'd attempted in the last ninety seconds.

The fundraiser. Courtney.

The pieces fell into place with the fragility of boulders rolling off a cliff. "Max's girlfriend was Courtney Ward? Of the 'Courtney Ward MADD Benefit?'"

Quinn nodded solemnly.

Hannah's head felt like a balloon—light, unsteady, and floating away from her body with no telling where it might roam. Her eyes burned with the promise of tears on the horizon, and she blinked rapidly as she tried to process what she'd learned. She didn't know all the details, but she knew enough: three years ago, Courtney Ward was crossing the street to enter a restaurant for a celebration. She was struck by a vehicle driven by a drunk driver. She died instantly.

And she was Max's girlfriend.

Quinn came to Hannah's side of the table and looked at her through watery eyes. "We have the benefit every year in her memory. The whole thing was Max's idea."

"That doesn't surprise me." She sniffled. Though shocked by everything that she'd learned in the last three minutes, she was in no way shocked Max had taken an opportunity to help others, even under such awful circumstances. The hurt he must have felt was unfathomable, yet he pulled something positive from the tragedy. It was just like him to seize an opportunity to care for someone other than himself, even when he needed care more than others.

"I'm sorry I threw all this at you." Quinn gently covered Hannah's hand with hers, and Hannah felt them both tremble. "I'm not sure why he didn't tell you. He must have had a good reason."

She thought back to the night she told him about her mom. He'd turned as white as a ghost when she said a drunk driver had hit her mom. And she thought she saw him wipe a tear from his eye. No wonder he was so emotional. She had unknowingly rehashed one of the worst nights of his life.

When she wondered why he hadn't told her about Courtney's accident, another dose of reality smacked her in the face. He most likely kept his past a secret because he was too busy helping Hannah deal with the ramifications of hers. And while that should have frustrated her because she was perfectly capable of handling things on her own— with the help of her therapist, of course—a feeling she'd never experienced overcame her. Her stomach felt like a home to no fewer than a thousand butterflies, her heart flopped inside her chest as though it forgot its rhythm, and her body felt a warmth akin to stepping outside on the first warm day of spring.

What did it say about a person who purposely withheld pain to help someone else through theirs? When she poured out before him the details of the darkest parts of her life, he gave her the attention and care she needed. He never pulled the attention his way, though he had every right to.

Maybe Max would never open up to her, but she needed to at least let him know she was aware of his past. And she needed to assure him he could talk to her. Like two parts of a broken bone, perhaps they could heal and be stronger *together*. He always kept her best interests at heart, and she wanted to do the same for him.

Chapter Nineteen

Hannah and Max spent every day together in some capacity over the next week. She came over for meals, bringing a side or the main course, whichever he hadn't made. He went to her place and watched TV in the evenings, and they always snuggled on the couch with the blanket wrapped around them.

The live boot camp class went off without a hitch, except for the incredibly sore muscles he had for about three days following. He'd never admit that to her, though. There was a chance he overexerted himself to impress her, because she seemed a little more distant lately. Like something was bothering her. He wouldn't pry, of course. If Hannah wanted to talk about it, he'd made it abundantly clear she could always talk to him about anything.

Now he sat, working on a project for work that was both unfulfilling and incredibly boring. If only he could channel his technology expertise into something less soul-sucking. He'd have to put a pin in that thought, as his cell pinged with a text from the woman he couldn't stop thinking about.

Hannah: I'm about to go live with another Zumba class, but are you up for another binge-session of Friends *tonight?*

He ground out a sigh. Well, more like a frustrated growl. Now he'd have to finish out his workday knowing that she was hypnotically gyrating on just the other side of this wall. *Wonderful.* But he was happy she reached out. He was definitely up for hanging out with her, especially since he was working up the courage to ask her something important.

Max: Absolutely. Could I interest you in some chips and guacamole for the occasion?

Hannah: Hmmmmmm … let's go back to our "this or that" game we haven't played in a while, shall we? This or that: chips and guac or carrots and celery sticks? Because the latter is all I have right now.

Max: Is this an actual question? Guac all the way!

Hannah: I like the way you think, Mr. Robertson ;)

His cheeks warmed. A winky-face was techy flirting, right? Since she'd shut down any signs of interest in him lately, he'd take what he could get. Though she was always friendly, he was craving more than friendship. And he hoped that's what would be on the menu tonight.

HANNAH WAS certain of one thing—she was screwing things up with Max. Epically.

When Quinn told her about the tragedy with his girlfriend, it stunned her. And since Quinn must have contracted diarrhea of the mouth, she kept spewing out details Hannah was sure her uncle would rather keep quiet. Hannah wished she had Ursula's powers to temporarily steal Quinn's voice, because there was no way to stop her. Quinn even told her he hadn't been on a date in over three years—or been on a first date in almost ten.

148

"I don't even think he's talked to a woman in that long." Yeah, he definitely wouldn't want Quinn disclosing that piece of information.

But the last tidbit kept her awake that night. What did it mean that he had not only talked to her, but they'd also been spending part of everyday together? She had feelings deeper than friendship for him. And with the evidence in front of her, she'd safely bet he felt the same. So, naturally, this meant she needed to put space between them. At least that's what her brain told her as part of Operation: Keep Hannah Safe.

It made no sense—it didn't even make sense to Hannah. But her gut told her that whatever was going to happen between them now weighed much heavier than she once thought. If he'd waited this long to be with a woman —to even kiss someone else—doing so with Hannah would really mean something to him. It wouldn't be a casual first kiss. And while that thought caused a tingle throughout her body, it also scared her. A lot.

She didn't have any doubts about kissing him. He was the quintessential definition of eye candy, and she was dying for a taste. But she also had deep feelings for him. Once she got past his hard shell, she now found he had a sweet center that was even more appealing than she could have imagined. A kiss with him would hold more meaning for her as well. And that was scary. How did she go from swearing off men to taking things slow to now possibly kissing a man she was pretty sure she was falling for? She was on a rollercoaster without a seatbelt. This was so dangerous—but equally thrilling.

And now she was back to scared. She'd driven this coaster right off the rails. Instead of nestling into his side like she usually did when they watched TV together, she kept half a cushion between them. Instead of flirting, she was friendly. If he noticed the changes, he didn't say

149

anything, and that disappointed her. What if he was content taking a step back? The thought sent a shiver down her spine and left acid churning in her stomach.

She knew she was a goner when she looked at graphic tees for men online and imagined his reaction to the cheesy slogans. She clicked "order now" on one that featured a cartoon avocado standing on the steps of the Philadelphia Museum of Art. The avocado's arms were raised, and the caption "Guac-y Balboa" was scrawled at the bottom. It arrived yesterday, and she couldn't wait to give it to him. She hoped he'd see it less as a peace offering for being chilly toward him this week and more like a subtle hint that she had been thinking about him all week. Despite the way she acted. And how ironic that he suggested chips and guac for their TV snack tonight.

Hannah knew she needed to let him know what was going on in her head. But that meant bringing up Courtney, a topic that he'd had the opportunity to broach and hadn't. Would he ever? She just had to wait for the opportunity to present itself and hope it did sooner rather than later.

Chapter Twenty

"Hi-ya, neighbor." Hannah cheerfully greeted Max at his apartment door. She seemed so elated to see him, and that made his shoulders drop below his ears for the first time all week. He chuckled softly when he caught sight of her shirt, featuring peas in a pod holding up two fingers with the words "Give Peas A Chance" stretched across the top.

She caught him looking at her tee. "You totally crapped on my vegetable snack suggestion for tonight. I had to let veggies represent in some way," she said with fake hurt in her voice.

He held up the bag of chips and container of guacamole. "I mean, you're more than welcome to feast on rabbit food. Just know I'll be sitting next to you, chowing down on the snack of champions."

"Ah, you wore me down, Max." She winked as she took the food and padded to the kitchen. He bit his lip once she walked out of view. That was the human version of the winky-face emoji she sent earlier, right? Definitely flirty.

Most of his family hunted. Max did not. But he knew

if you got too close to a deer, it would run away faster than Quinn used to when his sister tried to wipe food off her toddler face. He thought about how distant Hannah had been this week and decided to apply the deer strategy: see how things went, let her take the lead, and move slowly. Very, very slowly.

His intentions were good. Well, until she pulled the elastic from her hair. Such a simple act. But when she whipped her head side to side like she'd just gotten out of the shower in a shampoo commercial, he worked hard to keep his tongue from hanging out the side of his mouth like a canine deprived of water. The cascade of golden waves fell softly down her back and over her shoulders. It only reminded him how beautiful and out of his league this woman really was. And his palms slickened.

"Max? Are you ok?"

She had no idea that taking her hair down had nearly undone him.

"Uh, yeah. I was just looking at the rain outside." He pointed to the window he was looking nowhere near just moments ago. At least he had the sense to realize it was storming.

"Yeah, they're calling for some really nasty stuff tonight." She extended a small gift bag in his direction and nodded for him to take it.

"What's this? It's not a holiday or anything."

"I know. It's just something I saw that made me think of you." Her smile was now more than triple the size of any she'd given him earlier this week. Relief immediately filled him.

"But I didn't get you anything. This isn't fair."

She shook her head. "If it'll make you feel better, consider it a thank you for being in the live boot camp workout. I couldn't be more grateful that you were willing to help."

He would have done a hundred more workouts with her if she asked. Not back-to-back, though. He could raise his arms above his head without wincing for the first time since the class. How on earth could she teach the number of classes she did each week? She was superhuman.

"Fair enough, but it was my pleasure to help. And it's an ongoing offer to do whatever you need me to do."

Though not meant to be suggestive, her grin showed she definitely took it that way.

"Noted."

When he opened the bag and pulled out the T-shirt, he barked a laugh so loud, tenants on the first floor probably heard. His unabashed reaction earned yet another huge smile from Hannah.

"You mentioned you're a fan of the *Rocky* movies, but it was a total coincidence that you suggested guacamole tonight."

He set the bag down and started to lift the hem of the shirt he wore.

"What a ... what are you doing?" Her eyes looked like they were going to pop out of her head.

He released the shirt and brought his hands up, palms facing her in surrender. "I was just going to try it on."

"Oh, yeah." She waved her hand, acting like her eyes hadn't nearly plopped onto the floor a moment ago. "Go ahead."

He wondered if she knew her mouth hung open. When she slammed it shut and looked down at the floor, he realized she did now. The side of his mouth tipped up. He wasn't ashamed of his body and was wearing a tank top underneath, but he turned his back to Hannah. He didn't want to look like he was starring in a male revue. When he turned back to face her, her stare burned his chest. After a hefty exhale, she broke the silence.

"That, uh, fits really nice."

It *felt* really nice. The shirt had that perfect blend of cotton that was unbelievably soft, like it had been washed several times already. It reminded him of her. She was relatively new in his life, but like this shirt, she made him comfortable in ways reserved for people that had been in his life far longer.

"I love—it." He inhaled sharply. He'd almost blurted out "you" at the end of the statement. *What the heck was with him?* He liked her. A lot. But this wasn't love. It couldn't be. They hadn't even kissed yet. And at that thought, his eyes homed in on her plump lips.

"Well, you mentioned only having one graphic tee. Now, I've doubled your inventory." She patted the couch, inviting him to sit next to her. As he stepped in her direction, lightning flashed in the dark sky. A deafening blast of thunder boomed shortly after, causing him to jump a little higher than the noise warranted. Excuse him for being a little on edge this evening. He didn't need anything else making his pulse race. Hannah was doing a good enough job of that, herself.

She nudged him with her elbow, and a tingle radiated from the point of contact. "Afraid of a little thunder, are we?"

The thunder, the violent pounding in his chest, the moisture collecting on his palms that could soak a cloth— all of it was a little concerning right now. "Something like that." He shrugged and leaned back on the cushion. "I wanted to ask you something." He swallowed hard and took a breath to buy himself a second. He summoned every bit of courage he had to finish this thought. "My friends and I put on a fundraiser each year for Mothers Against Drunk Driving. It's usually a big deal, a couple-y kind of thing." *Couple-y? Ugh! Could you be any less smooth right now, buddy?* He mentally slapped himself but soldiered on. "I was hoping that maybe …"

He trailed off, unable to finish his request. Hannah's eyes, flirtatious and cheerful just seconds ago, swiftly turned down. Her lashes, which he'd always admired, now fanned across her cheeks, an indication she wasn't looking at him anymore. But why couldn't she look at him?

Oh, this was going to kill him. Rejection was a knife to his chest, and her look twisted it slowly.

"I'm on the planning committee for the event, a late addition, actually. They put me in charge of promoting it." She looked at him with eyes that conveyed … sympathy? Why? She must have felt bad about the impending rejection.

"I know about Courtney."

"Well, yeah," he replied. "She's who the event is in memory of. Such a sad story, isn't it?"

She reached over and laced her fingers with his, understanding passing over her features. "I *know*, Max."

Her rounded blue eyes begged him to say something. Anything. But he was too surprised.

He cleared his throat. "Uh, how did you find out?"

She shrugged. "That's not important."

It wasn't, but he needed to say something to fill the silence, and that's the first thing that came to mind.

"Why didn't you tell me?" she asked.

Despite how hard it must have been to talk about, Hannah was very honest about her past. He felt he owed her the same courtesy.

"It was a very hard time for me. It was hard enough seeing reminders of Courtney all around town. Add to that the fact that everyone here knew what happened. People showed me pity at every turn. You know, it's been over three years since the accident, and I think you're the first person who hasn't looked at me like I'm completely wrecked."

She shook her head. "You're not wrecked," she whis-

155

pered as she grabbed his hand once again. The gesture, though simple, immediately cut the tension in his body by half.

"I know. But I didn't want you to pity me like everyone else. I wanted to put that chapter in the past and move on with someone who hadn't read it."

She tilted her head and looked at him through squinted eyes. "But how can someone reading your book understand it if they don't start at the beginning?"

"I, uh, I dunno." He scratched the top of his head. "I guess I was hoping you'd be more than just a reader of my story. I kinda hoped you'd be in it." He watched his foot tap out an irregular rhythm, too shy to make eye contact with Hannah.

When she lifted his chin to meet her gaze, her blue eyes shimmered like the purest water, fitting because the way his stomach flopped, he felt like he was at sea.

"I'd love nothing more than to be in your story, Max. But if you'll let me, I want to know all of it. The good, the bad, the sad … is it a lyric poem kind of story? I've apparently got the rhyming part down."

With Hannah snuggled tightly into his side, providing him both warmth and courage, he told her everything. How he and Courtney were friends since grade school. How they dated for a decade. How he was minutes away from surprising her with a marriage proposal when the accident occurred. And when he was through, they spent several moments in total silence, save for the sniffles coming from both of them.

Their breathing synced into a relaxing pace as they watched Mother Nature's spectacular light show. Then Max remembered he had a mission he still needed to accomplish. He leaned back so he could look at Hannah and did something he hadn't in over ten years.

"I've always gone to this event alone. And I know it's not a big deal this year since it's being held virtually, but would you be interested in going with me ... as my date?"

"It would be my absolute honor to go with you, Max."

Chapter Twenty-One

By Max's estimation, the rest of the evening was perfect. Like a summer sky with intermittent flickers of light from fireflies zooming about, little sparks glinted between them throughout the night, their chemistry as undeniable as the bolts of lightning that streaked outside the window in front of them. A brush of a hand that lingered, a moment of eye contact that lasted more than a few blinks. All the little things Max missed so much this last week were now happening again. And they came more organically than ever before.

The wind picked up intensity now, and a weather alert came across Max's phone. As he reached for it to get a closer look at the message, the lights went out. They stared at one another for a couple of seconds, waiting to see if the electricity would spark back to life.

It didn't.

"So much for binge-watching TV tonight," he said with a shrug.

Hannah sprang from the couch like she spawned the idea of the century. "Wait right here!"

Where exactly was he going to go? Well, he supposed a

good guardian would check in on his niece. He no more than finished shooting off a text to Quinn when Hannah walked into the living area, armed with a large candle, a lighter, and what looked like skewers for kabobs.

"Okay, light this, and I'll be right back." She hummed on her way back to the kitchen, spirits clearly not dampened by the lack of electricity. He did as she asked, not wanting to quell her enthusiasm for whatever she planned. She got so excited about the smallest things, and it warmed a place deep inside him to see her filled with such joy. When she returned with a sack of marshmallows and graham crackers, he solved the mystery.

"S'mores." She waved her loot in the air with a little dance. "I'm about to show you how we city folk make this campfire delicacy."

Max could easily guess how it was done, but there was no way he was stealing this moment from Hannah. She was obviously eager to teach him. And he was certainly a willing student. "I'm all ears."

She put the marshmallows on the skewers and held them over the flame. The amber light illuminated her features in an ethereal way. His breath caught in his lungs as he watched the light dance across her face. She was beautiful.

"Whatcha lookin' at over there, Max?" She playfully nudged his arm with her elbow.

"You," he whispered.

"Oh, geez. Do I have food in my teeth?" She covered her mouth and turned away.

He shook his head and chuckled. "No, Hannah."

He figured the moment, however minor it was, passed. But to his surprise, she sat her skewer down, half-melted marshmallow still attached, and grabbed his hand. It immediately burned with a heat so warm, he looked to make sure it wasn't in the flame.

159

"You need to hold it a little closer if you ever want it to finish," she said, pulling his hand closer to the candle. "It'll never finish the way you're holding it. Aren't you hungry?"

Starving.

They both stilled. Neither looked at the task in front of them, only each other. He reached with his free hand to slowly pull the marshmallow from the wooden stick. Holding it, the near-liquid center slowly ran down his thumb, warming it and mimicking the heat that spread throughout his body.

His breath quivered as he inhaled. The smell of caramelized sugar mixed with the heady citrus scent of Hannah's shampoo calmed him, though his hands still shook. He sat the marshmallow on a plate and turned, fixing his eyes on hers. With a touch as soft a butterfly landing on a flower, he raised his trembling hand to her face and caressed her lower lip with his thumb.

She parted her lips and licked the marshmallow away. When she did the same to the marshmallow on his thumb, his heart thudded in his chest. He stared at this woman, washed in candlelight, impossibly gorgeous and looking at him in a way that made him feel much too weak to resist the pull into her orbit. He brushed a strand of her golden hair out of her face and took one last look at lips that offered an invitation to make them his. He couldn't fight the pull anymore.

He lightly touched his lips to hers, barely more than a brush, as he tried to take in every second of this moment. He knew at its inception it was something he'd want to remember forever. This kiss, though delicate, was much more powerful than the act itself. It was all the things he wanted to hear but never realized until he heard them. It was a whispered secret that only he was lucky enough to know—one he'd hold close to his heart for the rest of his life and protect like a priceless treasure.

Everything was building to this very moment. Every minute of heartbreak, every night spent alone wondering how he could move on, every day spent in the warmth of Hannah's presence—it all inched to this very moment. A moment Max felt something he hadn't in over three years. He felt alive.

As he deepened the kiss, his heart hammered so loudly, he had no doubt she could feel it. He knew she felt the effect she had on him. Every touch of her lips was a breath of life that found its way to the depths of his soul, awakening parts of it that had been asleep for so long, all the coffee in the world couldn't wake something that tired. But her kisses were the best kind of morning brew: smooth and comforting, with enough heat to jolt him from his romance hiatus.

He pulled back slightly, looking at her hooded eyes and swollen lips. While he took a minute to catch his breath, she did the same.

"Max," she breathed, "that was ..."

"Perfect." The moment the words left his mouth, Hannah roared to life. She took his face in her hands and mashed their lips together with no inhibition. Her mouth left a trail of kisses, sampling Max's neck, his jaw, until they found their home on his waiting lips. It was needy, it was hungry, and it was sexy. Hannah was on fire.

Whoa—wait!

Hannah was literally on fire!

HANNAH HAD SUSPECTED Max was too hot to handle. She never imagined they'd literally start a fire the first time they got physical.

What came over her? She pounced on him like a wild animal, poised to devour him in a single bite. The primal

161

noises he uttered let her know he didn't mind the ferocity of her attack. He gripped her waist and rolled her onto the couch. But in doing so, her foot knocked over the candle on the coffee table, immediately setting the bag of marshmallows ablaze. For a moment, she wondered what ingredient in the candy made it so ridiculously flammable—whether something so combustible was safe for human consumption. She'd circle back around to that another time. They had a fire to put out.

Max jumped to action as though he put out coffeetable fires regularly, and she wondered if he had some incendiary hobbies she didn't know about. At first, he thought she was on fire, but his swift response was still critical to saving her burning coffee table.

Once the flames were out, he used his spare shirt to waft the smoke. With each flap of the garment, his forearms flexed, and her hands ached to touch them. Clearly the fire hadn't quelled her lusty desires. How could it? His cotton shirt hugged him in all the right places, and he looked so hot, she worried that *he* might catch on fire next. Just as the thought popped into her head, in an outrageous coincidence, alarms blared through the apartment complex.

The next thing they knew, they were standing outside in the rain with their grumpy neighbors, waiting for the fire department to arrive. Though not possible, Hannah swore her neighbors knew they caused the glorified fire drill. Did they have a scarlet letter on their chests that matched the crimson flush of their cheeks? Only, in this scenario, the A would stand for Arsonist.

Hannah gaped at her best friend on her tablet screen. She cackled without restraint, and Hannah could see halfway down her throat as her mouth hung open. The summary of the evening's events was apparently the funniest thing Angie had ever heard.

"So, let me get this straight—it got so hot between you two, you dang near burnt down the building, did ya?" She continued to laugh, and she dabbed her eyes to absorb the onslaught of tears. The girls were supposed to be enjoying a little "self-care sesh" with their clay masks and soothing music. Nothing about this conversation relaxed Hannah. In fact, it brought to mind way too many memories of the evening that made her contemplate turning on the air conditioning in her apartment.

"I will hang up this video chat right now if you don't cut it out, Angelica DiBenedetto." The whole incident really was too ridiculous not to laugh about. She got very little sleep last night. They stood outside while the firemen checked every square inch of the building, which made for a late night. Despite the lack of sleep, she was in the best mood she'd been in for as long as she could remember.

Angie smirked. "Why am I not buying your threat?"

"Because I'm too damn happy."

Angie's mouth fell wide open, and her hardened mask cracked slightly near her jaw. "Hannah Banana, look at you with that potty mouth. My dream of rubbing off on you is finally coming true." She raised her arms in a victorious pose, made even more ridiculous-looking with the green goop smeared on her face.

Hannah rolled her eyes. "Saying 'damn' is hardly grounds for saying I have a potty mouth. Anyway, when are you gonna visit me again?"

Her friend's face fell a fraction as she told her that soon she might have all the free time in the world. "Rumors are flying that my school might consolidate with another for the next school year due to low enrollment." She rubbed her temples and then grimaced when she saw the mask now all over her fingertips. "I'm the least tenured person at my school, so the writing is on the wall for me."

"Oh, Ang. I'm so sorry."

"Ah, what good will worrying do? I might not be able to pay rent in a couple of months, but I'll work something out if it comes to that." For as strong and sassy as her best friend seemed, Hannah knew she had a fragile center. Seeing her friend filled with so much doubt was as common as seeing a scowling Santa.

"You always have a place here."

"I know, hun. Anyway, I have some lesson plans to put together, you know, while I still can." She chuckled mirthlessly.

"You know ... exercise is a great way to boost those happy hormones. I have another boot camp class this evening if you're free."

"Is the fireman in this one too?" She waggled her brows.

"He sure is."

Angie punched the air and whooped. "My day has been made. I can't wait to see the dynamic duo in action. I still can't believe I missed the last one."

"Then I'll *see* you soon!"

Hannah signed off and did some quick mental math. Only four more hours until boot camp class. Four more hours until she got to see Max again.

Chapter Twenty-Two

"Yo, Adrian!" Max shouted as Hannah opened the door. She turned away and snorted a laugh when he started shuffling like a boxer. "I'm just trying to get amped for this boot camp class." He gave the air a couple boxing jabs.

"Did you have yourself a little *Rocky* movie marathon this afternoon?" She laughed openly now, unable to contain it like before. It was melodic, and like a favorite song, he wanted to hear it over and over. "And was that supposed to be a Philadelphian accent?"

"Ouch." He grabbed his chest, feigning hurt. "If you have to ask, it must not be that good."

"I had to ask." She smirked and motioned him into her apartment. Right away, he noticed her shorts. She'd never worn that article in front of him before, and he'd definitely remember. She mostly wore yoga pants for her workouts. He thought they were his favorite article of clothing she had. But now that he caught a glimpse of her strong, sculpted legs, he'd have to bump the yoga pants down to second place. He tried so hard not to stare at her during the last boot camp class because Quinn was there.

Plus, he and Hannah were only friends at that point. Now that they were … well, what were they now? He knew they'd moved past friendship because he'd never kissed any of his friends like that before. And the sight of any of them in shorts had never rendered him motionless. It was okay to check her out, right? He sure hoped so. It wasn't like he could help it.

She couldn't help it, either. He wore another cutoff shirt. It was the only thing he had that was clean. He didn't think anything of his wardrobe choice, but the way her feverish eyes spent more than a passing glance on his exposed arms made him glad he picked this shirt.

"You ready to go?" she asked.

Oh, you have no idea.

He cleared his throat … and the flirty thoughts swirling in his mind. "Um, yeah. Are we doing the same circuits as last time? Or did you want me to come over early to go over something new?"

Her thick-lashed eyes grabbed him with an unrelenting grip. "There was one *position* I wanted to practice." Why did she say that word like that? She moved toward him, stopping when they stood toe-to-toe.

"I don't think standing this close gives us enough room to work out," he said, praying she wasn't about to do an exercise right now. He was unexpectedly breathless.

"I don't think we're close enough to do what I want." She erased the small space between them, and he finished the job, wrapping his arms around her small waist and crashing his mouth to her full, pursed lips. His hands ran up her toned arms and cradled her neck. As he deepened the kiss, her opened mouth invited him in. Forget boot camp—this was his new favorite workout. And given their panting, it was a really good one.

He needed to stop. But he couldn't. But he *had* to. In thirty minutes, nearly a hundred people were going to tune in for a workout. How would it look if they saw them red-faced and sweating before the workout even began?

"Hannah, I …"

"We should stop," they both said, chests heaving for breath that couldn't enter their lungs fast enough.

Her cheeks reddened, though Max couldn't understand why. "I'm sorry. I don't know what came over me just now."

"I do. I'm guessing it was the same thing that came over me the second you opened the door and I saw you." His eyes traveled down her body and slowly made their way back up to her face, which glowed brighter than the fire they accidentally started last night.

"I think you're right." Her arms met behind his neck, and she rested her head on his chest. His chin sat on top of her head, and his arms held her tighter. If music played, they'd be in the textbook position to dance. He inhaled her familiar citrus scent, the first full breath he took since he entered the apartment.

"Hannah, do you have any plans for Memorial Day weekend?"

She looked up at him, and his stomach fluttered. "Well, we've spent about every day together for nearly the past two months. I sorta figured my plans would somehow involve you." Her voice softened. "At least, that's what I was hoping."

He figured the same but didn't want to assume. "I was hoping you'd spend it with me … and my parents. Every year, we have a picnic and watch fireworks together. It's at Oglebay Park, by the way, and I know you've been saying you'd like to go there. So, if my company isn't enough to get you to come, I thought maybe the location would do the trick. They usually have a big shindig with all sorts of games and entertainment, but because of the pandemic, all that's canceled. But they're still having the fireworks."

167

Like a dimmer switch that turned up steadily, her eyes illuminated with a glow unmatched by anything he'd seen before.

"I'd love to come." She ensnared him in an embrace so tight, he might need the jaws of life to get out. Thankfully, he never wanted to.

"Great. I've been able to see my parents a few times to drop off groceries. We'll still mask-up for their benefit. They're just so excited to finally get to meet you in person."

She leaned back to look at him. "In person?"

"I mean, they've been watching your workouts ever since you started putting them online. At first, they tuned in to boost your viewership so the gym would keep the workouts coming. Well, that's what they said, at least. I have a sneaking suspicion they were spying," he said, rolling his eyes.

"They watch my workouts?" She clutched a hand to her chest.

"Oh yeah. They have perfect attendance, in fact. Haven't missed one since you started 'em."

She tilted her head to the side and stilled for a moment. "No one's ever supported my classes quite like that. Well, aside from you, of course. I—I'm, I dunno ... I'm touched. Truly." A visible flush developed on her cheeks. "I can't wait to meet them." She pulled him in for another hug. He'd never get enough hugs from her.

"They couldn't be more excited. My dad keeps telling everyone he's never met a celebrity before." He couldn't see her face as held her close, but he felt the quiver of her chuckling against his body.

"You ready for this?" she asked.

He knew she was talking about the impending boot camp class. But if she was asking about whatever it was that was blossoming between them, the answer was the same.

"Absolutely."

~

"WHY DIDN'T YOU STOP?" Hannah wrapped an arm around Max's waist while he limped to the couch. She thought she saw him roll his ankle during the burpee/jumping-jack set, the last of the class. He acted unaffected by the incident. Until now.

"I'm fine, Hannah."

He didn't look fine. In fact, the way he hobbled like a pirate with a pegleg looked the exact opposite of fine. He raised his leg to rest on the stack of pillows she'd piled up. His ankle already looked a little swollen.

"I'll be the judge of that," she said sternly. She loosened the laces and pulled off his tennis shoe. "You broke it four months ago. This isn't something to mess with, Max."

He was grinding her gears now. Why was he chuckling?

"This isn't the ankle I broke."

Oh. This piece of information, paired with the half-smile he wore, alleviated some worry, but she still felt responsible.

"Why were you going full-throttle like that? You were supposed to be demonstrating modifications for the exercises, not hulking out like a contestant in a strongman competition." She tried to act annoyed, and truth be told, part of her was. It was just so hard to stay mad at him when he gave her that smoldering look with his eyes. So, she stopped looking at his face.

But that didn't help. Her eyes quickly locked on his rugged arms that he unintentionally flexed as he rested his hands behind his head. On second thought, the cocky grin

169

plastered on his face suggested the flex was definitely deliberate.

"Max sad," he said in a deep voice, impersonating the green, muscle-bound comic book character, his pouty lip on full display.

"You're ridiculous." The smile on her face contradicted her words. "I'm going to grab some ice."

She padded to the kitchen and groaned when she saw the empty ice tray on the dry rack. She should have filled it after their last margarita night. Too late now. She did the next best thing and grabbed a pack of peas from the freezer. "Here you go."

"Aw. Give peas a chance, Hannah," he moaned, referring to the shirt she wore last night.

"I'm giving your ankle a chance. You could end up with two bum ankles once this is all said and done, you know?"

His nostrils flared and he bit his bottom lip. Was he trying not to laugh at her?

"Why aren't you taking this seriously?"

He placed his hand on hers. She stopped fussing with the peas and looked up at him. "I'm not going to end up with two bum ankles. After the break, the doctors assured me that it would heal even stronger than it was before. And that one"—he gestured to the ankle Hannah tended to— "is going to be fine. I barely rolled it. So, as much as I am enjoying the Florence Nightingale treatment—and I am *really* enjoying it—you can ease up a little. I'm gonna be fine, Flo."

He was probably right. Putting weight on it likely meant he didn't break it. But since it happened during her class, she felt accountable, and the over-the-top care she gave assuaged her guilt. "I'm sorry." She looked down at the frozen peas. "I still think you should keep something cold on it to keep the swelling down."

"Agreed. Can you prescribe anything else that would make me feel better?" His darkening eyes homed in on her lips. They'd transformed from milk chocolate to extra dark in a blink.

"Max." She gently pushed his chest in protest. *Well, dang, that's a hard chest.* "Knock it off." She rapidly shook her head as though it was an Etch-A-Sketch and moving it back and forth would erase the thoughts of his perfect upper body.

"Fair enough." He raised his hands in surrender. "I know medical professionals can't fraternize with their patients. It's *forbidden*." He bit his lip, moving his eyebrows up and down suggestively.

She pointed a stern finger. "No hanky-panky until we make sure your ankle doesn't get any worse."

"Maybe just some hanky?"

"I can't offer you a handkerchief, but I'm sure I have tissues around here somewhere." She pretended to look around her apartment when his arm reached out and wrapped itself around her waist like a frog's tongue snatching its prey. She crashed alongside his upper body. His eyes danced all over her face as she ran her hand through his tousled hair, still damp from the workout.

"I'm gonna go shower really quick. My stank is more than I can handle. You stay put."

His kissable cheeks flushed. "I happen to like the way you smell. Almost as much as I like the way your lips taste. Although you've made it clear you're content to let me starve this evening." On cue, his stomach growled loudly, sending them into a fit of laughter.

"Even so, I'm gonna hop in the shower. Why don't you order some food and let me spend the rest of the evening taking care of you?" She could see the gears turning in his head. He'd rather spend the evening doing other things, and so would she. But his health came first.

"You have yourself a deal … under one condition."

"Max, we're taking it easy tonight, I told you no—"

"Have dinner with me."

She crinkled her brows. Did he suffer a blow to the head she didn't know about in addition to the ankle injury? "We *are* having dinner together. I *just* told you to order something."

"I know that. I mean, another time. Out of the apartment. At one of the restaurants that reopened with outdoor seating." He shrugged. "I'm just wondering if you'd like to go on a date with me."

Her heart took off on a sprint. Though they'd spent so many evenings together and shared so many meals, the prospect of an actual date with him had her flying. "You have no idea how much I'd like that."

She peeked over her shoulder to get one last glimpse of him before entering the bathroom. The heat of his glare shot warmth through her entire body. She suspected he really *did* know how happy he'd made her, because she had a feeling he felt the same.

Chapter Twenty-Three

Hannah gave her hair one last tousle, making her beachy waves look a little more, well, beachy. Although, she usually looked like a crazed poodle at the beach once the humidity wrapped its clutches around her hair, so she wasn't sure where the name for this style came from. Nonetheless, it suited her.

She studied her reflection in the mirror and nodded in approval. Max said they were going someplace casual. Hopefully, her pale blue sundress would fit in wherever they went. Its light, cottony fabric was ideal for the warmer-than-average weather today, and the flirty, feminine way the garment danced with her every move made her feel pretty.

Excitement percolated inside her all day, making her unable to sit still. She decided to get ready earlier than necessary. When her phone pinged with a text from Quinn about a half hour later asking if she could meet before her date to look over a paper she was working on, Hannah was thankful she'd gotten a head start.

"What brings you by so early? I thought I was coming over to your place," Max said as he opened the door to his apartment. He wore a fitted undershirt tank top and khaki shorts, obviously getting ready himself. Was there was any place they could go where his wardrobe would be acceptable? She certainly wouldn't mind looking at him in that tight, white shirt all night.

"Quinn asked me to look at her English paper before we left." She pressed her hands firmly to her sides as she walked past him. They ached with desire to touch every inch of skin visible on his body. His exposed arms in particular whispered, "Touch me, touch me," as they stared right at her. She savored him with her eyes but thought better than to push things any further. Quinn could appear any minute. How awkward would it be to help her with homework after she caught her making out with her uncle? Uh, super awkward.

"Ah, now see, Quinn is ruining this whole vibe I was trying to create." Who knew someone so brawny could also be so cute?

"Just pretend I'm not here." She covered her face with her hands.

"Not possible," he responded with a rumble in his voice.

The side of his mouth tipped up into a half-smile as he wrapped an arm around her waist and lightly pressed his lips to her cheek. He took a step back and his dark eyes traveled slowly up and down her. "You're absolutely beautiful." The deep timbre of his voice caused her knees to buckle. His tightened grip around her middle—which kept her standing—also caused a fluttery sensation in her stomach.

Quinn, who Hannah just realized was sitting on the living room couch, had her hands clutched to her chest. She looked at them with her head tilted, a cheesy smile taking up much of her face. "Aw, you guys are couple goals."

Max rubbed his chin. "Is that a good thing?"

"Most definitely," Quinn answered, nodding repeatedly.

The two girls sat on the couch, and Max padded down the hallway to finish getting ready.

"He really likes you," Quinn whispered once her uncle was out of earshot.

"The feeling is mutual." Hannah grabbed the paper and began reading.

Just after they'd gone over the assignment, Max reappeared in the hallway looking even better than when he'd answered the door. His dark blue button-down shirt stretched snuggly across his broad chest and hugged his biceps in a way that made them look even larger than usual. She'd never thought of a button-down as super sexy, but something about the way it looked on him made her fingers itch to undo the pesky fasteners. One by one.

From behind his back, he presented her with a small potted plant.

"I was going to bring this when I picked you up, but since you're already here ..."

"Calla lilies ... how did you know?" She glanced at Quinn as she left the room, sharing a wink with her uncle as she disappeared down the hallway.

"I may have had help," he admitted. "But you did mention how you always felt bad when cut flowers died so quickly. And the other night, you said you wanted to get some flowers for your balcony. So, I thought this could be the start of your outdoor oasis."

She took the pot from his outstretched hands and looked at him through glassy eyes. She'd said all that weeks ago. "How—how did you remember all that?"

He shrugged. "I remember everything you tell me." He said it like it was no big deal, but to her, it was.

She looked at the flower from all angles. "I think I'll name it Max."

"Gee, I don't know if I'm worthy to be among those other hunky plants you've got at your place."

"See, that's where you're wrong," she answered as she intertwined her fingers with his. "They're not worthy to be around you."

He brought their hands to his lips and gave hers a soft kiss. "Ready for our first official date?"

With a smile that had enough wattage to light an entire city, she answered him. "I've never been more ready for anything in my life."

MAX PULLED into the parking lot of one of Hannah's favorite restaurants in the city. She'd never mentioned that to him before, but somehow, he always knew what she liked. Outdoor seating was the only option available, but she didn't care. Dining al fresco was incredibly romantic on a gorgeous night like this.

Tables and chairs, spread farther apart than usual, filled the space, providing a little more privacy than restaurants typically offered. Soon, globe lights that wrapped around the railing of the raised deck would add to the ambiance as the sun tipped behind the trees. Warm air blew past the handful of seated patrons, the sound of it through the nearby woods the perfect soundtrack for the evening. A large speaker's humming drew her attention to the slightly raised stage at the far end of the floor.

"Is a band playing tonight?" she asked.

He looked toward the stage. "Well, what do ya know? I guess there is." His poor acting skills didn't fool her. He knew she was a fan of live music and probably planned to bring her here for that very reason.

"Oh. My. Goodness." She gasped and turned over a card on the table which pictured a decadent milkshake in all its sugar-filled glory. "Okay, don't tell this to anyone at the gym because I'm supposed to encourage healthy eating habits. And while it's a fact that healthy foods make you feel good, I'll fight anyone that says a good milkshake can't make you just as wonderful. I mean, not like every day, obviously."

"You don't say?"

"Oh, I definitely do say." She licked her lips as saliva pooled in her mouth.

A masked server approached their table. "What can I get you two this evening?"

"A water for me," Hannah replied.

"Same for me," Max chimed in. "And two of these." He pointed to the milkshake Hannah still couldn't tear her eyes from.

"I really shouldn't," Hannah said, but she didn't mean it. She was as bad of an actor as Max.

"Hey, it's nutritionist-recommended."

"I'm not a nutritionist." She chuckled.

"Whatever the case, you better believe I'm getting you anything that puts a smile like that on your face." He reached across the table, brushing his soft palm against her cheek. It warmed immediately against his touch as she took a slow, deep breath. Her love of milkshakes was true, but even the sweetest treat couldn't compare to the taste of him on her lips.

"Too bad you're not on the menu then." She giggled but sucked in a breath when he uttered a guttural growl and pinned her with a gaze that explored her all over.

The waitress plopped two ginormous milkshakes on their table and took their food order. Hannah scooted her milkshake closer, a trail of condensation following behind. The rich scent of vanilla combined with the sweet smell of caramel flooded her senses as she took her first sip. It was cold, smooth, and sinfully delicious, just as it appeared on the menu. She raised her gaze to Max and noticed him sitting back with arms crossed and milkshake untouched, beaming in her direction.

"Good, is it?"

She blushed. "Were you watching me?"

"Maybe. It's hard not to look at someone who's enjoying something so much."

She gestured to his glass. "Take a sip of yours, and join me in euphoria, will you?"

He obliged with a long, slow slurp of the straw. "Well, that's every bit as good as I expected."

"Milkshakes have always been my favorite. My dad was no kitchen whiz, but he could make a mean milkshake." She missed her parents every day, and lately she wondered what they'd have thought of Max. Looking across the table at the man sporting a milkshake mustache, she was certain that they'd approve of him.

"I wish I could have met him." He stroked his thumb over the back of her hand, causing goosebumps to travel up her arm.

She reached across the table to wipe the ice cream from his upper lip. "You two would have gotten along well, I think. But speaking of parents, I should probably know a little about yours since I'm meeting them next week."

"Where do I begin?" He stroked the perfect dusting of stubble on his jaw. "Well, my dad's name is Gene. You know those people who are total wallflowers and never quite settle into social situations?" Hannah nodded. "Well, he's the complete *opposite* of that. He'll have you laughing until your stomach hurts. Oh, and he's massive," he said, holding up a hand to show that his father was even taller than Max. "He's a real hoot, though."

"And what about your mom?"

"Well, her name is Shelby, and she's just the sweetest."

Hannah couldn't help but notice the soft tone of his voice when he spoke of his mother.

"Obviously, you've noticed that I don't have a southern accent. Most people from northern West Virginia don't. But Mom's from Boone County—way down south—and she's got an accent that's thicker than gravy. Didn't lose an ounce of it since moving north. And she's just got the biggest heart." His eyes brightened as he looked at her. "She's going to fall in love with you."

His hand stilled on hers, and suddenly the deck, which had filled with a constant breeze, was without air. The way he said that—why did she feel like he meant more than his mother would love her? No, she was putting words in his mouth. This was wishful thinking to the highest degree. She felt things for him, sure. But love? It was too soon to be throwing that word around like candy at a Christmas parade.

"Here ya go," the server said, interrupting her thoughts. She plunked two plates of entrees on the table. "Enjoy."

They ate in comfortable silence, spending more time looking at each other than at their meals. Hannah considered it a miracle she hadn't dropped any food on her lap.

"Max Robertson?" an unmasked, middle-aged woman asked more than stated as she approached their table—staying six feet away, of course.

"Mrs. Ripley, how are you?" he asked, politely.

"I haven't seen you since ... well, it's been quite a while. How are you doing? We all miss Courtney somethin' terrible."

Hannah noticed the tilted head and the sympathetic look she gave him. It was just like Max described—everyone in town pitied him.

"I'm doing really well lately. Thank you for asking."

For someone inquiring about the well-being of another person, this lady sure seemed shocked that he was happy. Was this Mrs. Ripley expecting him to stay in mourning forever? That wasn't fair.

"Mrs. Ripley, I'd like to introduce you to my girlfriend, Hannah."

That statement caused two things to happen: 1) Mrs. Ripley folded her arms against her stomach as the rest of her body froze—who did she think Hannah was, sitting here with him?—and 2) Max's eyes bugged out of his head as he bit his bottom lip so hard, Hannah thought she might see blood drip down his chin. Frankly, he looked as shocked as Mrs. Ripley.

The woman turned to Hannah, making eye contact with her for the first time since she approached the table. "It's quite nice to meet you." Why did Hannah get the feeling she didn't mean it? "And it was good seeing you, Max." She turned on her heel and walked away.

Hannah waited until Mrs. Ripley was out of earshot before she spoke. "What was that about?"

Max wiped his palms on the front of his shirt and started sputtering. "Geez, I know! I don't know what I was thinking. We've never discussed it, and here I am blurting it out to virtual strangers. Hannah, I …"

"I hoped I was your girlfriend."

Max did a double take as he looked at her. "Really?

"Really. But that's not what I'm asking about."

He looked in the direction of their visitor, like he might not want her to hear what he was about to say. "Okay, well, Mrs. Ripley is the mother of one of Courtney's best friends —who must want me to stay single forever." He shook his head and chuckled dryly. "I mean, I tried that already. Didn't work out very well."

His sarcasm was a cover Hannah could see right through. "Max, are you okay?"

"Hannah, it's been a long time since I've even been *close* to okay. But now, I've reached a level of okay I didn't think was possible. And that's because of you."

It was hard not to believe him when his slow smile brightened to the amped-up version he now sported.

When they finished their meals, she saw three men walk onto the small stage. After a few audio tests, the air filled with the sound of their music.

Hannah dabbed the corners of her mouth with a napkin. She couldn't remember the last time her stomach was so full. She could say the same about her heart.

"That was absolutely delicious." She sat back in her chair as Max scooted around to her side of the round table. They sat shoulder-to-shoulder, and every point of contact sent a tingle throughout her body. The waitress cleared the table and came back to top off their water glasses, an invitation to stay a little longer and enjoy the music on this beautiful late-spring evening.

"I've loved every part of this evening so far." He took a sip of his freshly filled water, and she watched the movement of his throat as he swallowed. He touched his hand to the top of hers, and she instinctively turned it palm up, allowing their fingers to intertwine.

She noticed the way his eyes danced around the room. If she didn't know better, she'd guess he was nervous. Was he bracing for impact should another unexpected visitor stop by their table?

His gaze finally settled on the stage, and he shared a look with the lead singer. When the band finished their rendition of an upbeat Counting Crows song, one of her favorites, she felt his knee bouncing up and down against hers. His hand also felt clammy. *So, he is nervous.* Why now, though? She thought they'd shared a wonderful evening. And he seemed very comfortable, save for the brief encounter with his classmate's mom.

When the applause died down, the lead singer came up to the mic. "So, we're gonna slow things down a bit. This one goes out to someone special in the audience tonight. Now, this isn't a song we usually play, but hopefully she still likes it."

The opening chords were unmistakably familiar. This wasn't just any song. It was the one that played the night of her impromptu birthday party, when they almost kissed for the first time. This wasn't a coincidence—they'd dedicated the song to *her*. The glowing cheeks and yearning expression on Max's face confirmed her suspicion.

"Max," she began as a knowing grin spread from cheek to cheek. "What did you do?"

He feigned a "who me?" expression and then relaxed. "It's possible I called in a favor to a friend." He and the lead singer shared one of those head bobs guys always gave each other.

He rose slowly from his chair and extended an open hand to her. "May I have this dance?"

She gazed at the empty floor. They'd be the center of attention, but she didn't care. When a man looks at you like you're the only thing he sees, remembers every single detail that relates to you, and thinks of every possible way he can make you happy, you dance with him every chance you get.

"Always." She put her hand in his and walked to the center of the floor.

"You're full of surprises, Mr. Robertson."

"As are you, Miss Jenkins."

They danced under a sky that mimicked navy velvet with pinpricks of light poking through, and she couldn't imagine a moment more perfect than this. All they needed was some music, some starlight, and each other. He pulled her closer and pressed a light kiss to her temple, his lips lingering near her ear.

"Hannah," he whispered, the deepness of his voice making her feel as steady as standing on water. "I ... I think I'm ..."

The final note of the song played, and applause broke them both from the spell they were under. Max's down-turned mouth and the rapid rise and fall of his chest gave her hope that he was about so say something more meaningful than, "I think the song is almost over."

She hoped so, at least. Because as sure as she was standing there, she knew she was falling in love with Max.

Chapter Twenty-Four

"Maximus, good to see ya, bud!" Johnny shouted from across the field.

Max shook his head and offered a bemused smile. "As I've told you over and over for the last twenty-five years, that's not my real name."

"So you say, and yet I've never seen proper documentation supporting your claim."

Max laughed. "You're a nimrod." He walked over and gave his friend a hug with a firm smack on his back. When he pulled back, he noticed Johnny wearing one of the WVU-themed masks Hannah made especially for the two of them. She delivered over 250 masks all over town last week and made sure to leave Max with enough for his family, as well.

"Your girlfriend is quite talented and extremely thoughtful," Johnny said.

Max rubbed his neck and released an approving sigh. "You've got that right." Despite the chill in the air, he felt warmth spread throughout his body.

"You're a lucky man, Maximus Robertson."

"Not my name."

"Maxine?"

Max groaned. "You're right about Hannah, though. I feel like I'm luckier than any guy has a right to be."

"Hey, you deserve all this and more, bro." He gave his buddy another firm pat on his back. "Now, let's play ball."

They were hardly about to "play ball." But this was as close as they could get, given they only had two guys, two gloves, and a ball. He was just grateful Johnny invited him out to get some fresh air and have a catch.

They spread apart, and Max took off his mask. He breathed in deeply; the smell of his old, leather mitt and the wildflowers scattered on the nearby hillside filled his nostrils. They were a stark contrast of scents, but together, they reminded him of the countless hours he spent on this very field.

He walked past the old, wooden benches that looked like they could use a fresh coat of paint, and the metal fence appeared much rustier than he remembered. Rustier than his arm? He'd find out soon enough.

But when he dug his feet into the grass of the outfield, it was like no time had passed at all. He could almost hear his dad cheering as he struck out the last batter to advance his team to the state tournament his senior year. He had so many memories attached to this field. It felt both like a life-time ago and yet only yesterday since he'd taken the pitcher's mound for the title game.

Johnny pulled a ball out of his duffel bag and pounded it in his glove a few times, as though it needed broken in. The glove was as old as Max's and as pliable as it could be.

"So, how have the virtual training sessions been going?" Max asked as they threw the ball back and forth. He had flashbacks of college days, when they'd warm-up for practice and games, exchanging notes on their day in the process.

"My schedule is as filled as it was when I could train

185

people face-to-face." He smiled, a look of satisfaction on his face. "I even took on a couple new clients whose schedules didn't allow for training appointments at the gym with childcare issues and work schedules. Being able to keep doing this has been a blessing." Everyone was getting creative out of necessity because of the pandemic, making a lot of lemonade from the overabundance of lemons this year had delivered.

"That's awesome, Johnny. Maybe I should start training with you." He figured two ankle injuries in less than six months was a sign his body wasn't in the peak physical shape it once was.

"From what I've heard, you've already got yourself a trainer." Johnny gave him a knowing smirk.

"First off, Hannah is an exercise instructor, not a trainer. She has personal training credits but not a license to prescribe programs to clients."

The ball smacked Johnny's glove as he stared at his friend and cocked a brow.

"I mean, you know that already," Max mumbled, looking at the ground.

"I do. I didn't know *you* were such an expert on her credentials, though." Johnny bit his lower lip, failing to hide a smile.

"I'm not. I just appreciate what she does. And … and she's really good at it," Max asserted with his chin high and shoulders back. He wasn't sure why he felt the need to defend Hannah to Johnny—it wasn't like he was attacking her. It probably had something to do with the way she talked about her ex. That buffoon, Pete, claimed her passion was a silly hobby, one he hoped she'd someday shelve in favor of something more important. The jerk obviously had no idea the training, planning, and dedication it took for Hannah to do what she did. What she gave to her clients made every aspect of their lives better.

But Johnny already knew this.

"I'm sorry. I just—" Max scratched his head.

"Love her?" Johnny guessed, completing his sentence.

The ball plopped out of Max's glove as his wrist went limp and the rest of his body stilled.

"Johnny, I don't … I mean, I can't …"

"Don't lie to me," his friend interrupted, raising his gloved hand. "I've known you almost our entire lives. I probably know you better than anyone else. And I know every time I mention Hannah, your face lights up brighter than that Christmas tree everyone goes to see in New York City."

"The Rockefeller Center tree?"

"No—I mean, yeah, that's it. I just mean no, that's not what we're focusing on right now." He stepped a little closer. "What I'm wondering is why you won't admit to yourself that you love her."

Max blew out a large breath and tossed the ball back to his friend. He almost slipped and confessed big feelings to her the other night while they danced. But that would have been wrong. Because he wasn't in love. He couldn't be. Love ended in heartbreak, and he wouldn't survive another blow like that. Besides, it was too early to be thinking about love. Wasn't it? "I don't know."

"I think you do."

"Okay, you're right." Max threw his hands in the air. "I have feelings for her. Feelings I don't know how to identify. Feelings I don't know what to do with. Feelings that scare me so much, I just—" He looked down at the grass and ran his foot back and forth over a dead spot. "I don't know what to do."

"Uh … telling her might be step one. And then showing her for the rest of your life is step two." Johnny shrugged. "Pretty simple if you ask me."

"But it's not," he grumbled, still digging at the dirt with

187

his foot but more forcefully now, leaving a small hole in the ground. "And the rest of my life? Don't you think it's a little too soon to be thinking about the future? And I don't even know if she's into that. I don't want to get into too much, but she's had a rough go of it lately, Johnny."

He crossed his arms. "Okay. But so have you, as I'm sure you'll recall."

Max lifted his baseball cap and ran a hand through his hair before he yanked it firmly back down on his head. "What if I can't give her enough?"

"Enough what? Love?"

"Well, I guess, yeah. I mean, not love. I can't be in love with her already. But enough of anything. Enough of me. I mean, I gave my heart to someone and never really got all of it back." He dug at the grass some more and noticed how much of the dirt he'd exposed. The metaphor wasn't lost on him at the moment because that's exactly how he felt right now—exposed. "What if I can't give her all of me because I don't have all of me left to give?"

Johnny scrubbed a hand down his face. "Where is this coming from? Because every time we've talked, you've been slowly and steadily moving on. Why are you pumping the brakes all of a sudden?"

He sighed loudly. "We ran into Mrs. Ripley the other night at dinner, and uh, she seemed miffed that I was out with Hannah."

"Oh please." Johnny threw his hands up in the air for the second time. "That woman's always sticking her nose where it doesn't belong. And I'm pretty sure she was the originator of the resting you-know-what face. Do a Google image search—bet you she comes up."

"Johnny!"

"Sorry. That's more than a little disrespectful. But, damn it, Max. Knowing she made you feel like this is more than a little upsetting." Now it was Johnny's turn to dig feet in the dirt. But with the force he exerted, he'd be ankle deep in the soil in no time.

"Only I'm accountable for how I react to others. It's not Mrs. Ripley's fault."

Johnny's eyes rounded. "It definitely is. Look, you've been happier these past couple months than I've seen you in a long time. And I know you're always thinking about everyone else—their feelings, their needs, their problems. It's one of the things that makes you such a great guy. But it's also the thing that's kept you from moving on with your life."

Max's eyebrows pressed together as he looked at his friend. "I, uh ... I'm not following."

Johnny drew in a deep breath and forcefully blew it out before he spoke. "When Courtney died, you made sure everyone was okay. You worried yourself sick over how her parents, sister, and friends handled her death. Don't get me wrong—that was incredibly noble. But what about you, Max? Did you let anyone check in on *you*? In the months after her death, you organized fundraisers for the community. Again—very honorable—but did you let anyone do anything for *you*? You put everyone else's needs, emotions, and grieving ahead of your own, and now that you're happy for the first time since the morning of your twenty-seventh birthday, you're still worried how what you're doing impacts people closest to Courtney, when *you* were probably the closest. If you're everything to everyone and you're no one for yourself, how are you supposed to heal? You can't be so busy living for everyone else that you forget to have a life of your own. We're all rooting for you. In fact, I ran into Josie on the hiking trail the other night, and she heard about you and Hannah."

"Really? How's she doing?" Guilt churned in his stomach because it had been a few weeks since he'd reached out to Courtney's sister, something he'd done regularly since the accident. She'd always treated him like family.

"Not great. Between losing her sister and her broken engagement, I think she's just doing what she can to make it to the next day. But she couldn't be happier for you. And I know she meant it."

Max bit his lip and tried to control his emotions. Crying wasn't allowed in baseball.

"Everyone has moved on," Johnny continued. "We didn't want to, but we *had* to. No matter what we do, Courtney isn't coming back. And as far as not being enough for Hannah? You've been more than enough for this whole community. You collect coats for the homeless in her memory every November. You had dinner with her parents weekly the entire first year after the accident because they'd thought of you as a son. You told me you didn't want them to feel like they'd lost two children the night of the accident. You helped plan nearly every detail of her funeral because her folks were too wrecked to handle it. So, when you stand here and tell me you're convinced you don't have enough love to give someone because of what's happened in your past, I can't even process that. Because, Max, you've given more love to more people in the past three years than most people give one person in their lifetime."

Max looked up to the sky, hoping the sun's warmth would dry the moisture pooling in his eyes. He squeezed his eyes tightly shut to suppress the tears. "You're supposed to be the one I come to for comedic relief," he choked out with a chuckle behind a sob.

Johnny rubbed the back of his neck. "I know. I'm even a little shocked, myself."

"Thanks, bud. Those are all things I needed to hear, but I've been refusing to listen to any of it for the past few years."

"Ain't no thang," Johnny said, attempting to break the tension that covered the baseball field like a dense fog. "Just remember, even heroes have a right to be happy."

He shook his head. "I'm hardly a hero."

"Not if you ask anyone in this town who isn't named Max Robertson." He tossed the ball back to Max.

He smiled and returned the throw. "Keep me humble, buddy."

"You do too good a job of that on your own."

They threw back and forth a few more times, Max's anxiety lessening a little more with each toss. "You know, I've always *shown* people how I feel better than I've been able to say with words."

Johnny looked around, and his eyebrows rose to his hairline. "Are you about to grand-gesture me, Max?" He batted his eyelashes and pursed his lips, a moment of comedic relief Max appreciated.

"Not a chance. In all seriousness, I was wondering if you could answer a couple of questions for me. I've got an idea, and you're just the guy to help me set it in motion."

"Whatever you need. You know I'm always here." Johnny then looked around the field, a sly smile emerging. "Follow me," he shouted over his shoulder as he jogged to home plate. Max followed until he saw his former battery-mate crouch behind the dish and hold his mitt as a target.

"Hit me!" he shouted.

Max shook his head. "There's no way I can throw like I used to. I'd rather not embarrass myself anymore." He jerked his thumb over his shoulder. "I already sobbed in the outfield."

"Humor me," he yelled as he raised his mitt chest-center and readied himself for a throw.

Max swung his arm around in a circle to warm up a bit. He'd already suffered a broken ankle and a twisted ankle in the last six months. *Let's not add a dislocated arm to the list.* He pounded the baseball in his glove a couple times as he strode to the top of the mound. He leaned in like he was receiving a sign from his catcher to amuse his buddy, wound up, and released the ball. It sailed through the air with a velocity that shocked him. The smack of the ball hitting Johnny's glove echoed throughout the field.

"Oh yeah!" Johnny shouted, holding up his glove with the ball inside. Max watched his friend run to him, and the image transported him back to every time they'd played together as pitcher and catcher. When Johnny caught the final out, he always met Max at the mound with a giant hug.

Some things never changed. His teammate and best friend still cheered him on all these years later. And he'd need that kind of support if he was going to show Hannah how much she meant to him.

Chapter Twenty-Five

T he day of the big Memorial Day picnic arrived. Well, it was big in the sense that Hannah was meeting Max's parents today. She couldn't remember the last time she'd "met the parents," and while her palms moistened every time she thought about that, excitement bubbled inside her at the chance to finally meet them.

She gathered supplies and ingredients to take to Max's place. After teaching two classes yesterday back-to-back and another early this morning, the contents of her living room were now in her kitchen area, so Max let her borrow his kitchen. She wanted to make something for the picnic, but she didn't want to move furniture again—she had another class tomorrow. Despite him telling her a million times she didn't need to bring anything, she refused to show up empty-handed. Plus, Quinn wanted to learn how to make her homemade Chex Mix, and she certainly enjoyed spending time with his niece.

"Come on in," Quinn greeted her at the door. "Hannah's here," she yelled down the hall to Max. He came barreling into the kitchen, swallowing her in a hug so large, calling it a bear hug wouldn't do it justice. After a quick kiss on the cheek, he stepped back.

"There are children present, you two." Quinn snickered.

Hannah blushed, and Max sighed loudly. "Turn away then," he responded, pretending to shield Quinn's eyes. "I'm happy."

"Well, that makes two of us," Hannah smiled back.

"This is all very cute, but we have some Chex to mix, right, Hannah?" When did the sixteen-year-old become the mature voice of reason in this apartment?

"That's right. It'll need some time to cool, so we'd better get started." Last night, Max told Hannah they'd leave for the park a little earlier than needed because he had a surprise for her.

She put the ingredients on the kitchen island and gestured to an open laptop. "Max, what do you want us to do with your computer?" He'd already gone down to his room, and she wondered if she could just move it herself. She caught a glimpse of what looked like a website design on it. He'd never shown her any of his work before, but this looked really well-done.

"Oh! Hey! I forgot I left it out," he squeaked, his voice high in both volume and pitch. He scuttled into the room and shut the screen with a thud. When met with narrowed eyes zeroed in on him, he cleared his throat and simply stated, "It's just a project for work."

"Some top-secret government work?" Quinn half-joked. But with the urgency with which he'd closed the laptop, it was a valid assumption.

"Tee hee." He tucked the computer under his arm and carried it to his bedroom, like he hadn't just thrown himself on the kitchen island to close it.

"I mean, he didn't say no," Quinn stage-whispered to Hannah, and they both laughed.

194

"Let's just focus on the mix." Hannah finished organizing everything and measured the ingredients as she dumped them into a huge bowl. She tried to forget whatever it was Max didn't want her to see on that screen. His work was his business.

After they mixed the ingredients, stirring gently so they wouldn't crush the cereal bits, they put the giant bowl in the oven and set the timer. "We have to stir it every fifteen minutes, so we have a little time to relax."

When they walked into the living room, Hannah noticed a couple packed boxes and a suitcase stacked along the wall.

"What's going on here?" Sweat dotted the back of her neck. Surely Max wasn't just up and moving. No. Just because that's what Pete had done didn't mean Max would do the same. It was ridiculous to even jump to the assumption, but that's what anxiety could do to a person. The sudden thought of history repeating itself sent a chill down her spine.

"I'm moving out," Quinn answered.

"What?" She was relieved Max was staying, but she didn't want Quinn to move, either.

"School ended Friday, so I don't need Uncle Max's supercharged WiFi anymore. I'm gonna live with my grandparents so I can help out. You know, mow grass, help Pap with his garden, do housework for Gram, and maybe have some friends over so we can hang out in the backyard."

She seemed happy, so of course Hannah was happy for her. "Well, I'll miss you, neighbor."

A small smile crept on Quinn's face as she looked down the hallway to the room her uncle currently occupied. "I have a feeling we'll be seeing a lot of each other—and hopefully for a long time." She offered an exaggerated wink.

As scared as she'd been about jumping into something serious, Hannah noticed her resolve deteriorating quickly. She held up two hands with crossed fingers for good luck. "I sure hope so."

When the oven beeped, they worked together to scoop the mix into the snack-sized plastic baggies with red, white, and blue fireworks Hannah found for the occasion.

"I think we're all set," Quinn said when she saw all the baggies filled to the brim.

"Thanks for all your help. Are you meeting us at the park?"

Quinn crossed her arms and rubbed her elbows, avoiding eye contact with Hannah. Her eyes glistened under the fluorescent apartment lighting. "Yep. I'm going to drop a load of stuff off at Gram and Pap's first. We'll, uh, pick up the rest tomorrow morning." Her voice cracked a bit on the last word.

"It's been nice having a sister for a couple months." Hannah sniffled. She closed the gap between them and wrapped her in a tight hug while she softly stroked her hair.

"I know. I always wanted one." Quinn stepped back and rubbed her nose with her hand.

"Me too."

Max softly cleared his throat from the hallway, and the girls choked out a garbled chuckle.

"You ladies are going to see each other in an hour. Two tops." He walked over and brought all three of them into another big hug.

"Alright," Quinn interrupted. "I need to get moving, and so do you guys."

"I'll grab these boxes, and we'll follow you down." Max grabbed two labeled "school books" and lifted them so easily, they could have been labeled "feathers."

Once Quinn drove out of the parking lot, Hannah and

Max got in his truck and turned on the A/C. It wasn't a particularly hot day, but hauling boxes down three flights of steps made them a little sweaty. She wasn't sure what her excuse was because he did all the heavy lifting. Watching him flex his muscled arms as he hefted the boxes couldn't make someone that sweaty, could it?

"Okay, so what's this surprise you're keeping from me?"

"Let me explain to you how surprises work: if I tell you, it won't be one, now will it?" That darn half-smile was back to its usual tricks, and now not only was she sweating, but she felt her cheeks burn, as well. When he reached across and grabbed her hand, she melted completely.

Chapter Twenty-Six

Max recalled one of the first nights he and Hannah sat on their balconies and talked. She said she'd like to visit Oglebay Park and see what else it had to offer besides the Christmas light display they had each holiday season. When he looked at her now and saw the smile that reached her wide eyes, he knew he'd made the right choice to bring her to the park early to show her around.

"Like what you see?" Stupid question. The answer was written all over her face. Her eyes blinked rapidly as she stifled a small gasp at the flowers so vibrant and colorful, not even an artist with every color at his disposal could recreate the beauty spread before them.

"Like it?" She chuckled softly. "This is absolutely gorgeous. Thank you for bringing me here."

He reached for her hand and led her to a wooden bench beside a large fountain. The soothing sounds of the water trickling and the birds chirping as they flew between the trees of various heights were a soothing soundtrack to the moment between them. Something told him this was a moment he wouldn't soon forget.

"Isn't it beautiful?" She motioned to the scenery surrounding them.

He didn't see any of it. Didn't care to. None of it compared to her.

"Breathtaking."

He pushed an errant hair out of her face and placed a soft kiss to her lips. He felt hers upturn to a smile, and he summoned every ounce of strength he could muster to keep from deepening the kiss. He teetered on the edge, and if he leaned any further, he wouldn't stop. And he had to because he couldn't kiss her like he wanted when they were in public.

"This would be a beautiful place to get married," she said after he pulled away.

"Hmmm?" he answered hazily, unsure what she'd asked.

She pointed to a bride and groom posing for photos in front of the Oglebay Mansion, the cornerstone of the entire park. Because of the pandemic, they didn't have a wedding party with them. Just a lone photographer.

As he watched the couple pose in a variety of positions, Max couldn't help but imagine the two of them in their places. Hannah would make a beautiful bride.

Wait ... what?

Why was he picturing Hannah as a bride? It was way too soon to think like that. He wasn't even sure he loved her yet. His heart clearly didn't care, judging from its frantic gallop at the picture-taking place in his mind, featuring Hannah next to him in a gown as white as fresh-fallen snow.

The sound of kids yelling in the distance woke him from his daydream. "I know they do a lot of weddings here. It's beautiful twelve months of the year, so they keep busy."

"I bet." She looked at her watch. "What time are your parents expecting us?"

He checked the time on his phone. "Any minute now." He stood and offered her a hand. "We can leave my truck here and walk to the picnic site. It's not far."

"Perfect."

Perfect. If ever there was a word to describe this woman, this feeling he felt for her, and her place in his life, there wasn't a better choice.

~

THE TWO OF them walked through a wooded area, the crunch of gravel and the chirping of birds overhead the only sound they heard. Max figured he should be nervous introducing Hannah to his folks. This was, after all, a big step in a relationship. But the feeling that pumped through his veins wasn't fear—it was excitement. As they walked through the park to the picnic tables his parents reserved, her wide grin and the bounce in her step made him think she felt the same.

"Big Max!" a booming voice echoed through the hillsides of the park. Yes, at six-feet, four-inches, Max was a big guy, but his father had a good two inches on him. At least.

"Dad." Max waved from the bottom of the hill. He squeezed Hannah's hand, which she met with a small squeeze of her own. Because of his parents' ages, everyone wore masks when they were within a close distance of one another.

"They're wearing the ones I made." Hannah beamed with pride. She'd dropped the masks off a couple of weeks ago when she and Quinn made stops around town. He hadn't seen them, but when his mom called to tell him how sweet his new girlfriend was (although they weren't official yet), she mentioned that they had the West Virginia University logo on them. Just like his.

"Oh, honey, of course we're wearing them. Bless your heart," his mother said, accent as thick as molasses, as they walked up the gravel pathway. "Now get in here," she said as she smothered her in a hug.

"Hannah, meet Shelby and Gene Robertson," Max introduced.

"Please, just call us Mom and Dad," his father responded. "I mean, no pressure or anything like that. I just mean, that's what all his friends call us, and you're his girlfriend, which is a step up from that, so, okay then."

"Smooth, Gene." His mom snickered, jabbing a playful elbow in his side.

"You call us whatever you dang well please. We answer to anything, sweetheart." His mom was clearly already a fan of hers. How could she not be?

His dad pointed to the cooler. "There's pop, water, and beer in there, and I've got Beanbags set up, so you can have a go at that if you want."

"Cornhole, Dad," Max corrected with a chuckle.

"Listen here, Maxine," his dad began as he put his son in a good-natured headlock. "I'll call it whatever I want." They both laughed loudly. It was so good to see his parents in person.

"I'll go with your mom and drop off the Chex Mix, and then I'll definitely give *Beanbags* a try," Hannah said as she looked back at Max. Though her mask covered her face, he knew from the crinkle of her eyes she shot a smile in his direction. Likely a mischievous one after that comment.

"I like her." His dad's raised voice was loud enough for Hannah to hear as she walked to the picnic table. She flashed a thumbs-up in their direction.

"So do I, Pops," Max said in a voice a smidge louder than a whisper.

He watched his father's eyes raise to the sky with a deep exhale. "You know I'm the furthest thing from a mushy guy. And I'm not—how do they say—*with the words*. But you don't know how happy I am to see you like this." Together, their eyes traveled to the picnic area where his mom and girlfriend loudly laughed as they pulled supplies out of a picnic basket. They were like old friends sharing a memory they'd enjoyed at least a hundred times before. His dad gave him a couple pats on the back, and they joined the women at the table.

Max hung back a few steps, watching his mom interact with his girlfriend. When his father joined them, he had Hannah cracking up within ten seconds of coming to her side. How was that even possible? And how did it seem like she'd known his family far longer than the twenty minutes or so she had?

The crunch of tires on gravel shifted his attention. If Hannah was happy before, she was going to be ecstatic once she saw who exited the vehicle.

"Nobody better be burning my burger!" the loud voice reverberated through the wooded area. Hannah's head whipped faster than the swing of a homerun hitter's bat. Max didn't know how she stayed upright.

"Renee?" Hannah clasped her hands to her chest. "What are you doing here?" She looked around, and Max's grin gave away his involvement in this surprise.

"Well, everyone knows it's not a party until I'm here," Renee answered, arms raised above her head in a pose that said, *Here I am.*

Hannah's eyes danced from his parents to Max and back again, looking for answers.

"Mrs. Morris is our next-door neighbor," his mom supplied. "She mentioned a lovely young girl at the gym who taught her water aerobics class, and after talking to Max, we put two and two together. My son thought you might enjoy seeing her, since you mentioned missing your gym family."

Max's lips twitched, attempting to suppress a smile, which wasn't necessary since he still wore his mask. He sensed pure elation in Hannah's eyes, and before he knew it, she hugged him with such force it knocked the wind out of him.

"You did this for me?"

"Of course. I told you I'd do anything to make you happy," he whispered softly in her ear. He saw goosebumps pop up on her neck and heard her small, satisfied hum. Suddenly, he wished they had a little more privacy.

"You never stop amazing me." She pulled down her mask to kiss him quickly on his cheek. Too quickly. He wanted more than just that half-second of bliss. She paused like she might say something but then looked like she changed her mind. She instead grabbed his hand, pulled her mask over her face, and dragged him over to Renee, who was also the recipient of a WVU-themed mask from Hannah.

"It's so good to see you!" She hugged Renee, and his insides warmed with the happiness that radiated from these two. They had a grandmother/granddaughter dynamic, and since Hannah didn't have any family left, he was glad to include Renee in today's festivities. "I had no idea you knew Max."

"Oh please, I've known this guy ever since he was about this high." She gestured with her hand, holding it as high as her hip. "I watched this kid grow up. I still remember seeing his tush in my window that one summer."

His eyes bulged, and his eyebrows shot to his hairline. No one ever knew what would come out of Mrs. Morris's mouth, but time away from her had caused him to forget how loose of a cannon she could be.

"Oh my God, Max! You mooned Renee?" Hannah snorted as she laughed.

"NO!" he shouted. Loudly. A little too loudly, now that he thought of it. Exactly how someone who *had* mooned their elderly neighbor would respond. "Let me explain. I was four years old. My dad and I were outside doing yard-work near the woods behind our house. We both needed to pee, and we didn't feel like walking all the way back to the house, so he taught me how to relieve myself outside. I thought it was so cool, later that night when I had to go again, I snuck out the side door to do my business between mine and Mrs. Morris's houses."

"Next thing we knew, we got a call from Renee askin' us if we knew our little Maxy was outside with his pants at his ankles," his mom finished the story, and everyone laughed. Well, everyone but Max. He was too busy dying of embarrassment.

"Yes, yes. Thank you for that lovely memory, Mrs. Morris," he said through semi-gritted teeth.

"Oh, Max, that's so cute," Hannah said as she rubbed his arm.

Max shrugged. "Public urination stories are always a hoot, I guess." How could he be all that embarrassed when Hannah laughed with such joy? Nah. Forget it—he was still embarrassed, cute laugh or no.

"Wait." Hannah looked at Renee. "Why didn't you tell me you knew Max?"

Her eyes looked at the ground to her right. "Well … I would have. I should have. But I decided I'd rather play cupid, instead. I knew from the second I met you that you'd be perfect for each other, but I couldn't be an impartial matchmaker if you knew he and I went so far back." Renee's brows raised and lowered more than a couple times as she continued. "From the looks of it, you two didn't need my help at all."

Max usually wasn't a fan of meddling, but as he wrapped an arm around Hannah's shoulders, he decided he didn't care how they got to this place. A place bursting at the seams with happiness. He was willing to let the interfering slide. This time.

"Alright," his dad interjected. "Who wants to listen to some music?" He held up a wireless Bluetooth speaker and wiggled his hips.

Max looked at him quizzically. "Dad, you know you need Bluetoo—" He stopped abruptly. His father, a man who refused to get WiFi in his home, who still had slow-as-molasses internet, pulled a smartphone from his back pocket. "What?" If his dad pulled a tiger out of his back pocket, Max would have been less surprised.

"Now, don't be jealous, Max. This is a highly-sophisticated piece of equipment I've got here."

"I'm well-aware, Dad." He shook his head, a smile of disbelief on his face. "I work with technology for a living—and I've been trying to talk you into getting a smartphone for years."

"Yeah, well, you were always talking about socializing apps and the Instant-gram and mumbo jumbo like that. We have one Gram here. That's enough." He winked at Max's mom. "You never told me I could clip coupons … on my phone!"

Ah, yes. He should have known his audience better. He'd have made a terrible salesman.

His father smiled at Hannah. "How else do you think we got to see this brilliant girl's classes on the line?"

"Online, Dad," he corrected. He set his parents up with a Facebook account several weeks ago so they could watch. "I just assumed you saw it on your computer."

"Not with that slow internet. Poor girl would still be

standing frozen on our screen with that sorry excuse for technology."

Mr. Robertson wasn't wrong. That's why Max kept begging them to upgrade. But it was like speaking a foreign language to them.

His dad tapped his phone a couple of times. Before Max could wrap his head around the image of his father operating a piece of technology he swore he'd never get, a familiar country tune filled the air.

"Hannah, why don't you and Mrs. Morris catch up while Max and I grab a few more things from the car? Gene, you start up the grill, and I'll send Max over once it's ready."

Max smelled it from a mile away—this was his mom's chance to separate him from the pack so they could chat. When she declined Hannah's sweet request to help, he was certain.

"So …" his mom started, her long southern drawl as present as ever. She pulled a checkered table covering and grocery bag from the trunk. This wasn't a two-person job, but he played along.

"So …"

"Oh, don't start with me, Max." His mother laughed, and it warmed something inside him. She laughed with the same joy in her eyes as Hannah whenever Max made her giggle.

"What do you want me to say, Mom?"

"I don't really *need* you to say anything, honey. I'm just giving you the chance to confirm what I already see, plain as day." She winked and then nodded her head to the picnic site. Max followed her gaze.

He closed his eyes and shook his head to make sure his vision wasn't playing tricks on him. But there it was: his father and his girlfriend, dancing a two-step to one of dad's favorite country songs while Renee clapped in time with the music. He could hear his dad singing the lyrics, which he bellowed above the volume of the speaker. Hannah's movements were so seamless, it looked like the two of them had practiced this routine hundreds of times. When she spun, her hair mimicked a golden river, following behind her in a fluid motion. And when his dad dipped her on the last beat of the song, their laughter was even more melodic than the song that played.

His mom placed a hand over her heart. "She's really something."

Max was almost too breathless to speak, so he bought himself a moment with a thick swallow. "Yeah. She really is, Mom."

A weightless gaze from his mother said without words what he had yet to admit to himself: *You're in love with her.*

AFTER A DAY FILLED WITH BURGERS, storytelling, and so much laughter, Hannah doubted the picnic could get any better—that is, until she snuggled up with Max to watch the fireworks. Her back met his solid front and she cocooned herself inside his large arms. He took full advantage of the proximity of his head to her ear.

"I had a wonderful afternoon with you, Hannah." His breath tickled her ear, and a chill ran down her spine. He followed the trail of goosebumps on her neck with the light touch of his finger, and more popped up on her skin.

She tipped her head back to see his face. When he brushed his lips on her forehead, she melted into him. "Your parents are really something."

"They feel the same about you. You fit right in, already."

Another chill ran rampant through her body. Was it too soon to think about being part of his family? Too bad. This afternoon brought her to a place she hadn't been in years. She felt like she belonged. And it felt as wonderful as she remembered.

Her mind took off like a horse from the chute. Images of the fun they'd have together at holidays and other family gatherings galloped along, playing like a highlight reel of the future. And she wanted so badly to be part of it all. Was she jumping the gun a tad? Probably. They'd only been officially dating for a short while. But trying to quit thinking about it was like hitting the brakes on an icy road. She was helpless to control it.

After the fireworks, they walked to the truck, the warm breeze blowing through her hair on the summer-like evening.

And just like that, the air stopped.

She gasped for breath but couldn't catch it. Her eyes, large and unblinking, now burned from the threat of oncoming tears. Because there he stood. The man who broke her down to a shell of a human being—with his arms around the woman he left her for. She'd recognize his curly blond hair anywhere.

"Slow down, honey." Max yelped as she practically dragged him to the opposite side of the truck. She had to hide. Or disappear. Sure, she could walk over and confront them. Show that she, too, could be happy. But what would that accomplish, exactly? She *was* happy. Happier than she'd ever been in her entire life. She needed no validation from them, no acknowledgement that she'd moved on. Still, that didn't mean she wanted to see him. She slammed the truck's door quickly ... and loudly. So loudly, Pete turned around.

But it wasn't Pete.

What?

Hannah blinked rapidly and rubbed her eyes. They were fooling her, right? She was sure that had been him.

But it wasn't. She sat, shoulders slumped and head hung low.

Why had she acted this way? She didn't need to prove a thing to Pete. For the first time, she truly didn't care what he thought of her. And that was a huge accomplishment. Look how far she'd come. But look how much farther she had to go. Things with Max were, although perfect, moving quickly. Maybe he deserved someone with a little less baggage.

"I'm sorry," she said as Max slid onto the bench. She glanced at him from the corner of her eye.

He moved slowly toward her then stopped. "Everything okay?"

She flashed a too-quick smile, nodding her head. There was no way he bought it. But because he was a man who put her needs and feelings above all else, he didn't pry.

The ride home was quiet, save for the light music on the radio and the intermittent swish of the windshield wipers that cleared the sprinkles of rain that started falling shortly after they got into the truck.

Hannah walked past his apartment door to hers when they got in the building. "Where are you going?" he asked.

The near-Pete experience left her longing for time alone, and their plans to watch *Friends* and snuggle were no longer appealing to her.

"I think I'm turning in. Long day." She fished for the keys in her purse and looked up when she heard his footsteps. Max ruffled a hand through his hair. Despite the emotional hurricane churning in her gut, she wanted to reach out and do the same with her hand.

"I, uh—I thought it was a good day."

The slight slump to his posture broke her heart.

Ugh. She didn't want him to think this had anything to do with his family. Because it didn't. "It was a wonderful day, Max." She took a step toward him and gave in to the urge to tousle his locks. "It was perfect." Her hand trailed down his face, and she gently cupped his cheek.

"Then why is your face saying the opposite?" His eye contact intensified as he closed the gap between them.

"Let's not do this in the hallway." She grabbed his hand and led him to his apartment. He slowly closed the door behind them, never breaking either his eye contact or the hold of her hand.

Her insides quivered as much as her lower lip. She bit it as she braced herself for the question she needed to ask.

"Why do you want to be with me?"

His face fell slack as his mouth dropped open. "Why do I want to be with you? I ... I just ... I want to." He shook his head lightly. "Where is this coming from?"

"Max—ugh! I have a lot of baggage." She ran both hands into her hair, grasping her scalp out of frustration as she stared down at her feet.

His soft hand gently cupped her jaw, lifting her head so they were face-to-face. Her gaze locked on his throat as it bobbed with his large swallow.

"I've made it very clear I have a lot of baggage, as well, Hannah."

"Well, see—that's the thing. I'm a lot to handle, Max. I mean, after all you've been through"—she blinked back oncoming tears—"don't you think you deserve to be with someone, I don't know ... easier?"

His eyes rounded as he cleared his throat. "Uh, easier?" A small quiver of his lips momentarily broke through some of the tension in the room.

"Oh, you know what I mean." She shoved his shoulder, and it was no surprise to her that he didn't even budge.

"Hannah." His voice turned gravelly, a touch deeper than she'd ever heard, and her breath quickened. "I want to snuggle with you on the couch and watch sitcoms, but I also want to hold you when life gets too rough. I want to be the one you run to when you get good news, but I also want to be the one who scoops you up when you find it hard to stand on your own. And I want to help you get stronger even though you're already so much stronger than I'll ever be." He moved closer, taking both of her hands in his. The warmth of his breath on her face both soothed and riled her. "I don't want easy, Hannah. I want *you*."

Her lips crashed into his so quickly, her brain hadn't yet caught up to what she'd started, but it caught on quickly. Her arms encircled him with power, with purpose, and their chests collided with a force that only added to the urgency of the kiss. As she ran her hands up and down his broad back, she felt each dip and valley of his many—oh, so many—defined muscles. They tensed suddenly, and her feet came off the ground. He lifted her with ease, and the hold his large hands had on her legs made her feel safe. He'd never let her fall.

He carried her to the couch and gently lowered her on the center cushion. She readied herself for what was next, but he surprised her by taking a step back. The breath moved in and out of his lungs at the same frantic pace as hers, but when he dropped down on one knee, hers stopped. When he quickly dropped his other knee to the ground, relief came over her. But there also remained a smidge of disappointment.

With slight shake to his hands, he ran them lightly up her arms and over her shoulders, where they found their home entangled in her long hair. He tipped his head down so their foreheads touched, and they paused a beat to catch their breath.

"Thank you for making me feel like part of your family today," she whispered.

"Of course. I wouldn't have it any other way."

"And I'm sorry I got weird earlier. The truth is, I thought I saw Pete at the park—"

Max pulled back. "He was there?" he asked with a primal growl to his voice.

"No, no. I just thought I saw him. And it threw me off. After all that's happened, he still gets to me. And I hate that I let him. Or his doppelgangers, too, apparently." She chuckled cheerlessly. "But seeing him—or thinking I saw him, in this case—only makes it more clear to me what I really want." She touched her hand to his chest and felt the steady pounding underneath.

"What's that, Hannah?"

"You."

Max reached his free hand up to his chest and covered hers with it. "I don't deserve you."

"What a coincidence."

He rubbed his forehead. "Huh?"

"Lately, I've been thinking that I don't really deserve you, either."

He scooped her into his side and pulled a blanket over them. They spent the rest of the evening in each other's arms. A small kiss here. A longer one there. She couldn't imagine a feeling more euphoric than the one she felt right now. It was, to her, abundantly clear: Max was what she wanted—for the rest of her life. And while he hadn't yet put those feelings into words, she thought he felt the same.

Chapter Twenty Seven

The sound of birds chirping and the warmth of morning sun beaming through the living room window woke Max from a restful night's sleep. The irony that nature mirrored the feeling inside wasn't lost on him. He and Hannah kissed themselves senseless last night, and he made sure to savor each brush of her lips on his. Every kiss was like a song that he'd never heard before. And he was more than happy to listen to it over and over. So, he did. A lot.

His fingertips touched his lips as he thought about last night. They felt like sandpaper and were in serious need of some lip balm. Unfortunately, he kept that in the room where Hannah now slept.

He never imagined she'd fall asleep so quickly. As they snuggled on the couch last night, the feel of her on his chest was as soothing as a weighted blanket. And while he could have stayed like that forever, he feared the position would take its toll on her neck if she stayed like that the rest of the night. So, he gently carried her to his bedroom and put her in his bed. Digging through her purse for her keys and going from one apartment to the other would have woken her. And, if he was honest, he liked the idea of her sleeping in his room.

"Hey there."

He turned toward the hallway and froze while pouring his coffee. When Hannah entered the kitchen, he nearly overflowed his mug. He'd never seen her first thing in the morning, bedheaded and groggy. Tendrils of hair escaped the messy bun that sat atop her head, and the makeup she'd worn yesterday was long-gone. She'd found the hoodie and gym shorts he'd left her on the nightstand. He'd seen her in everything from a sundress to a bathing suit. And who could forget those tempting yoga pants? Max sure couldn't. But seeing her like this—in his clothes —well, she'd never looked sexier to him.

"Good morning, beautiful. How did you sleep?" Why did his voice choose this moment to crack like a prepubescent boy?

"Great. That's the comfiest mattress I've ever slept on."

He made a mental note to thank his mom for the recommendation. She reached her hands above her head to stretch, and the tiniest sliver of skin winked at him just above the waistband of the gym shorts—which caused him to choke on his coffee.

"Hot," he blurted between coughs.

She quirked a brow at him, and his cheeks heated.

"The—the coffee," he corrected, pointing at the mug. "The coffee is hot. Careful when you drink it. Don't want you to choke too." *Nice save, buddy. Not.*

She looked at the pillow and folded blanket on the couch. "Did you sleep out here last night?"

"I did."

"Oh, geez. I'm sorry. You should have sent me home. You're too big to sleep on the couch."

"I assure you I was properly worn out and had nothing but sweet dreams all night long."

214

A silly grin crept up her face. "Same here."

He walked to her and lowered his head to hers.

"No way," she interjected, covering her mouth and squishing his plan like a bug. "None of that right now. My breath could stop a train."

He didn't mind, but he obeyed. She wrapped her arms around him, offering a hug as compromise. Her messy bun tickled his cheek, and the smell of citrus still lingered in her hair. He breathed the scent, a welcome fragrance that complemented the happiness he felt with her in his arms. But a sudden knock at his door broke him of the spell far sooner than he'd wanted.

"Uncle Max, you up yet?" a muffled voice passed through to their side of the door.

Uh-oh.

While he was busy admiring Hannah the way most people stared at a beautiful sunrise, he'd forgotten about Quinn and his parents stopping by to pick up the rest of his niece's belongings.

"Be right there."

Hannah's eyes widened. "Don't let them in yet. They'll know I stayed here," she whisper-yelled.

"I'm fine with that. I mean, nothing happened."

"I know, but that's what it looks like—literally the night your niece moved out, I moved in. It's just, I dunno, awkward." She cringed and ran her hand through her hair, making her messy bun even messier. "Plus, look at me. I'm disgusting."

Could he have presented a whole case against that last statement? Absolutely. But there wasn't time. And it's not like he'd be able to convince her, anyway.

"Okay, okay. Gotcha. Go back to my room, and I'll make sure they don't know you're here. All Quinn's stuff is in the cloffice, anyway."

She scampered down the hall into his room, and he opened the apartment door.

"Took you long enough. Were you hiding a body in here or something?" Quinn joked, elbowing her uncle in the ribs. He tried his best to suppress his guilty smile. *If they only knew.*

"Oh sweetie, we were just talkin' about how much we love Hannah. We're all so taken by her. Just the sweetest!" His mom gave him a hug, and he wondered how much of this Hannah could hear down the hall.

"Speaking of Hannah, have you shown her your project yet?" his dad asked.

"No, no. It's not the time yet. I'm not quite ready. There's still a lot to work out, and I want to have everything in place before I let her in on it," he answered with a lowered voice. He was trying to keep his project under wraps for the time being, but his father's booming voice threatened to blow it.

"I'm proud of you, son. I know you've put a lot of work into this, and it's been fun to watch where your talents are taking you."

"Thanks, Dad."

With the last few boxes loaded, he waved goodbye to his parents and walked down the hallway to let Hannah know they'd gone.

He was officially the sole inhabitant of his apartment once again, but it felt far less lonely than it had nearly three months ago when he'd moved in. His job was opening doors he didn't even know existed, and his heart was full for the first time in years. And he owed all of it to the woman behind his closed bedroom door.

Chapter Twenty-Eight

Hannah's life brimmed with activities these days. Her classes were so well-attended her boss asked if she'd be willing to add more to her schedule.

"Absolutely!" she shouted to her boss on the phone, excitement pumping through the one-word response. "I'm willing to add as many classes as I can." The more people she could reach with her classes, the better. Exercise was her life's passion, and she was proud of what she could offer others during the pandemic.

"I've got another favor to ask. Since the fitness center is the gala's biggest sponsor, I usually say a few words at the start of the night. Max Robertson also shares a few remarks at the event each year since he's the chief coordinator." At the mention of his name, Hannah smiled. "Would you be willing to speak on my behalf? I heard you and Max are attending the event together, so I thought, this way you could share the light and microphone and save the center from purchasing two sets of the equipment for two separate locations." She knew her boss loathed public speaking and suspected that was the primary motive for getting out of the task. Regardless, she was happy to help in any way needed.

"Not a problem at all. Just let me know the gist of what you'd like me to say, and I'll take care of it."

"Thanks, Hannah. If I haven't said it before, we're lucky to have you at the center."

Over the next couple days, Hannah kept to her busy schedule of teaching and worked on her speech for the gala. She never shied from a crowd but speaking at the event meant there would be a lot of eyes on her. And she faced a problem every woman realized when they had someplace to go—she had nothing to wear. As just an attendee of the gala, she planned to wear a fancy top. It wasn't like anyone would see her from the waist down, anyway. But that wouldn't work now. So, Max had an idea. Tonight, she was off to his place to do some online shopping together. Turns out, he didn't have anything to wear, either.

Ever since she mentioned speaking at the gala, he hinted about a surprise he had in store for her this evening. For the life of her, she couldn't imagine what it could be. Maybe it had something to do with whatever his dad mentioned when she hid in Max's bedroom the other morning. They hadn't known she was in the apartment. But Max had. And he lowered his voice when he spoke of it. Clearly, she wasn't meant to know the details. And while secrecy would have worried her in the past, she trusted him with every fiber in her body. Whatever he was hiding, he'd share with her when he was ready. The way he dropped hints about this evening, she might not have to wait long.

❧

"THANKS, AGAIN." Max closed his apartment door and wheeled a rickety clothing rack to the center of his living

218

room. It wasn't much sturdier than the noodle container on wheels at the pool that time Hannah almost fell in. He smiled at the memory when he thought about how far they'd come in such a short amount of time.

Hannah expected to shop for a dress online with him tonight. He couldn't wait for her reaction when she saw the rack of gowns he'd arranged to be delivered. There were many perks to living in a small town like this one. Graduating high school with someone who now owned a boutique and was willing to lend a gown for the gala was a big one today.

At five o'clock on the nose, Hannah knocked on his door.

"Close your eyes," he yelled before opening it, hoping to conceal the surprise as long as he could.

"Um, okay," she responded, a touch of trepidation in her voice.

"Don't worry. I'm not gonna pop out and scare you or anything. Got 'em closed?"

"Yep."

He opened the door slowly just in case she was peeking. She covered her eyes with one hand, so he grabbed the other and guided her through the door.

The shop owner was a member at the gym and had attended many of Hannah's classes. She seemed confident she could guess Hannah's size when Max had talked to her on the phone. Hannah could wear a paper sack to the event and still be the most beautiful woman there. These dresses would only enhance the beauty she already had.

He centered her in front of the rack and released her hand. "Okay ... open 'em."

With eyes wide and glowing, Hannah stood slack-jawed as she looked at the rack in front of her. She drew a hand to her mouth as she slowly moved closer to the gowns. "Max! What did you do?"

219

"I called in a favor to a friend. I hope that's okay. I thought having dresses to try on was better than online sho—"

She jumped into his arms and kissed him until they were both breathless. Who knew dresses would garner this response? He needed dresses waiting for her every visit.

Stepping back, she laid a trembling hand on her heart. "I ... I just can't believe this—you. I can't believe *you*, Max. How much thoughtfulness can be wrapped up in one person?"

"Not nearly as much as you deserve."

A visible flush appeared on her cheeks. "That's a load of, well, I'm not going to curse in front of these classy gowns. They deserve better than that." She ran her fingers over the various fabrics, gasping at some and whispering *oh my* at the sight of others. "Can this be like an awards show? Would it be alright if I switched outfits throughout the evening?" she joked.

The thought of Hannah changing in his apartment made his lungs stop working for a second. "Uh, whatever you want," he croaked.

Putting this together at the last minute took a little work, but he was happy he'd done it. When a few of the volunteers mentioned how much extra work Hannah had done for this fundraiser, he knew he wanted to do something special for her. And when she said she had nothing to wear, he knew just who to call. "So, you think something here will work then?"

"Absolutely." She squealed as she grabbed three dresses and skipped back to his bedroom. He settled on the couch and prepared himself for his first fashion show.

Fabrics of every color of the rainbow and every texture imaginable paraded through his living room. The gowns were beautiful, of course. But he was blinded to all else but Hannah's larger-than-life smile.

"How about this one?" she asked with a twirl.

"You look beautiful."

"What do you think of this?" she asked when she appeared moments later in a different gown.

"Again. Beautiful."

"And this one?" she asked, this time donning a light pink ensemble. "Let me guess ... beautiful?" She crossed her arms and tapped her foot.

"Hannah, you're short-circuiting my brain. You look drop-dead gorgeous in every single one of these dresses. I mean, I'm just trying to keep my wits about me. It's taking everything in me to stop myself from barreling over to you and mauling you like a horny fifteen-year-old."

She opened her mouth to reply, then stopped. "I'm flattered." She said it more like a question than a statement, and he chuckled.

But he wasn't laughing for long. The next gown she modeled sucked so much air out of him, he couldn't have laughed if he wanted to.

"How's this one?"

"I ... wow ... whoa ... Hannah," he stuttered.

"What happened to your go-to adjective?" She smiled. No, she glowed. As modest as she was, even *she* had to know how stunning she looked right now.

It was a gown the color of the purest tropical water imaginable. The kind you see on brochures inviting you to the most gorgeous beaches in the world. Her bright blue eyes popped against it. The smooth, satin fabric had an opalescent sheen that reflected light in a hypnotic way. The straps draped off her shoulders, offering a view of her open collarbone. His mouth watered at the sight. Satin hugged her curves in all the right places as it pooled to the floor like a cascading waterfall of fabric.

And when she turned, he nearly came undone. The back was open—and, well, quite low. It showed off a place on her body he'd never seen. But he'd never forget it after tonight.

She faced him and placed a hand on her hip. "What do you think?"

See, that was the problem. He *couldn't* think. In fact, a coherent thought was nowhere near the vicinity of his head. He gawked at her and swallowed to relieve the dryness in his mouth. Having it hang open for minutes on end did that to a person. But he couldn't help it. He touched her wrist and slid his fingers down to her hand and pulled her close.

"That's the one," he said, his voice higher than normal. Maybe he actually was a horny fifteen-year-old.

She bounced on her toes and clasped her hands under her chin. "I think so too. Oh, I could stay in this forever." She did a half turn and watched the small train of fabric follow behind. "But I'm gonna take it off before something happens to it. That would just be my luck."

She changed quickly and appeared in the hallway, gown slung over her arm, and a wide smile splayed on her face. "Are we doing takeout tonight?"

"Sounds good to me. There's a pile of menus on the kitchen island. See what looks good to you. I'm gonna use the restroom real fast. Let me know what you're in the mood for. I'll order, and you can run the dress over to your place."

When he came out to the living room, she was nowhere around. He took a seat at the island and drummed his fingers on the countertop, waiting for her return. Several minutes passed, and he was just about to text her to see if everything was okay. *Dropping off the dress shouldn't take this long* Just then, his phone lit with a text.

Hannah: Hey, I'm sorry to do this, but my stomach feels weird, so I think I'm gonna skip dinner at your place tonight.

He wrinkled a brow. Not even five minutes ago, she'd

seemed perfectly fine. Then again, maybe she had some sort of feminine issue she didn't want to discuss with him via text. Quinn's tampon fiasco was still a fresh memory. *Ugh.* Whatever the case, he hoped she was okay.

Max: Do you need anything? I'd be happy to order you something light and easy to digest if you'd like. Or would you like some company?

Hannah: That's not necessary. I'm just going to rest. I'm better off alone right now.

Something about that last line didn't sit right with him.

I'm better off alone right now.

He was probably reading too much into it. But he couldn't shake the feeling something was wrong. And it had nothing to do with her stomach. What else could he do, though? She said she wanted to be alone. There was really nothing he could do but sit and pray that the suspicion that churned inside him was unwarranted. His stomach suddenly felt kind of sick now, as well.

Chapter Twenty-Nine

"I'm the most naïve idiot in the world, aren't I?" Hannah looked at her best friend on the tablet screen. She caught a glimpse of herself in the corner and immediately wished she hadn't. Her hair stuck out, the dark circles under her eyes were more pronounced than ever, and her eyes had cried so many tears, they'd probably stay this pinkish-red hue forever.

"You're not an idiot, Hannah. You're someone who's in love."

She scoffed and rolled her eyes. "Tell me the difference between the two." She ran a hand through her uncombed hair and winced as she snagged it on several knots. "I just can't believe I'm back here again."

When she showed up at Max's apartment the other night, she thought the big "surprise" he kept was the rack of gowns. But when he asked her to look at the take-out menus, she couldn't believe her eyes. An opened letter from a web design firm in Dallas fluttered out from the pile and landed at her feet. They thanked him for applying for a position at their company and congratulated him on a project he'd done. Phrases like "benefits package" and "final round of interviews" jumped off the page and smacked her in the face. They'd even included some housing options and the number of a local realtor he could call.

Her breath quickened, and she got lightheaded as her mind replayed events from the past few weeks. Like Max quickly closing his laptop and stammering a reason why Quinn and Hannah couldn't see what he was working on. Like the conversation she'd overheard with Max and his dad about something he needed to share with her but wasn't quite ready to yet. And then the last piece of the puzzle clicked into place—the job acceptance letter she found the other night. It all came into view.

"Are you sure this is what it looks like though?" Angie asked. Hannah got vertigo with the swiftness of the role-reversal. *She* was usually the overly optimistic one in their friendship.

"It's pretty damning evidence, Ang." Her face burned with anger when she thought how her relationship with Pete ended the very same way. He dropped her like a hot potato and skipped town before she cooled. "I just thought Max was different." She rubbed her temples and her head pounded with every beat of her broken heart.

"Now, don't get upset with me, but I think he really is different." The hope in Angie's eyes was apparent but not contagious. Hannah was too confused and jaded to feel even the slightest bit of hope. "Did you at least talk to him about the letter?"

She hated confrontation. There were instances when she needed to stand her ground, demand answers, and make herself known. She supposed this was one of those times. She just couldn't bring herself to ask the questions she needed answers to the most.

Why do you want to leave me?

Didn't our time together mean to you what it meant to me?

225

And the one she dreaded the most: *Aren't I enough?*

"No. We've texted back and forth the past couple days. I just said I've been swamped at work, which isn't a lie."

Angie nodded. "So, you're avoiding him, then? How long do you think you can keep doing that?"

"Not much longer." Hannah blew out an audible sigh. "We have that gala in two days, so I'll be going over for that."

Angie's eyes widened. "You're still going to that with him?"

"I kinda have to. I've gotta speak on behalf of the gym, and they're sending the video equipment to his place. I don't want to explain issues with my personal life to my boss. Besides, it's a cause I believe in. I need to be there." Max or no Max, she was doing this for all the victims of drunk driving, like her mother and Courtney.

"You're a good person, Hannah Banana."

"Ha! Look what that's gotten me." She pushed the heels of her hands into her eyes. "Why didn't he tell me, Ang?"

Her friend sighed. "So, I just wanna get this straight—we hate him now?"

Hannah looked up, her vision blurred from the threat of tears collecting in her eyes. "No. I couldn't hate him if I tried."

"Can I say something, though?"

Hannah chuckled. "When have I ever been able to stop you from speaking your mind?"

A soft smile spread across her face. "Good point. Okay, I think he's a good person. I really do. I feel it in my bones, Hannah. Everything you've told me about him—bad guys don't do those kinds of things. You need to talk to him. And I think deep down, you know that. If for no other reason than to advocate for yourself."

She wanted to believe she was stronger. That the past

wasn't something that kept her from doing what she needed to do in the present. She should have talked to him the night she found the letter. Isn't that what most people would have done? But, once again, her fight or flight instincts told her the runway was clear for takeoff.

But she knew what she had to do. For the first time in her life, she was going to ask the hard questions, knowing she might get answers she didn't want to hear. She had to show she was someone people couldn't cast aside like junk mail that didn't deserve a second glance. She needed the words to come out of his mouth. If he didn't want to be with her, she needed to hear it. And she deserved to know why.

~

MAX SAT on his couch and stared at a blank television screen. He didn't feel like getting up to turn it on. It's not like his mind could focus on a show right now, anyway.

Hannah didn't come over last night. And she replied in clipped messages all day, a major red flag. He ribbed her regularly about her paragraph-long texts.

Just a couple days ago, they spent an afternoon together, and he'd never felt closer to her. But now? He felt miles away from the woman on the other side of the wall. And he had no idea why. There were no signs that anything was wrong. But something was definitely off.

A light knock on his door pulled him out of his inner monologue. When he saw Hannah through the peephole, his shoulders dropped from below his ears. This was the longest he'd gone without seeing her face.

"Can I talk to you for a minute?" She walked past him, a waft of her vanilla-citrus scent following her. While she normally glided, her gait was more like a march. She stood in the space between the door and the living room, a sign she didn't plan to stay long.

"Sure. What's up?"

She fidgeted with the spinning ring on her finger and fixed her eyes on the floor three feet in front of her. "Are you leaving?"

He looked down at his bare feet then arched a brow in her direction. "Uh, no. I'm staying in tonight."

She shook her head. "No. I mean, are you leaving Wheeling?" Her chest rose and fell at the same pace it usually did after one of their make-out sessions. But now they stood several feet apart.

He scratched the stubble on his chin. "No. What gave you that idea?"

She walked to the kitchen island and held up a paper with a trembling hand. "I saw the other night next to the takeout menus." She inhaled shakily. "So, I need to know —are you leaving?"

His long stride quickly ate up the space between them, and he looked at the paper in her hands. She'd seen the job offer.

He shook his head. "I'm not leaving. The company offered me that position last week."

She placed the paper back on the table, and for a minute, he thought he'd diffused the conversation. But when she looked up at him, he sensed an impending explosion.

"Why do you still have the paperwork?" Her lip quivered. Whether from sadness or anger, he wasn't sure. Neither case sat well with him.

"What do you mean?"

"If the company offered you the job a week ago, and you turned it down, why do you still have the papers?"

Max slowly moved his head from side to side. "I didn't turn down the offer."

She didn't blink. She didn't speak. Only the sound of her deep breath filled the room as she stared at him with glassy eyes. "So, you're leaving." It wasn't a question.

"No. I told you I'm staying."

Her brow quirked. "Then why didn't you turn down the offer? Are you considering accepting?"

"I was."

Her head tilted to the side. She didn't look like she believed him. "Okay."

"I just needed a backup plan."

She jerked back like she'd been stung. "A backup plan?"

He blew out a long breath. "Well, sometimes things don't work out, and you need to prepare for … that."

She put a hand on her hip, and her brows drew together. "What kinds of things? Us? Did you need a backup plan for us?" She paused and pinned him with her stare. Then her fierce eyes softened. "Or was I the backup plan in case you didn't get this job?"

Oh boy. He didn't like the way all this sounded. In his head, his logic seemed smart. Responsible. Safe. But when she put it like this? Well, it didn't sound good. At all.

"Okay. So, I reached out to a headhunter before we even met. I was ready to leave Wheeling because I couldn't take the sad memories and people who remind me of those memories constantly. When this company reached out, it was tempting. But then you came along."

"And you were thinking about going anyway." Again, this wasn't a question.

"No." He ruffled a hand through his hair. "Maybe. I told them I needed some time to figure things out."

She looked up at the ceiling, blinking rapidly. Was she trying not to cry? He hadn't meant for this to upset her. He hadn't meant for her to find out at all, actually.

"Why do I get the feeling what you're trying to figure

229

out has nothing to do with your job?" Her teary eyes met his. "When do you have to give them an answer?"

"Next week."

Something in that answer flipped a switch, and her eyes lit with fire. "So, let me get this straight. You were giving us a couple weeks to, in your words, 'figure things out' before you decided to either stay with me or dump me and take a job several hundred miles away."

Sweat collected at the base of his neck, and his breathing became shallow and quick. "I—I didn't know what to do then. I don't know what to do *now*." He clenched and unclenched his fists. "Courtney left me, and that was it. She was gone, and I was empty. What if that happens with us? I need a plan to fall back on in case you aren't in my life anymore. For whatever reason. Do you realize how terrified I am of that happening to me again?"

She stared at him and said nothing. But the silence screamed things he'd rather not hear.

"Hannah, you've gotta understand where I'm coming from. You don't know what it's like to have someone just vanish from your life in the blink of an eye."

"Don't I?"

His breath stopped. Why did he say that? Of course she knew how that felt. Pete disappeared just as fast.

"Hannah. I'm sorry." He reached for her, but she stepped back, stumbling over her own two feet.

"I don't need your sympathy." Tears now poured down face. He knew she wouldn't let him wipe them away. Watching them stain her face was his penance for being a jerk. "I need you to trust that I won't hurt you or leave you. I need you to be there for me, completely. And I need you to walk with me, without a safety net. Because if we're in this together, I need you to be in it one hundred percent."

"I *am* with you."

"I don't think you really are. When someone is totally

committed to someone else, they don't have a backup plan." She looked to the side for a breath than met his stare. "I don't think you can give me one hundred percent."

That line hit like a verbal punch in the gut.

This was his chance to convince her. His chance to say what he was feeling in his heart. To tell her everything he'd been feeling for the past few months. To tell her that since he'd met her, the job was something he no longer wanted. That what he wanted now was her. But he couldn't.

Why couldn't he?

Flashes of the last couple years raced through his mind. Days of barely being able to get out of his bed after Courtney's accident haunted him. The memory of him standing on the dance floor with Hannah, unable to say the words he hadn't told anyone since Courtney died, sparked a startling realization: he was broken. And here he stood before a woman who had the capacity to break him even more. If he fell any further for her, he'd live through that pain all over again because endings were inevitable. He learned that the hard way.

Who was he kidding? He was more damaged than he let on, and she'd figure that out eventually. She'd either stay with him out of pity—and he couldn't take any more pity from people—or she'd leave him for someone she deserved. And she deserved to be with a man who loved her, totally, and wasn't haunted by the ghost of his past relationship. It was exactly as he'd feared from the start, and what Hannah just said was true: he couldn't give her one hundred percent because he didn't have one hundred percent left to give.

This was it. He had to let her go before the damage was too great to handle. Before either one of them would end up as broken as he once had been. And still was. He was doing her a favor and sparing her the sadness he still

231

hadn't recovered from. The road to their inevitable heart-break had an exit ahead. If he wanted to take it, it was now or never. He knew what he had to do. He hit the gas pedal hard. And he never looked back.

"The job is still up in the air, but it's a possibility. A good one. It's a chance for me to grow and expand on what I've been doing here."

"So you're thinking about it."

"Yes," he lied.

She walked slowly past him, eyes trained on the floor, and stopped just short of the door. When she turned to look at him, her face lacked color. Surely, she hadn't fallen for him already. He was trying to spare her the pain, not cause it.

"So, this is it?"

He looked down at his feet, unable to bring himself to look at her again. He'd lose his nerve if he did. "I think this is better for both of us."

She opened the door, and by the time he looked up, she was gone.

He stared at the closed door for several minutes before he moved, still processing what happened. He stood by his choice. Getting out before anyone got hurt was the right call. Though, if he'd done the right thing, why did Hannah look like that when she left?

Chapter Thirty

Hannah stared at the trash heap in front of her. Technically, it was her work desk, but she hadn't been in her office in three months and people kept dumping mail on it with no semblance of order. The gym reopened a couple weeks ago, but her water classes were still canceled until further notice, and she was able to do the rest of her work remotely. She hadn't needed to come back. Until today.

With the gala one day away, she had a lot on her plate. Calling to confirm a few last-minute details, running a couple more promo ads, and taking care of a host of other errands occupied much of her time. There was a lot on her shoulders. But what she had on her mind was a much heavier load to bear.

After her chat with Angie, she knew she needed to talk to Max. Unfortunately, she had all the confidence of someone asked to perform a choreographed routine to a crowd of thousands without ever having heard the music. She knew *what* to do but hadn't a clue how to do it. And now that he'd admitted what Angie was so certain couldn't be the truth, Hannah wished she could travel back to a time when they both were happy.

"Hannah, I didn't know you were coming in today." Johnny's eyes lit with excitement and surprise to see her, which meant he hadn't talked to Max about her recently. She needed to wrap this conversation up before the topic arose.

"Johnny, how are you? It's so nice to see you in person again. I wanted to thank you again for your help with the boot camp classes."

"No problem. I was happy to help. I've heard all your online classes are a huge hit."

"The reception was unexpected and amazing, that's for sure." It still thrilled her that the classes were so well-received.

"And what does my boy Max think about dating a local celebrity?"

Ugh.

She glanced sideways, as though the way to handle this awkward situation would magically reveal itself in the corner of the room. Spoiler: it didn't.

"I ... uh ... I'm afraid we're not together anymore."

He froze as though she'd shot him with a stun gun. The mask he wore probably kept his jaw from hitting the floor.

"I ... I'm sorry, I guess? This is just ... man ... unexpected." He rubbed his forehead. "Are you okay?"

Johnny might have given off the impression of being a playboy or a major flirt, but she knew him better. And the fact that he asked how she was, without knowing any details or choosing sides, showed he was a good guy.

"I've been better, actually." She didn't want to get into the details and figured short responses to his questions were the best way to get him to stop asking them.

"He didn't mention anything the other day."

There's a lot he hasn't been mentioning lately.

234

Johnny narrowed his eyes. "What hasn't he mentioned?"

Oh geez. Did I say that out loud?

"I'm sure he's told you all about his new job opportunity and the big project that got him the position. But, I'm sorry, Johnny. Look, you just need to talk to Max. I'm running late, and I've gotta go."

She scooped up the papers she'd come for and bolted for the door so fast, if she was a cartoon character, a trail of smoke would have appeared behind her. There was no place she needed to be, but the air in the room had thickened tenfold at the mention of Max's name. Leaving Johnny that way wasn't right, but she couldn't talk to him about this. She actually couldn't talk to anyone about it right now—every time she heard Max's words replay in her mind, she fell to pieces.

And she needed to put herself together quickly because she had to look presentable for the gala tomorrow night.

MAX HAD EXPERIENCED HEARTBREAK TWICE in his lifetime, though under very different circumstances. In one case, it'd shattered him. In the other, he'd done the shattering. In both, he'd never felt so miserable.

He hadn't seen Hannah since the night they ended things, but she mentioned in her latest text that she was still coming to his place to attend the gala. He assumed it was out of obligation. The hollow look of her face when she left, the one he'd never forgive himself for causing, haunted his every thought. She didn't owe him a thing.

He was no better than that ex of hers. Sure, Pete had manipulated her. Max wanted to pound him into the ground for every time she'd say something about how Max was too good for her, and she didn't deserve him. Or the

235

night she said she was too broken for him, and he should find someone with a less messy past. His blood boiled even now. Hannah was the dream, the girl you conjured up in your head, knowing you'd never find someone so close to your fantasy in real life. To him, she was everything, and he let her go. His tactics and Pete's were different, but the result was the same.

He didn't know how things would be between them at the gala tomorrow night, but he couldn't think about that today. He checked himself in the mirror, though he didn't know why. His red eyes and slack expression weren't going away any time soon. He rubbed a hand on his chest and swore it felt hollow beneath his palm, though he knew that was impossible. The ache was conceivable, though.

Shuffling through the living room, he grabbed his keys and a mask. He snatched his sunglasses—which he rarely wore—but he didn't want anyone to see him like this. He didn't care that the mask/sunglasses combo made him look like he was incognito. In a way, he was.

After a quick stop at the local flower shop for a sprig of forget-me-nots the florist had waiting for him, he drove his truck up the hill to his destination.

His hands trembled as he grabbed the flowers and got out of the truck. The sound of his heart pounding in his ears tarnished the silence that hovered over the hilltop. No matter how many times he did this, it never got easier. People told him it would. People lied.

He slowly followed the gravel path, rocks crunching under his boots. Birds and chipmunks went about their day in a playful manner, a direct contradiction of their surroundings. The thrum of a lawnmower ran in the distance and filled the air with the scent of fresh-cut grass.

He stopped and looked around. Not much had changed since the last time he'd been here. He bent and placed the flowers down on the ground and blew a deep breath to steady himself.

"Happy birthday, baby."

He sniffled and took a seat on the bench nearby. How had it been over three years since he'd last seen Courtney?

"I know I haven't been by in a couple of months. But that doesn't mean I've stopped thinking about you. Uh, quite the opposite, actually." He sucked in another deep breath and exhaled shakily. "I, um, actually started moving on a little. I hope you're not too disappointed it took me so long to do that. I've hung out with friends, and I've left the house for more than work. Finally got my own place. Boy, that was a biggie. I worried I'd be too lonely. I was supposed to be moving to a place with you, after all." He bit his bottom lip and fidgeted with his fingers.

"I started seeing someone. But, uh, that's over now." His knee bounced faster than the passing hummingbird flapped its wings. "Courtney, whenever I needed advice, you were always the person to give it." He scrubbed a hand down his face. "And, man, do I need you now."

He raised his mask and wiped his nose with a wadded-up tissue he had sense enough to pack when he left home this morning. "But I guess if you were here, I wouldn't even be in this situation, would I? I'm still not used to navigating life without you. I'm not sure when I'll ever feel like I am. Seems I've messed up the best thing I've had since you. And I'm not sure I can fix it."

"Sure you can," a gruff voice echoed from behind, startling him. Max quickly shot from the bench, standing ramrod straight, facing the man he wasn't prepared to see. But he should have been.

"Colonel." Max nodded respectfully, though he'd been told a million times that wasn't necessary.

"Max." The man shook his head. "You almost became

my son-in-law. Will I ever have to stop reminding you to call me Mr. Ward?"

Mr. Ward was more decorated than the Griswold house at Christmastime, so there was little chance Max would ever address him as anything other than the title he deserved to be called. The older man took a seat at the opposite end of the bench, far enough from him that he could lower his mask. Max did the same. If the Colonel noticed his watery eyes and quivering lip, he didn't say anything. But it was nothing he had to hide from him. He'd seen his daughter's boyfriend in much worse shape. Many times.

"So, how are you going to fix this?" Courtney's dad asked with a growl to his voice. It was gruff enough to frighten anyone who didn't know any better. But Max knew this was his natural tone.

"No disrespect, sir, but I doubt you want to hear about this," he said, nervousness apparent by the shake in his voice.

He chuckled dryly. "Then why the heck did I ask?"

Max rubbed the back of his neck to buy himself a little time. How should he approach this awkward topic? Discussing problems about the woman he was dating with the guy whose daughter was once the love of his life—this had all the makings of the soap operas he always caught his mother watching on summer afternoons when he was home from school.

"I met a woman."

"Yeah, Hannah."

Max shook his head. "How did you know that?"

Courtney's dad chuckled heartily. "Max, do you want me to waste time explaining how small towns work?" His smile gave Max just enough courage to begin.

"Okay, well, things were going really well. Too well. And then I blew it."

The older man raised his brow. "Who says you're to blame?"

"Oh, I'm sure. If you're placing bets on who blew this relationship to smithereens, put all your money on me."

"Does she know you love her?"

Max looked at everything around him except Courtney's father. "I, uh, what, I dunno what you mean."

"It's okay, son," he said, his face softening. "I can see in your eyes this woman is something special. You love her, don't you?"

His eyes burned as the Colonel's face blurred. He was about to admit something he'd been feeling for weeks but had never admitted out loud to anyone. Not to Hannah. Not to Johnny. Not even to himself. He was about to say something that he'd so badly wanted to admit to her the other night but couldn't.

"Yes. I love her." His eyes dropped to the ground, and a tear fell from his face, wetting the dirt below.

"Did you tell her?"

It was on the tip of his tongue so many times, but he couldn't say the words. He'd tried to show her in as many ways as he could without uttering the words. They were words he hadn't told anyone since he'd said them to the woman who now rested six feet below the place where he sat.

"No. I tried, sir. So many times. I just can't. She deserves someone who can love her the way she deserves to be loved. Someone who can say what she needs to hear. She deserves more than I can give her."

"Says who?"

"Sir, I'm not the same man I was when I dated your daughter."

"You're right." Courtney's dad gave an understanding nod. "You're a better man now."

Max's head flinched back slightly. "What?"

239

"If I may—telling Hannah you love her won't make the love you had for Courtney any less, Max." Could he actually see the exact thought swirling in Max's head? "But keeping yourself from moving on with your life is the kind of thing that's really gonna tick my daughter off, ya hear? And she was as easy-going as they came, so don't go riling her up, son."

They shared a chuckle. Then the Colonel continued.

"If there's one thing I know about my daughter, it's how deep her love for you was. And because of that, I know she's not only up there wishing for your happiness, but she's cheering you on now that you've found it." His eyes glistened under the glow of the morning sun. "Because that's what love is, Max. It's beautiful, unselfish, and wonderful. But it's also painful, difficult, and often-times inconvenient. But we do it anyway. We take the chance we were afraid of taking. We make the leap that causes our stomachs to drop to our ankles. We give our hearts to a person who has the capacity to destroy us because we realize we're not living if we do the opposite. We love, despite all the obstacles, because love is why we live, son.

"And of course, you're a different man now. That's why I know you have more than enough love to give Hannah. You'll love her with more than anyone could because you know how fragile life is. You know how to value time with someone because you've felt the hurt of having those minutes unfairly ripped away. You didn't lose half your heart when Courtney died, Max. You gained a new appre-ciation for every minute you get to spend with the person you love. And because of that, you'll make those minutes count."

Both men wiped their cheeks, now slick with tears.

"So, I guess I need to talk to Hannah," Max said after wiping his nose with more tissues. He thought he'd be brought to tears for an entirely different reason when he packed them. He had no idea the turn his morning would take.

"You're a smart man. You'll figure it out. Do one of those epic gestures they're always talking about in the movies."

Max smirked. "A grand gesture?"

"Eh, same idea. Although, something tells me this woman might be worthy of something more epic." The older man smiled.

Max nodded. "You might be right, sir."

He waved a dismissive hand. "Then, go get her."

After they bade each other farewell, Max made the short walk back to his truck. He sat behind the wheel for a minute, letting the sage advice of the Colonel settle in his brain. He'd made a lot of good points, but what if he'd hurt Hannah too badly? She might reject him. She certainly had every right to. But she at least deserved to know how he felt, or he'd regret not telling her for the rest of his life.

He was just about to put the key in the ignition when his cell phone rang.

"Max, buddy," Johnny said hurriedly. "Can you meet me at your place in fifteen? We have to talk ... now."

Chapter Thirty-One

The last lock of hair fell from Hannah's curling iron and cascaded over her shoulder, blending with the others. It had been a while since her last trip to the salon, and her hair was quite longer than she usually kept it. But she wasn't hating her pandemic 'do. In fact, she rather preferred it to her regular style. It made her feel feminine, pretty, and with the addition of a rhinestone clip to pin hair away from her face, she felt like a princess.

Of course, as she slipped into her silky gown, she thought she might even look like one. When she thought about the way Max looked at her when she first tried it on, her stomach tightened. No one had *ever* looked at her like that, and the feeling it gave her when he did wasn't something she'd soon forget, if ever.

She rubbed her now-clammy palms on a bathroom towel and grabbed the final touch to her look: the perfect shade of lip stain—not too red and not too pink. The rest of her makeup she kept light, save for the bold lip. It's not like she and Max would engage in any activities that would rub it off. Now, eye makeup? Well, there was a strong possibility he'd ruin that by night's end. Hopefully not until

Hannah was safe in the confines of her own apartment, though.

With a shaky hand, she brought the lip wand to her mouth. She willed herself to calm down, if for no other reason than not wanting lip stain running down her chin.

Surviving the night with a man who broke her heart was going to be impossible. She grabbed a tissue to blot the single tear that threatened to wreck her makeup and sucked in a deep breath.

She still couldn't shake the feeling that something didn't add up. And it wasn't just because Angie had said the same when they last talked. Hannah felt like something just didn't fit.

Max never gave the impression he was looking for a way out of their relationship. Never alluded that he might be leaving. They shared their deepest thoughts and darkest moments, yet he never brought that up. The whole thing felt like a puzzle she was so close to finishing. But she couldn't because the final piece didn't belong in this particular box and the one that did was missing. She hoped to find that piece tonight. And while she knew she might not like the picture once complete, she needed to at least see the finished product.

Max asked her to arrive a half hour before the event was set to begin. He'd mentioned something about his speech, and she assumed he wanted to practice it one last time.

"Okay," she breathed. "I'm brave, I'm strong, and I can do this." She repeated the mantra one more time. The more she heard it, the truer it would become, right? With shoulders back, chin high, and eyes dry for the first time in the past few days, she gave herself one last look in the mirror.

She turned off the light and walked next door.

WHEN SHE STRODE down the hallway, she was surprised to see Max's door propped open with the deadbolt. A small note taped to it said, "Hannah, come in." Now, Wheeling was a friendly city and virtually crime-free. But that didn't mean people left their homes unlocked on a regular basis. Hannah immediately wondered what was going on.

The door creaked quietly as she slowly opened it, the rain pelting the windows the only other sound. With the storm outside and all the lights turned off in the apartment, it was uncharacteristically dark for five-thirty on this early June evening.

"Max?" she asked as she gently closed the door behind her. He was nowhere to be found. Not that she could really see much. Only his laptop that glowed from the coffee table at the far end of the living room. She took another step forward and heard a crunch.

"Ah!" she gasped. She hoped it wasn't a small rodent that snuck in through the door he'd left partially ajar. "Please don't be a critter. Please don't be a critter," she repeated in a whisper as she reached for the light switch. She shielded her eyes, not sure she wanted to know what was beneath her high heel.

She managed to find the light switch in the darkness and gasped even louder than she had just seconds ago. Under her foot was an origami flower, identical to the one Max gave her in a bouquet on her birthday. Well, she'd totally flattened this one. But the squished one wasn't the only one in the apartment. Dozens scattered on the floor made a trail leading to the opened laptop. As she followed the flowers, she remembered Max mentioning how long it took to make one of these flowers. He must have worked on these for days. She picked up each one she passed and

244

admired the intricacy of the art form, turning it to see it from every angle.

By the time she reached the table, she'd gathered enough to make a whole bouquet of origami flowers. They varied in shades of blue, ranging from dark to light, turquoise to something close to violet—the perfect complement to her gown. Angie's words replayed in her mind as she looked at the folded flowers: *Bad guys don't do these kinds of things.*

Her vision blurred as tears, which she swore to herself she wasn't going to shed until she'd made it home, made an early entrance.

And then she looked at the laptop screen.

"What?" she whispered to herself, eyes wide and brows knit together. She bent to get a closer look and still couldn't believe what she saw. It was a website full of links to workout videos. All featuring her.

She rubbed her head and stared openly at the screen. The site was beautifully designed. A work of art, really. Every workout she'd done live was catalogued according to type, duration, and props needed. She'd always imagined a platform where she could share workouts with people, but she'd never had the courage to share that dream with anyone.

"Did Max really do this?" she whispered to herself.

"I did."

She whipped around so fast, the headrush nearly caused her to lose her balance.

"Max," she murmured, her throat thick with emotion she couldn't define. He stood before her, looking more handsome than any man had a right to. He'd styled his hair and sported a black suit that looked custom made for him. And for the second time in less than two minutes, she found it hard to breathe.

He strode forward slowly, keeping a generous distance

between them. Like he was waiting for permission to enter her space.

"What is this?" she asked.

She watched him wet his lips and audibly swallow.

He gestured to the origami bouquet in her hands and cleared his throat. "This is me trying to woo you."

She smiled back, shyly, still unsure of what was going on.

"What is this?" she asked, angling her body toward the screen on the table behind her, never breaking contact with his eyes.

His chest visibly rose and fell before he answered her. "This is me trying to support you."

She covered her mouth with a trembling hand, touched by the gesture that meant more to her than he could have known. All she'd ever wanted was someone who realized that her dreams were her own, as serious as anyone else's, and worthy of the same respect she gave others. She never expected anyone to go to such great lengths to show their encouragement for her dream.

She was just about to tell him when he pulled his hands out from behind his back and held up a piece of paper Hannah knew well. It had haunted Hannah's nightmares for the past several nights. It was the one she'd found that made her question everything about the man she thought —no, was *certain*—she knew.

"And what's that?" she asked with a frostier tone to her voice than usual.

With eyes unblinking and locked on hers, he ripped the paper in half and let it fall to the floor.

"This is me telling you I love you."

His chin quivered as he moved another step forward, closing the space between the two of them.

"Hannah, I love you. In fact, I think I've loved you since the moment I saw you at the gym. And I should have told you. Repeatedly. Because even if I'd said it a million times since then, you still deserved to hear it so many more.

"But I got scared. I couldn't bring myself to say the words because I was afraid they'd come back to hurt me. The last time I felt this way about someone, it almost killed me. So, I held back. Or I tried to, anyway. But your hold on me was something I couldn't resist. So, I broke it, instead." He reached out slowly, tentatively for her hand. The warmth of his touch heated her entire body. "I thought if I let you go, if I let you find someone who hadn't been torn apart and pieced back together again, it would be better for both of us. You'd find someone worthy of you, and I wouldn't stand in the way of your happiness. I didn't think I could give you all of me. But it seems you'd already taken it."

He looked down at the paper he'd torn. "I was *never* going to take this job. I lied to you, and I shouldn't have. I take that back—I actually lied to myself. You see, I put out feelers for a new job back in February, before we'd even met. I thought I needed a fresh start. A new home. A place where I could be happy. But, Hannah, *you* make me happy. Turning these guys down the other day was the easiest decision I've ever made. Well, the second easiest." A cautious smile came across his face. "Hannah, I'm choosing to be with you. For however long you'll have me. It's the easiest decision of my life. That is, if you'll still have me."

She couldn't wait another second. She reached her hands around his neck and gave him a kiss unlike one they'd ever shared. It was full of passion, of course. Their mouths crashed together like they hadn't met in years, not just a couple of days. But in this kiss was so much more. It was a promise, a vow, that through it all, she'd be by his side, as he'd promised to be by hers.

247

"I love you, Max. So much." She panted as she tried to catch her breath. "You've always been more than enough for me. This week has been hell. I didn't know how I was going to get over you. You mean more to me than anyone I've ever met, and I don't want to be where you aren't. I've always wanted to be with you, wherever that is—I just figured I wasn't invited."

"I'm not going anywhere. I don't want to leave my family. My friends. You."

Tears welled behind her eyes with the release of tension that came over her body. She held him closer. Part of her felt like this was all a dream and if she didn't hold him tight enough, this would all slip away.

"So, what's this website?" she asked, realizing they'd never discussed it.

"Well, that was the surprise you overheard me talking about. I got a little guidance from Johnny. He told me you found out about it—or you thought you had. This had nothing to do with the job offer, and I'm sorry you thought I was working on this project to get me out of town behind your back."

"Johnny." Hannah forgot she'd run into him yesterday. In her defense, she'd been walking through much of this week in a fog.

"He actually helped fold the flowers with me last night … and this morning. He earned a six-pack or twenty, that's for sure."

She looked down at the bouquet still in her hand. At least two dozen flowers made up the bundle. "How long did this take you guys?"

A smirk appeared on his face. "A little bit of time." He chuckled. Then he turned back toward the laptop. "So, I talked to Johnny, and with the success of your online classes, I thought your boss might be open to making it something more permanent. Johnny got me a meeting with him a few weeks ago, and he was ecstatic. Once this part of the site officially launches, members can log on with their membership number and either do a live class or view one of the archived ones."

"Max, this is amazing."

"You mentioned wanting to reach more people, get them moving and make them happier. I think you'll be able to make a lot of people happy with this website.

"This is unbelievable."

"Well, I believe in you, Hannah." He took her hands in his and stroked her knuckles with his thumbs. "I believe in *us*."

He brushed her lips with his, just for a moment, and then pulled away while still holding her close.

"You're it for me, Hannah Jenkins. I'm content calling you my girlfriend. In fact, it's an honor to be able to do so. But know it's only temporary."

Hannah inhaled sharply. That last statement felt like the ground had crumbled beneath her.

"What?" she asked, her eyes the size of saucers.

"I just mean at some point, I might like to call you my fiancée—and if I'd be so lucky, one day I'd call you my wife."

She looked into his eyes—eyes that saw her at her best but had also seen her fall apart. She touched her hand to a face that had given her smiles that made her insides melt. Her hand ran down a solid arm that had held her when she needed the comfort of someone who loved her. When her hand found his, she grabbed onto it and made a promise to herself to never let this man go again.

"Max, whatever name you give me is fine. But just promise to always call me yours."

"Always."

Epilogue

A little over six months later...

"Holy cannoli! It's so cold out here, my goosebumps are getting goosebumps." Hannah stepped out of Max's truck, snow crunching beneath her boots. "Makes it a little more festive, though." Her smile was warm enough to forget it was the end of December. He came prepared for the elements, though, and pulled out a thermos of hot chocolate from behind his seat.

"You didn't!" she exclaimed as she grabbed one of the travel mugs he handed her.

"I know how to warm you up," he said in a suggestive tone with a wink. They laughed as he poured the steaming beverage into her cup. She took a sip and closed her eyes.

"I don't deserve you." She slid her free hand into his.

He took a swig of his hot chocolate and smiled at her. "I believe with my whole heart it's the other way around."

"Agree to disagree." She playfully nudged him with her elbow and blinded him with a smile brighter than all the Christmas lights that surrounded them.

The truth was there were a lot of reasons to smile these past several months. Her section of the fitness center's website, now known as Jenkins' Gym, was on fire. No, not like the time they almost burned down the apartment in the throes of passion. Although Max recalled that being pretty fun. The site was helping hundreds of people attend fitness classes every day. After the success it had with gym members, her boss told Max to open the site to patrons nationwide. Hannah now reached thousands and inspired them to move daily, something she'd always dreamed of doing. The paid memberships through this venture provided quite a financial boom for the gym, one they were happy to share with Hannah since she'd spearheaded that part of the website. But her generous heart refused to keep it all. She donated a large percentage of her new paycheck to MADD in memory of her mom and Courtney.

She continued going to therapy. And while her good days far outnumbered the bad, Max made sure he was there for her in any way she needed. Shouldering the weight of mental illness was something he wouldn't wish upon anyone. He admired the tremendous strength his girlfriend showed whenever she admitted to needing a break because her anxiety was creeping in. He was more than happy to hold her for as long as she needed, physically or metaphorically. And he was always there to remind her that she didn't need to be fixed—because she wasn't broken.

This gave her an idea to expand the website, as she continued to help even more people with her caring spirit. Now, Jenkins' Gym wasn't just a place for people to get physically fit. It also became a place to foster good mental health habits. She added meditation classes and offered online seminars hosted by local counselors, her therapist included. It was a place people could get the help they, or someone they knew, needed. She thought this was even more valuable than the site's original intended purpose.

And that was only the beginning. Though he insisted it wasn't necessary and he hadn't designed her website for his own publicity, Hannah insisted that his name appear somewhere on the site. She wanted people to see it.

And see it, they did.

Many small businesses reached out to hire him for freelance web design work. In addition to Hannah's workplace, he was now the chief webmaster for so many companies, he considered starting his own business, something Hannah not only supported but also researched in what little spare time she had.

As for the two of them, things were great. With the help of therapy, Hannah accepted that she deserved all the happiness she felt. Contrary to what the past had taught her, not everyone in her life that loved her was going to leave. Max continued to participate in community service projects but delegated much of the chairperson work to others. He was still part of the organizations that he believed in but without the risk of burnout—something he'd learned in one of Jenkins' Gym's stress management seminars.

The pair spent more time together than ever before, which seemed impossible since they met during a quarantine. They even hosted their first Thanksgiving at his apartment. Only his parents attended, with the pandemic still ongoing, but it was a smoking success. Literally. Max was so caught up in watching Hannah and his mom in the kitchen laughing and sharing memories of holidays past, he forgot to keep track of the bread in the oven, the one job Hannah had given him. Next thing he knew, they were wafting smoke into the hallway. But like any challenge they'd faced these last months, they faced it together. With a smile.

So, yes, there were lots of reasons to smile lately. And tonight, Max hoped to add one more to the growing list.

"You were right," she said, interrupting his thoughts. "This is far more beautiful than I imagined."

He had the same thought, but he was looking at her. She stared at the Garden of Light, an area of Oglebay Park where they'd sat before she met his parents this past summer. Only now, flower-shaped light displays for the holiday season replaced the blooms of May.

"I thought you'd enjoy this." He squeezed her hand a little tighter because he noticed his shaking a little. He could blame it on the cold winter air that tagged along with them tonight, but he knew the real reason for the trembling.

They took a seat on a wooden bench, the same one they sat on that afternoon before the Memorial Day picnic. He thought she looked beautiful that day, her hair pulled away from her face in a patriotic scrunchie and a bright red tank top that showed off her toned arms and shoulders. The memory alone was enough to send warmth through his body despite the chilly weather. But tonight, skin totally covered save her beautiful face, she looked luminous under the glow of thousands of twinkling lights. Her beauty left him speechless. And that was a big problem. There was something he needed to do.

"Are you okay?" she asked, looking down at his leg. His knee rapidly bobbed up and down.

"Never better," he answered, the pitch of his voice betraying his words.

Hannah raised a brow. "I'm not sure I believe you."

"Well, would you believe me if I said I think you're the most gorgeous woman in the universe, and the love you have for others only makes you more beautiful?"

She blushed. "Well, that's quite sweet of you."

"Would you believe me if I told you that I want to be with you always because being apart from you is something that's becoming harder and harder to do?"

"I'd have to agree with you on that one."

"And would you believe me if I told you that I wanted to be with you for the rest of my life?"

Hannah smiled even bigger now. "I think that sounds like a pretty good plan to me."

"Well, that's a relief to hear." He stood, removing a black box from his coat pocket, and dropped to one knee in front of her. She clutched her hands to her chest.

"Hannah Rose, when you came into my life on my birthday, I got the greatest gift of all. So, now I'd like to give you something." He opened the box with his shaking hands, and she gasped at the sparkling ring inside. "Will you marry me?"

She dropped to her knees in front of him, grabbing his face between her hands, and crushed her mouth into his.

"Is that a yes?" He was pretty sure he knew the answer, but he still wanted confirmation before he gave himself permission to stop holding his breath.

"Max—that's a heck yes!"

They both still knelt on the cold stone path as she tore off her glove with the ferocity of a wild animal. With a hand that shook far less than it had just thirty seconds ago, he put the ring on her finger.

As he looked at his bride-to-be, he couldn't help but beam with gratitude for this moment. It had truly been a long, hard road to get to this place. But from this moment on, he'd never have to walk it alone.

The End

255

A note from Lindsey

Thank you so much for reading my very first novel. Reviews are very important to independent authors, so if you loved hanging out with Hannah and Max, please leave a review on Amazon, Goodreads, or wherever else you'd like. I'd appreciate it so much!

Acknowledgments

Sitting down to write the acknowledgements for my first books feels surreal. It also feels like the most important thank you note I'll ever write, so here's hoping I don't screw it up.

Mom and Dad, thank you for always supporting my dreams. Mom, I appreciate you reading my first draft and telling me it was good. I hope this version is *a lot* better than the one you read. And Dad, thanks for being my unofficial advertising manager. I don't know if you were walking around town with a sandwich board telling everyone about my book, but I feel like every time I saw you, you told me someone new wanted to buy it. That meant a lot.

Mom and Dad J, you've followed this journey from the beginning and have cheered me on. Mom J, thanks for being one of my betas. Your sweet words kept me plugging along in the early days.

Allison and Lindsay, you trudged through the rubble of my first draft and lived to tell about it. I learned so much from the two of you, and I'll never be able to express how grateful I am that you took on this newbie and pointed her in the right direction.

Megan, Sam, Julie, and Andrew, though we've never met in person, I feel like you've been important people in this whole process. You've given me advice when I was clueless, motivation when I was lacking, and a laugh when I needed it most. But above all, you've been some of my biggest cheerleaders. I hope you know how much I'm cheering you all on, as well.

Sarah, Katie, Loretta, and Emma, from reading early drafts to sending me texts and emails out of the blue just to say you're proud of what I'm doing, your encouragement always seemed to come at a time I needed it most. Thank you for being there.

To the Bookstagram community, wow. This little corner of the internet has been the support I didn't even know I needed. I've met some of the most wonderful people who were more than happy to share in this dream of mine. Every post you've shared, every message you've sent me, none of it has gone unnoticed or unappreciated.

To my girls, I love you so much. Thank you for being (mostly) quiet when I needed to work on some things. I hope I've made you proud.

And Rob, what can I say? I honestly don't think there would be a book if not for you. When I came to you and said I wanted to write a book, you were 100% on board. When I had mini freak-outs (and there were a few), you kept me grounded. And when I needed to talk out a scene, you were always there with a listening ear—and some interesting suggestions (sorry so few of them made it into the book). You'll always be my favorite love story hero.

Lastly, I'd like to thank God for the gift of gab and love of words I was born with. It made me the writer I am, and I hope I've used the gift to make Him proud.

Also by Lindsey Jesionowski

*Spend the holidays in West Virginia as Johnny helps Courtney's sister, Josie, find love in a novella coming in November 2022.

*And don't miss out on Johnny and Angie's story, *Shut Up and Dance*, coming in early 2023.

Visit my website to sign up for my newsletter. I'll share news, sneak peeks, and bonus content exclusive to subscribers.

https://lindseyjesionowski.wixsite.com/lindseyjesionowski

And follow me on Instagram:

https://Instagram.com/authorlindseyjesionowski

About the Author

Lindsey Jesionowski is a wife and mom who does most of her writing in her car in the school pickup lot. She's a native of West Virginia, a lover of coffee, and a fan of books with happy ever afters—so she decided to write one.

Lindsey's books are full of heart and humor with plenty of steam and no explicit content. Just lots of smiles. This is her first book.